THE
AGE

ALSO BY NANCY LEE

Dead Girls

NANCY LEE

THE
AGE

A NOVEL

McClelland & Stewart

Library and Archives Canada Cataloguing in Publication

Lee, Nancy, 1970–
The age / Nancy Lee.

ISBN 978-0-7710-5252-1

I. Title.

PS8573.E34845A64 2013   C813'.6   C2012-906080-1

This is a work of fiction. Any similarity between the characters
in this book and persons living or dead is purely coincidental.

Cover image © Anthony Hatley/ Millennium Images, UK
Book design by CS Richardson
Typeset in Garamond 3

Printed and bound in the United States of America

McClelland & Stewart,
a division of Random House of Canada Limited
A Penguin Random House Company
One Toronto Street
Suite 300
Toronto, Ontario
M5C 2V6
www.randomhouse.ca

1   2   3   4   5   18   17   16   15   14

For my mom and John

o o o

1

THE DAY GOES DOWN IN FIRE. Sooty clouds crush the sun to a red stain at the horizon. The dwindling light plays tricks, douses the mountains in shellac, casts hedges and stretches of asphalt as mirrors. Gerry squints against the glare, her grip on the handlebars part sweat, part tack of peeling tape as she races her ten-speed away from a half-eaten Sunday dinner and her mom's prying small talk, past split-levels and wide lawns.

She crosses into the park and coasts, shakes out her arms, swallows the pulse in her throat, lets the gravel drag beneath her tires. Ahead on the path, old men in suspenders and rolled shirtsleeves stoop over bocce balls. They cluck their tongues at her approach. Grandpas hooked by trailing hair and drain-pipe jeans, blind to her mud-splattered high-tops and frayed fatigue jacket. She pulls the cycling cap from her back pocket, twists her hair up and under. The old men moan, flap their hands in disappointment.

Dusk rises from wet grass, mixes with the scummy stench of the nearby pond. Below the slope of the path, down beside the running track, BMX boys huddle under the long shadows of willow trees. Gerry slows to watch them. Bikes strewn, they guzzle beer from stubbies, pose muscled bodies like angry cut-outs. Boys who have graduated but don't have jobs, who cruise the park in acid-wash and storm-riders, smoke dope and stab at picnic tables with pocketknives. One of them hikes a middle finger in front of his Ray-Bans, shouts, "Take a picture, faggot, it lasts longer." Greasy hair, open mouth, he reclines, knees spread in invitation.

She guesses at distances: from each of them to their bikes, from her spot on the path to the park exit, works up speed, ready to sprint past. At the last second, she skids out her back tire, sprays them with a fan of gravel, listens to it hit like shrapnel as she rides away.

"You're dead, you little prick!" one of them shouts. Somewhere behind her, a beer bottle smashes into a tree.

Under the fizz and tick of streetlights, she passes lit windows of houses where mothers tidy kitchens and fathers fold newspapers in front of the TV. She knows their daughters, bloodless girls who jostle her in the hallways at school, nick with warning glances. Preppy girls with chiselled bobs and frosted smiles like cotton candy over barbed wire. Rocker chicks with glazed eyes, who reek of cigarettes, Juicy Fruit, and Charlie, bitch-bags dripping feathers and rabbits' feet. Barricaded in their bedrooms, armed with mousse cartridges and hairspray, their skulls rattle with Tic Tacs. They tie up phone lines, assemble mixed tapes, inflict handjobs on boyfriends before doing their homework.

Always, it seems, Gerry's mind is full of them, girls, flitting and hovering. At school, they swarm beside lockers, drawn to one another but not to her. She scolds herself to ignore them. When they see her face on the evening news, that's when their gaping mouths will be worth imagining.

Windows blur into smears of yellow. She pedals faster, begins a mental countdown, imagines the air-scrape of missiles, the end of neighbourhoods, houses lit like balsa wood, each particle an inferno. She speeds downhill, abandons the useless daughters, the sound of their burning.

Apart from the TV's blue strobe in the living-room window, Megan's house sits dark. Gerry wonders if Megan's father has fallen asleep in his chair again, suit rumpled, shoes shined. She rounds the bushes to the half-buried septic tank, pushes up her sleeves, feels the rusty surface for a hold that won't cut her hand. She hoists herself, scrambles to kneel on the flexing metal, stretches to the window. Glass stucco grazes her arms. The ledge at her collarbone, she blinks, waits for her eyes to adjust to the dim of Megan's bedroom.

Megan's body offers itself on full display: legs an open V, triangle thatch of pubic hair, half-moon arcs of breasts, her shaved head hidden beneath the window. Ian lies on his stomach, naked from the waist up, arms hooked around Megan's thighs, face buried. Megan moves her hips in slow underwater circles that make Gerry shudder.

She mimics Megan's hips with her own, tosses her head as she imagines Megan doing. Low in Gerry's belly, secret muscles twitch and tense. The grit under her sneaker shifts with her rocking. Her foot starts a slow, easy slip. She steps back to steady herself but finds only soft, yielding air. As she tips, her fingers snatch at the ledge, her hands flail out, a sting catches her wrist. The ground slams up against her back.

She opens her eyes to dirty twilight, tall grass, and the bowed heads of dandelions. A sob burbles, then quells. She rolls onto her side and tries to breathe normally. When she can finally sit up, she finds blood, a dark dribble down the pale blade of her arm.

2

MEGAN'S LIVING ROOM IS ALWAYS STUFFY, like a hand over Gerry's face, heat that starts in the matted carpet beneath her socks, then rises to muddy the air. Gerry crouches in front of Clem, tries to catch his eye, holds up her wrist with its makeshift bandage, a wad of paper towel affixed with masking tape. She points to a small spot of blood leaking through. Her wounds are of no interest to him. He stares past her to the screen.

Behind her, the TV clatters with the giant slots of *The Joker's Wild*. She hates game shows, wishes she could watch the news, a second Soviet warship spotted in the North Atlantic, but Clem shouts at every channel change. Instead, Gerry studies the pits and lines of his skin. Some days his expression looks gouged out of clay or carved into leather; today it's traced on paper. If she took an eraser to him, she could make him disappear.

"Gerry Mouse!" Ian's voice jolts her. He stands in the hallway, bare-chested, T-shirt in hand. His open belt buckle dangles. A thin line of hair starts at his belly button and burrows into his jeans, his half-nakedness an insult, a dare.

She sniffs, unimpressed. "Don't call me that."

"Guess it was you making that racket." He stretches the T-shirt over his elbows, flashes his shaggy armpits.

Gerry cringes. "Surprised you could hear with your mouth full."

"Jealous?"

"Lark will be." The TV light cuts shapes in the dark of Clem's eyes.

"Fucking shut it about that, I'm not even kidding." Ian kicks at the doorframe to make his point. She ignores him, waits for him to leave.

No matter how hard she looks, she sees no trace of Clem's younger self. Nothing like the photos in the library microfiche, yellowed newspapers lit from behind, the X-rayed past: a pointy-faced man in heavy glasses, curly hair combed to a peak at the front of his head. Clem, who served twenty-five years for the death of a homeless man sleeping under a contractor's trailer at a dam site. The maximum because he refused to name other protesters, a detail that, in her mind, separates him from the toxic waste of adulthood.

She wonders if the dead man haunted Clem, if that explained his white hair, his bewildered expression, or whether prison alone did that to a person, whether she herself might go to jail a young girl and leave a hobbled old woman.

Soon Megan will move Clem to an old folks' home. Even if Gerry had the courage to tell him, he wouldn't understand. She presses her fingers to his papery wrist, holds her breath to feel his pulse.

She finds the four of them gathered at the kitchen table, Andri recapping the weekend's testing at Michelle's family farm. Gerry slips into the chair beside him, draws her feet up onto the seat, tries to picture Andri and pregnant Michelle in lab coats and goggles, marking results on clipboards as they watch things explode. What things, Gerry isn't sure. Andri fiddles with a tube of cough candy, peels the foil wrapper in short, exact tears, begins a mazelike explanation of trajectory effects, gravitational forces, momentum conservation. His rough Eastern European accent muffles in his beard. She follows the meaning of his words but not the message of them strung together.

Across from her, Ian glares, leans back in his chair, and wiggles a spastic squeak out of its metal joints. She avoids his gaze by watching Megan fold laundry, her long fingers pinching the seams of Clem's shirts. Megan's profile reminds Gerry of old statues she's seen in books at school, hard marble angles that taper into the pillowy curve of her lips. Her shorn head is a constant temptation, like a nap of fur. Gerry rubs her hands against her jeans, soothed by the friction.

As Andri speaks, Michelle nods in agreement. Her pregnancy makes Gerry feel both protected and protective. At times, she admires Michelle's peaceful reserve, so opposite to the frenzy Gerry feels as she waits for a chance to speak. Other times, Michelle's placid face makes Gerry sad, especially when she thinks of Michelle's family: her crazy brother alone on a farm, collecting guns, believing in flying saucers and people who live at the centre of the earth, their parents dead in a car accident before she graduated high school.

Ian belches, a deep, yawning echo.

Andri continues to talk, scrawls on the sheet of paper in front of him, equations and a diagram of the building, the street, arrows pointing off in different directions. Under Andri's trampled parka, the edges of his shirts and sweaters overlap. Gerry admires his weirdness, his fear of cold, his different-coloured eyes, arbitrary patterns in his thin, patchy beard. She loves his smell, the perfume of mentholated lozenges clicking against his crooked teeth. Lemons, but not sickly and artificial, green and sharp, like unripe fruit. His gruffness makes him seem an old man trapped in a younger man's body. In his home country, he had trained as an electrical engineer, perhaps that was what made him so serious. She studies the smooth stretches of skin above his beard and collar and wishes she could touch them, work out his true age.

Andri called the device "a cinch" when Megan first asked if he could build one. Gerry collects these snippets, joins their mismatched sides together whenever she's asked to leave the room. Twice, Ian has told her to stop coming around. She wears them out, climbs in through the windows, rises up from the basement, sits on the back porch and pounds her heels into the stairs. She tries to make herself indispensable by helping with Clem.

Andri catches her stare and smiles. She blinks at the table. He clasps her wrist, his grip warm and meaty. His thumb grazes the stained bandage. "Killing yourself?"

She snatches her hand into her lap, seesaws between pride and embarrassment, being thought capable, then incapable of suicide, shakes her head.

"Too bad."

"Andri!" Megan's disapproval prickles a flush into Gerry's face.

"What? When I was her age, we were always trying to kill ourselves. It was a gesture."

Gerry studies the creases around Andri's eyes. Ian is three years older than she is, Megan and Michelle will turn twenty-nine in the same month, but Andri remains a puzzle. "When were you my age?"

Andri feigns being hit by a bullet and collapses onto the table. Everyone laughs. Gerry smiles, uncertain in the wake of her accidental joke.

"Such cruelty," Andri says as he sits up.

Megan rises from the table to put the kettle on for Clem's tea and medicine. "What about the route?"

Ian's chair drops with a thud. A pressure settles over Gerry's foot. Ian's heel grinds down, pins her, his gaze taunts her to rat him out. "Done," he says.

"You've mapped it? Marked it? Timed it from beginning to end?"

"Well, duh." Ian says.

Gerry suckles the inside of her cheek, tries not to wince.

"Anyway." He lifts his chin. "Who cares about the route if we can't get into the building?" His boot eases off. Gerry curls her toes against a cramp.

Megan stares at him. "I'm still working on access. Maybe something tonight."

Ian's mouth flattens.

Andri snorts and chuckles, as if another joke has been told. His coolness makes Gerry want to reach under the table and squeeze his hand.

Ian and Megan stay in the kitchen to argue. The kettle whistles its own complaint. Gerry waits on the couch, hopes Ian will storm out, leave her to talk to Megan alone. With her stockpile of overheard facts, it's easy to cast herself in their plan. She has been to the building, stared into it from the sidewalk, peered through glass walls to the darkened lobby, where an empty security console hulked in front of two rows of elevators. The word *revenue* makes her wonder if they keep money there.

Out on the street, Andri's Chevette splutters. Gerry pulls an elastic through her hair. The band snaps back in her fingers and the sting makes her curse. She apologizes to Clem as she tucks stray wisps of hair under her cap.

"Ian'll drive you." Megan leans in the doorway, arms crossed.

"I'm gonna ride," Gerry says. She sidesteps to avoid a shove as Ian passes.

Megan shakes her head. "It's late. Make sure she gets home."

Ian yanks open the front door. A moustached man in a paisley shirt stands on the stoop, a case of beer under his arm, his hand poised to knock. Ian wrenches the doorknob back and forth. The metal clacking grates at Gerry. Night air drifts in and settles cold against her face. The man on the stoop smiles without blinking.

"Close the goddamn door!" Clem's voice is surprisingly loud.

Megan giggles.

Gerry grins, wishes she had turned in time to see his lips move.

They dodge awkwardly at the door. Ian and Gerry shuffle out, the man slips in.

On the grass, Ian foot-dribbles an invisible soccer ball. "Who do you think that was?"

"Magnum P.I.?" The dials of her bike lock jam under her fingers.

Ian snickers. "Yeah, it did sort of look like him, didn't it? Fuck." He steps backward to the sidewalk and cranes to see into the living-room window. "Here." He claps his hands together.

"I'll give you a boost and you tell me what they're doing." His agitation makes the world seem temporarily fair.

"What do you care?" Gerry backs her bike away from the house. "You've got Lark."

"So I do."

As she passes, he wings his shoulder into her. She ducks and elbows him, catches a patch of softness under his ribs.

"Jesus!" The strain in his voice pleases her.

From the sidewalk they watch the window. The glowing rectangle exposes only the TV's boxy back, a hazy ceiling light, the top edge of a far wall. Ian rocks on his heels. "What the hell is up with you, anyway? You're like a bitchy twelve-year-old. You finally get your period or what?"

"At least I'm not some stuck-up private school skeeze. She's like, my age, you know." Gerry drags the bike, wheels juddering over the curb.

He follows her onto the road. "Eat your heart out, Gerry Mouse. She's a year older and about ten years more mature." He holds the rim of her bike seat; his arm jerks, piston enough to push or pull her at will. "I've been babysitting you since kindergarten and that don't exactly pay dividends, if you get my drift."

"Then tell Megan about her."

His head sways back in exaggerated reaction. She wants to slap him, watch the shock blossom on his face.

"The little mascot has no idea what she's talking about right now."

"Fuck you." Her voice repeats tinny and off-key in her head. She sounds childish, even to herself.

"Come on." The words stretch, a whining complaint. He taps the seat post, points to his car. "Let's live to fight another day."

She steps hard and slow on the pedals, balances her weight, and turns a tight circle. "I'm going."

"I'm not chasing you."

"No shit." She sprints away, limbs fizzing.

Around the park's perimeter streetlights smoulder, but cutting through will get her home faster. Gravel pops, smooths to grass, then pops again as Gerry rights herself on the unlit path. The sky a moonless shield, she pedals blind, night air thick and silky, velour against her face and arms.

She is not afraid of the dark, she tells herself. She is afraid of spiders, of dying a virgin, of the new virus, detonators and plutonium, warships in the Persian Gulf. She is afraid of airplane sounds, the shape of certain cloud formations, gas masks, submarines, the electric squeal of the emergency broadcast system, farmers' fields that open to mile-deep silos. She is afraid of generals and admirals, and old white presidents. Of seeing her father, and never seeing him, of radiation sickness, and reincarnation, being vaporized only to return to an annihilated world. She tries not to think of Ian cruising home, stereo cranked, the coddling heat of his car.

Above the wind in her ears, a whir rises. She tries to place the sound, rhythmic and buzzy like a cloud of bees. She pedals faster. The lights at the edge of the park stay stubbornly fixed. Something snaps and flutters above her head. She shuts her eyes, flattens, chest to handlebars to avoid a brush of feathers or, worse, leathery skin. Her heart knocks near her throat. The whirring gets louder, breathy and mechanical. A man's laugh startles her with its closeness. Before she can turn, a weight on her back, a hard snag. Her bike flies out from under her.

Through blackness pricked with stars, she sees herself swan-dive, reach for a trapeze bar that floats beyond her fingers then falls away. She plummets, looks down for a net, but sees only the hard deck of an aircraft carrier. The grapple of hands on her body wakes her. Hurried words, *shit, wallet, motherfucker*. She plays dead, lies still, eyes closed. Silent with relief when the hands withdraw, she listens, waits for their retreat.

The first kick jolts her, crushes into her stomach, vacuums her lungs. The second spears her back, raises water in her eyes, triggers a dry, sucking gasp. Voices shout for her to stand. Her hands push at the ground. Beyond their legs, she sees her bike, frame contorted, wheels bent. She raises an elbow over the pain in her head, draws her knees to her chest. A hand cradles her jaw as if to comfort her, then lands two hard punches. A shoe clips the brim of her cap. Fingers reach into her hair. *It's a fucking girl*. The scuff of shoes, the scrabble of tires.

She tells herself to get up and run.

$$3$$

ON THE SIDEWALK IN FRONT OF HER HOUSE, Gerry
pauses to straighten her gait, tightens the right side of
her body, tries to lift her feet instead of drag. She makes
a *huh* sound to clear her throat and swallows a coppery slug of
mucus. Elbow clenched against her sharpened ribs, she turns
her key in the lock, braces for maternal hysterics.

Symphonic music swells as she steps into the foyer, the warmth
of the house consoling and exhausting at once. In the living
room, Randy's tall, broad back blocks Gerry's view of the couch.
Her mom's nyloned feet cross at the end of the coffee table, the
rest of her hidden, tucked down in front him. On TV, a camera
sweeps over craggy cliffs, pans a green field. Gerry holds the
front door, eases it into its frame.

"You're late." Her mom's hand waves from Randy's body.

"I know."

"Randy brought over his VCR. We rented a movie." The tip
of her mom's chin peeks out from Randy's arm. "Come watch
with us."

Gerry faces the coat hooks, fiddles with the pockets on her
jacket as she senses her mom about to turn in her seat, stretch
to get a glimpse of her. Gerry soaks her voice in sarcasm. "Um,

thanks, but no thanks." She punctuates with a snicker that fires a spark through her face.

Her mom sighs. "Suit yourself."

Gerry clings to a hanging sleeve, counts the seconds before she can turn around again. She checks over her shoulder.

On the screen, a blond actress in a hooded cape runs through a crowded train station; fevered music matches her steps. Randy's gaze catches Gerry by surprise, his stare, blank and stricken with alarm.

She tries to smile. Blood percolates behind her nose. She raises her shoulders in an agonizing shrug. Her index finger quivers as she lifts it to her lips, shakes her head in slow motion. "I'm going to bed now," she calls to her mom.

Her mom's fingers waggle in the air. "Sleep tight."

Steam churns inside the small room as the bathtub fills. She bends at the sink, water like needles, rinses her mouth and nose, the gash above her eyebrow. Just below her right eye, a gel sack of wine-coloured blood forms a grotesque supermodel cheekbone. She presses the taut, swollen surface, flinches, swallows the trickle that crawls down her throat.

The mirror steams over and her distorted self disappears. She smears herself back. They could have done worse. Panic shakes through her legs. She coughs, bows her head, and waits for the hot fist of her stomach to jam up in her throat, splatter the circling water with blood. Instead, a sob breaks in her chest and she bawls into the sink, the night rushing out of her.

A knock at the door dissolves in the tub's rumble.

"I'm having a bath," she shouts.

"Open up." Randy's beefy husk.

She splashes her face with water, grabs a towel and holds a corner of it over her nose and mouth, cradles the rest against her body. Standing as straight as she can, she opens the door, catches it with her foot. She tries to see past Randy's bulk filling the doorway. "Where is she?"

He looks over his shoulder. "In the kitchen. Making popcorn."

"Intermission."

"What happened to you? You need the hospital?"

"I got in a fight." She lowers the towel to give him a peek at her face. "Don't tell, okay?"

"Gerry." Randy groans, raises his arm on the doorframe, rests his forehead in his palm. His hand reminds her of a catcher's mitt.

She feels light-headed with the effort of standing. Her fingers search for the counter.

Randy reaches out to steady her, the mitt on her shoulder. "Christ," he says.

"I feel like shit right now, and I totally can't handle her flipping out." She has never looked at him this close. His face calms her, furrowed and toughened, yet round at the edges. "Just don't say anything, okay? And. I won't tell her you lost your job."

His hand drops from her shoulder as he leans away.

"I saw you at the doughnut place last week. You were circling want ads."

"I was looking for a car."

"She's dumped guys for way less."

His nostrils flare. His face reminds her of a cartoon bull and she imagines leading him by a chain, a large metal ring through his nose. Randy sighs and taps the door. "Yeah. Well." He nods as he turns for the stairs. "Don't die in your sleep."

She closes the door and shuffles toward the bathtub. As she passes the sink, she catches a glimpse of herself in the fog, alien, unrecognizable.

The Hurting scratches thin and twangy from the record player. Flat on her bed, swaddled in towels, she stares at the ceiling. Above her, Trinity's radioactive mushroom explodes in grainy black and white. A blink of tears blurs, then sharpens the poster. Her body trembles with the New Mexico sagebrush, the after-shock of overdue adrenalin. Air on her skin like chipped ice, she gathers the blankets around her.

They might have beaten her dead, left her on the path in a bloody heap. A carnival of police lights, a lullaby of sirens, her mom folding to the ground in grief. Gerry's mind, adept at substitutions, casts a TV dad in the obvious void. A dad who stalks off in the night with a shotgun or grips a baseball bat as he scours the streets. Who rigs traps of razor wire and spikes, then organizes work buddies with chains and crowbars. A dad who calls the police, then pays to take a lead pipe into the back of a paddy wagon. A dad who blames himself, finishes his days at the bottom of a whisky bottle.

She dabs her eyes with the bedsheet. A pulse throbs under the tight swell of her face. Eight years gone and her father has a house in Santa Clara, a swimming pool, a wife, and twin boys. It would take a miracle for him to blame himself. Instead, she has Randy, a lousy stand-in, rough and dumb, and even he couldn't care less, ready to tempt fate with his warning: a jellied clot blocking her windpipe as she dreams, a splintered rib slicing her heart, blood seeping from her brain into the nest of her skull.

The poster dissolves into particles, the great cloud fracturing over wasted desert while miles away, scientists, haunted already by ash shadows of children, sip champagne to dull their guilt. She eases a pillow under her neck, flexes a bicep, slowly, to feel the flare in her chest. The pain, predictable now, leaves her glassy and hollow-headed. She flexes again, imagines that overnight her muscles will fuse, harden over wounds, tighten around her like fleshy armour.

Dying in her sleep would be a blessing, a pardon. She knows her death comes prearranged, the end of a decades-long physics experiment: a bright, sunny day, a missile in the sky. She once watched a TV program on phobias, how people afraid of spiders should try to imagine spiders, a spider across the room, a spider at their feet, in their lap, in their hand, and somehow these thoughts would make them less afraid. So she rehearses. At first it was a view from space, the planet's watery curves retreating against a sea of pitch, surface drawn in impossible detail, undulating trees, mountain range scars, white-tipped ocean, and scabs of desert. On cue, soundless columns of fire would rise. Later, she pictured an old black-and-white television set, soundless atrocities from a camera's perspective, devastation contained behind the curved glass screen. Now it begins at a bus stop.

Her mind is mischievous. Primed for nightmares, disturbances, it casts her in the body of a boy. A slight boy, without bulging muscles or bristles of hair, a subtle evolution that unsettles her, heats her with shame and excitement. Her inner self still her self but distilled to only strengths, all her curves and weakness cut away.

o o o

IT HAPPENS WITHOUT WARNING. A sunny day. Nothing
on television. No escalating tensions, no rogue states in crisis,
no awkward catch in the morning newscaster's voice. Slouched
over his knapsack in the shade of a wooden bus shelter, the boy
in the mud-splattered high-tops plays with the frayed edge of
his fatigue jacket, nods to the urgent tide of "Eclipse" on his
Walkman. Beside him on the bench, a man in a short-sleeved
shirt and tie reads the paper. A woman in a sundress and high-
heeled sandals stands by the bus stop marker, denim jacket
hanging from her shoulders like a cape. She shimmies her legs,
rubs her powder white arms against the chill. The smell of her
morning routine, shampoo, hairspray, perfume, teases the boy,
helps him imagine her naked.

Pink Floyd's chorus swells inside him, then fades in a final
chord of voices. Beneath the trailing notes, an unfamiliar sound.
A low vibration that thrums in his head, then seems to push
up through the bench beneath him. He slips his headphones
down to his neck. The muffled world comes clear. Sirens rise in
a dizzy spiral.

Traffic continues, drivers busy with coffee, eyeliner, toasted
breakfast. At the bus stop, people turn their heads, faces posed
as question marks, curious, ready to reassure or dismiss. An
elderly woman opens and closes her purse. The sundress woman
smiles. The man in the tie folds his newspaper. They wonder at
the sky, look to one another and shrug.

The boy stands and something happens to his eyes. A sheet of
light flashed with purple, a dim milky haze, as if a circuit in his
brain has flared and fizzled. Confused, he blinks, then squints

to see. He expects people to stare, to ask, What is wrong with that boy? But no one looks at him. The man in the tie sits with his mouth open, the sundress woman squeezes the edges of her jacket, they stare at the horizon.

The sound shocks him. Thunder so loud and deep, he cannot imagine anything louder, until it sucks the breath from him, the moisture from his eyes, a massive, suffocating bass in his chest. The noise suspends him like water.

A cloud rises from the south, a funnel of fire, the horizon dwarfed beneath its expanding plume. Transfixed, he tries to guess its height in feet, office buildings, miles.

Traffic slows, then stops. Drivers climb out of their cars and gawk at the sky, others sit bewildered, punch buttons on their radios. A hand grabs his arm. The sundress woman shouts, Run! He wants to tell her, It's no good, you can't run from that. She pulls until his legs obey.

They run north as an equal tide of bodies runs against them. The woman glances back, second-guessing their route, trips on her sandals and tumbles forward. Her jacket catches over her arms. The boy waits for her to stand. The sky darkens, the air grows cold. He studies the cloud spread, miles wide. And as he tries to calculate the landmass below it, another flash-bulb explodes to the south, then one to the west, and another, and another.

4

SLEEP SETTLES COLD AND BLACK, pondwater at night. Submerged, Gerry shivers, liquid pressure aching in her chest and hands, her face thick with tangled weeds. She surfaces once, in the grey morning, her mom's soft knock on the door, a blade of light from the hallway. Gerry covers her head with the comforter.

"I have to go in early, someone tripped an alarm at the lab."

Too waterlogged to respond, she curls into herself, imagines floating.

"I don't want you wasting your day with Henry. Spring break or not, you've got chores to do."

"Light," Gerry moans. Through the blanket she feels the room go dim.

Her mom sighs in the dark. "Did you hear me?"

She wonders who her mom is talking to.

"Have a good day. I'll miss you." The door bumps in its frame.

Later, Gerry wakes to the hum of daylight, her face a mask of thorns and splinters. The sound of a faraway hammer thumps in her head. She lies still, teases crust from the corners of her eyes. A short, tentative sniff spears through her nose, into her temples. Her eyes water as she holds her arm to her ribs to sit up, tries to steady the filaments of pain in her chest and back, keep her breath shallow. She stands, tests her weight, limps a slow arc around the bed.

She opens her window, lets the morning rinse over her. Low clouds hang in a dingy sky. The hammer starts again, pounding on the front door that echoes up through the house. Across the street, her grandfather's brown Audi.

"I'm getting ready," she calls down. The words vibrate through her face, leave her nauseated.

Leather-soled shoes brush the pavement, Henry steps back onto the walk, grey hair a moulded shape, the lines of his suit pressed into tight corners. Hands in his pockets, he gazes up but doesn't spot her. He talks to the sky. "I'll wait in the car, then."

She takes her time in the bathroom, dabs dried blood with a warm washcloth to unveil the darkened skin beneath, brushes her teeth, hypnotized as the paste foams pink. With the tips of her fingers, she pats her mom's liquid foundation over the worst of it, tempers the angry purple with tawny beige. She leaves her hair down as camouflage, draws a brush through it, careful not to graze her scalp.

The door handle is cold and tricky in her fingers. The car unleashes an overheated waft of aftershave, stale old man, and FM classical. She keeps herself angled away as she settles in the passenger seat. When she turns to face him, Henry's brows crowd together like scruffy caterpillars. The edges of his mouth sink into his jowls. Then, like a cycle of bad weather, the expression clears. "Close your door." He puts the car into gear. His nonchalance impresses her. She tries not to smile as they pull away from the curb.

"Face like that usually comes with a play-by-play."

"I was in a fight."

"I'll have to tell your dad."

Gerry shrugs as she calculates what her father should know. "The other girl got it worse." The imaginary win buoys her.

"You see a doctor?"

"What for?"

Henry smiles. "Your father was scrappy. The first Mrs. tried to coddle it out of him, turn the other cheek and all that, but the instinct to fight is one hundred percent pure Cross."

She rolls down her window, reassured by the certainty of genetics.

Houses pass like a filmstrip. Ahead on the block, two figures perch on Ian's front steps. Ian and Lark kissing. As the car drifts by, Lark's sprayed-out hair glints in the sun, her skinny arms draped around Ian's neck.

"Friends of yours?"

Gerry slumps back in her seat. "As if."

Gerry doesn't mind the newsroom, the dreary chaos, the bell rattle of phones, desks clad in fake wood panelling, their narrow metal legs threatening to buckle under the weight of file trays and hooded IBM Selectrics, the chance to spin in Henry's chair. Scorched ashtrays send up trails of smoke, soot the ceiling tiles black. Near the far wall, a tile popped open like a hatch. Where news people go to die. Gerry pictures them climbing a tall, wooden ladder, crawling into the ceiling on their hands and knees. She imagines skiffs of bones overhead as she leans back against Henry's suit jacket.

Beneath a bank of wall clocks, each displaying a different time, Elaine, the weathergirl, perches at her desk, red lipstick, red highlights in her permed hair. She twirls a pen, glasses at the end of her nose. A red stiletto dangles from her stockinged foot. Gerry searches for evidence she's a lesbian as Henry claims. Perhaps the bony square of her shoulders, the chain on her glasses, the man-sized watch on her wrist. None of it seems like proof.

Henry's desk is a single, teetering mound of papers, files, and debris that date back to the Mesozoic Era. Time has compressed the layers closest to the bottom into a nondescript wad. Gerry pinches the corner of a pink, carbon-printed sheet near the middle, shimmies it slowly while monitoring the pile for the hint of an avalanche. The paper comes free and she raises her arms, makes a soft, airy stadium cheer in her mouth, then lays the paper on top, a flat pink cherry.

At the end of the room, Henry stands inside the news director's glass-walled office. Stripped of jackets, both men are stout, barrel-chested. They pace and lumber about, wave their arms to the sides, above their heads. They remind her of cavemen or gorillas. Each pauses to unbutton his cuffs, roll his shirtsleeves, shake his head, each makes the other wait for a reply. For a few seconds, they both yell at once, slap the backs of their hands into their palms. Her grandfather appears a stranger, made anonymous by the blur of his features, his perplexing resemblance to his boss.

The two men hulk out of the office together, sweaty and red-faced as if from a sauna. The news director cuts a sharp right. Henry stalks toward his desk, tosses a ruffle of papers onto the mound. Gerry holds her breath as the pages flutter and wobble, then settle to a perfect balance on the pile.

They park across the street from Henry's former house, a low, tidy bungalow in a neighbourhood of mansions with wrought-iron fences. An early spring drizzle scurries across the windshield as Gerry flips through a catalogue of spy equipment, infrared sunglasses, ashtray tape-recorders, microphones moulded into sun visors. Beside her, Henry presses binoculars to his face.

"These are cool." She holds up a page of men's dress shoes outfitted with cameras.

Henry snorts. "Prohibitively expensive is what they are. Nothing but junk in there."

His disapproval catches her off guard. She blinks at the catalogue pages. Despite their recent time together, he is difficult to please, erratic in his tastes and opinions. His seesaw moods leave her uncertain of when to argue, when to agree. She shoves the catalogue under her seat.

She'd always known the stiff, inflectionless anchor on the cut-rate local station as her father's father. For years, she associated the broadcaster's cheap set, a cityscape silhouette dotted with skyscraper lights, with her father's new life. The idea of contacting her grandfather took root in the hot, sticky boredom of summer holidays. She could always hang up on the old man, claim it a prank. The station receptionist connected her before she could finish saying his name. Henry answered on the second ring, and after she explained who she was, shouted, "Yes!" as if he'd been expecting her call. That same afternoon, he toured her around the newsroom, flip-flops slapping out her steps, held her shoulders and introduced her as "the granddaughter" while she craned to examine his face, tried to peel back the decades to see how her father might look.

Henry shifts in his seat. "You haven't mentioned your group in a while."

"It's not a group, it's just a few people."

"How do I know it isn't some FLQ or Symbionese Liberation Army?" The teasing in his voice makes her smile. "I'm pretty sure your dad wouldn't approve."

She welcomes her father's disapproval, imagines most dads disapprove of daughters with ideas. It thrills her to think of her photograph on the evening news, her small gesture marking a fulcrum in history. She imagines the replacement wife begging him to stay as he rushes to catch a flight to Vancouver.

"What if there's a hostage situation? I hate to break it to you, but you're no Patty Hearst. Police would as soon shoot you as negotiate your release."

Henry's words turn her reverie inside out: policemen chuckling as they fondle their warm guns, poke at her bullet-ridden body. She shivers.

"Door." Henry tosses the binoculars into the backseat and slouches down. Gerry ducks. On the stoop, knotted into a tan raincoat, Henry's third wife opens an umbrella. She strides down the path to the sidewalk, chin at a regal angle, folds into her grey Honda Civic, and drives away. Henry struggles with the gearshift, grips the steering wheel to follow. Fat drops of rain splatter the windshield.

When they first met, Henry told Gerry he had only one thing to offer: provenance, a word he explained as a sense of her rightful place in the Cross line. Her grandmother, Henry's first wife, Geraldine, had worked as a grade school teacher before marrying him. Petite and shrewd, a woman whose hobby was balancing their chequebook. Weakened by the shame of divorce, a phrase Henry muttered with a shake of his head, she died two years before Gerry was born. Gloria, a big-boned, opinionated painter, served as the second Mrs. Cross. Henry brightened with his descriptions of her walking around nude and enjoying a shot of vodka for breakfast, then practically shouted that she had moved to Fiji to live off her hefty alimony. Then there was Helen. The final descendant of a good family, she still lived in the house she and Henry once shared. She powders her face every morning, chooses her outfits the night before. She volunteers as a fundraiser and donates Henry's monthly cheques to charity. The polished, well-postured woman Gerry has admired only through a windshield.

They round a wide left onto King Edward. Gerry grips the plastic handle above the door, braces herself against the car's sway. Her seatbelt squeezes like a metal bar, flinty pain in her ribs and back. "Where do you think she's going?" The words hang pinched and dry in front of her lips.

Henry knocks the wipers on at a frantic pace, fiddles with the defogger. He yanks a wrinkled handkerchief from his pocket and rubs an arc in the steamy glass. A car honks as he changes lanes without signalling. "Job would be good. Boyfriend would be better." He cranes his neck to see around a minivan. The steering wanders with his gaze.

"Henry." She tries to correct him.

He jerks the wheel.

Traffic slows for a red light and Henry tries to hang back, but the lanes on either side have filled and they glide to a stop behind the Civic, Mrs. Cross's eyes framed in the rectangle of her rear-view. Henry lowers his head. "Shit."

The Civic's door swings open. Mrs. Cross emerges, umbrella in hand. Despite the rain, she leaves her door flung wide, strides past blinking taillights, through puffs of exhaust.

"Shit, shit, shit, shit." Henry cranks the volume on the radio. The cabin swells with a deafening overture.

Mrs. Cross's face looms in the streaky driver-side window, her silver pageboy, powdery skin, and mauve lipstick caught in abstract. She shouts, lips curled, teeth bare, arms flapping. Gerry can hear a few *damn*s and *fuck*s, but everything else gurgles beneath the music. Henry keeps his hand on the gearshift, stares straight ahead.

The light turns green. Cars creep past, slow for the spectacle. From behind, a mob of horns. Mrs. Cross steps away from the car, glances around as if alarmed by her surroundings. Gerry feels the urge to rescue her, to leap out and round the car, pull open a door, and gather the woman in.

Mrs. Cross lets loose with her umbrella. Both hands on the grip, she beats furiously at Henry's window, wet fabric glomming to glass. Gerry rears in her seat. Henry flinches, as if taking the blows himself. With one last single-handed *thwap*, Mrs. Cross stalks back to her car, peels away.

Henry reaches forward to turn down the music, rubs his hands on the steering wheel. Gerry struggles against a quake of nervous laughter. She coughs instead, spasms that splinter her insides.

The honking dies off. In front of them, traffic seams together like a zipper. Drivers glare as they pass. Henry flips the bird to someone beyond Gerry's window. "Family court has given me a date."

She nods, her voice coming back. "That's good." He often spoke about his "day in court," but she assumed it was an expression, an imaginary reckoning, like St. Peter at the gates of heaven.

"Tuesday next. A week today. Pre-hearing mediation in front of Judge Wilson Fennimore." Henry pauses as if he might ask her along, but then pinches his thumb and finger at the bridge of his nose. "That rumour I told you? Co-anchor?" He closes his eyes. "Not a rumour."

Her mind hurries from the courtroom to the newsroom. "It's not true?"

"No, it is. It is true. God, would it kill you to listen for once?"

She smiles to mask the sting of his words but feels her mouth fall lopsided, stares at the dash to keep her eyes dry.

"I'm sorry." He mumbles into his palm. "I'm an asshole. I'm sorry."

Her fingers play with the seatbelt buckle. The buckle pops open and the strap drags across her, eases the pressure in her chest. She sits for a while, tries to get comfortable, but misses the strap's cinching hold. She tugs the belt and pushes the tab until the buckle snaps tight. Outside, the rain has stopped. Toward the west, clouds thin, leave a trail of blue sky. She feels Henry watching her, his heavy gaze an apology. She stares ahead until he turns away.

"Looks like it might be a nice day after all. What I wouldn't give to be you, gliding around on my bike, not a care in the world."

Saliva pools under her tongue, her throat aches. She feels flushed and feverish, wonders if she might have caught a chill walking home. "Bike's gone."

Henry rubs at his eyes, then settles his hands in his lap, blinks. "Since when?"

She points to her face.

"I see." He squints at the windshield, takes a deep breath and puffs out his cheeks, blows a long, deflated sigh. "Well." His hands clap together. When he turns to her, he's smiling.

5

BY THE TIME GERRY COASTS UP Megan's walk, the
shock of Henry's extravagance has settled like sweetness in her mouth. She locks the bike to the back stairs
and admires its silver paint. The bright white handlebar tape
distracts her as she works out her story. She takes the steps
slowly, waits on the back porch to hear what they talk about
without her.

"–that it doesn't sound precise."

Though she hears Megan's voice, Gerry can only see three
of them at the table. Ian sits with his back to the door. Andri
shakes his head, scribbles on a piece of paper as he talks. "You
want precise? Take up archery."

"What about bigger, stronger?" Megan crosses to the table,
pulls out a chair, and sits on it backward.

"We said smoke and shattered glass." Andri rubs the fabric
dome of Michelle's belly. "Not a body count."

When Megan pauses, Gerry wonders if she's thinking of
Clem's homeless man. "What I'm saying is if we've got two
weeks, why not try to make it better?"

Andri nods. "Okay. Room for improvement. Technically, we
have eleven days, but, okay."

Ian props his boots on the counter as Gerry walks in. He sees her first, straightens in his seat. "What the fuck happened to you?" He sounds winded, empty.

She walks to the fridge and reaches inside for a can of beer. "I got hit by a car." She shrugs, cracks the top, and sucks the foam off the tab, fizz bitter on her tongue.

After barely a glance at her, Andri goes back to his doodling. "I hope the driver didn't report it. To. The. Cops."

Megan rises from her chair and circles Gerry. Her hands tilt Gerry's head, lift her elbow, gather her hair to see the back of her neck. Gerry smiles, stares at the linoleum's orange curlicues, self-conscious with the scrutiny. "I didn't get the licence plate. It was too dark. It was just like, *bam*, and he was gone."

Megan steps back. "This happened last night?"

"Did you hear me?" Andri asks.

Gerry milks the details as she sips her beer: amber haze of streetlights, a green sedan making a faulty left turn, a swerve, the clip, an endless somersault. No cops, she assures Andri. By the end of the story, a beer buzz flickers behind her eyes. The room is silent. Megan grabs the wooden napkin holder from the counter and hurls it at Ian. The holder bounces off the side of his head and clatters to the floor, a trail of paper napkins flopping like dead birds. "I told you to drive her home!"

"Jesus!" Ian touches his head. Gerry holds her breath.

Megan picks up a glass mug, draws back.

"That's enough." The sharpness of Michelle's voice startles Gerry.

Andri doesn't look up from his paper but bobs his head in a fervent nod. "Yes, it is."

Megan drops the mug into the sink, where it thumps, then

rolls. Gerry raises her chin, tries to show off her bruises, but no one is watching.

"Come on." Megan nods toward the bathroom. Gerry keeps her gaze on Ian. He winces as he touches the side of his head. For a second, he resembles his younger self: flitting eyes, a wounded half-grimace, stains of flushed skin that make him look either freshly slapped or on the verge of crying.

Before she can turn away, he catches her stare, rubs his nose with his middle finger, a private fuck you.

The bathroom is a cramped box of tiny pink tiles. Megan plants Gerry on the closed toilet seat. She fingers the matted plush of the toilet seat cover while Megan pulls bottles out of the medicine cabinet.

"Shirt off."

Gerry twists the edge of her T-shirt, lets it curl and uncurl. She thinks of the paper-thin cups of her elastic bra, nothing like the moulded foam contraptions she's seen strewn in Megan's bedroom.

Megan's hand overflows with cotton balls. "It's nothing I don't have."

Thinking of what Megan does have only makes it worse. Gerry gets the shirt and bra over her head with one hard yank. Her muscles tremor with cold, strands of hair tickle across her shoulders. She bunches the clothes in a fist, shields her small breasts with her forearms.

"Oh, for fuck's sake." Megan says it gently as she reaches down to lift Gerry's elbow. She skims the inky patches across Gerry's side. Her touch is warm and smooth, and Gerry wishes there was space enough in the bathroom to lie down and close her eyes.

Megan starts with Gerry's face, swabs raw scabs with a pungent liquid that stings. She cuts tiny strips of tape to close the dried split above Gerry's eyebrow, traces Gerry's swollen cheek with the pad of her thumb. Gerry jolts, the pressure like a knife in her eye.

"That definitely needs ice." Megan's body sways, knees hard against the inside of Gerry's thighs. Her stomach brushes Gerry's face as she bends to a cut behind Gerry's ear, her breasts weighty beneath the navy-and-white stripes of her top. Gerry imagines touching them, feeling the soft nubs of Megan's nipples. Gerry own breasts cling slack and purposeless, half-filled water balloons. As Megan leans back, Gerry reaches to touch the line of studs that curve up and around Megan's right ear, the silver cuff that bands the top. "Did these hurt?"

"Not really." Megan rubs a pungent ointment into each of Gerry's bruises.

Gerry's eyes tear up.

"Stinging?"

She lies, "It's the smell," looks around the room to keep her mind off the pain. On the far corner of the bathtub, a metal razor sits propped against canister of shaving cream. "Is that for your legs?"

Megan looks over her shoulder. "No, that's Clem's. It's easier to shave him while he's in the tub."

Gerry pushes away thoughts of Clem naked, a plucked bird, a shrivelled nest. Electric hair clippers dangle from the hand towel loop beside the sink. A cord trails up to the light bulb above the medicine cabinet where it plugs into a socket she has to crane her neck to see. "You cut his hair too?"

"My hair." Megan crouches in front of Gerry, reaches her arm around to massage ointment into Gerry's lower back. Gerry frees a hand from the tangle of her shirt, rubs her palm over Megan's shorn head. The texture is soft, just as Gerry had hoped. "Maybe you could do mine."

"It doesn't grow back overnight." Megan grips the sink to hoist herself up.

While Megan washes her hands, Gerry covers her nose and mouth with her fingers, breathes the sour apple smell of Megan's scalp.

"You'd look good with an undercut."

The new wave girls at school had undercuts, tucked their teased black hair behind their ears to show off shaved temples. "I'd want it all off." Gerry shakes her head forward, gathers her hair to examine the dry, wavy strands, winds them around her finger, marvels at how artificial and wiglike they feel.

"It suits you. It's pretty."

"I don't want to be pretty."

Megan smiles. "Boys won't like it."

The only boys Gerry knows are at school, their scrawled notes shoved into her locker, illegible except for *tits* and *cunt*, anonymous, grabbing hands in the hallway, pocket bulges during square dance lessons in gym class. She shrugs. "Who cares."

Megan lifts the clippers from the towel loop, tosses them. They land heavy and cold in Gerry's hands. She pushes the power switch and the clippers clack to life with a metallic purr. The machine buzzes in her fingers, numbs her, itches into her arm. She holds her breath and raises the clippers to her forehead.

"Wait!" Megan shouts, her face wide with laughter. She shakes her head and holds out her hands. "That's not how you want to do it."

Gerry follows Megan's instructions, leaves her jeans in a heap on the floor, climbs into the empty bathtub, skin turning to gooseflesh against the icy enamel. Megan combs out Gerry's hair, has her hold it in a mound above her head.

The sound is a million angry insects chewing through straw. The vibration shimmies through her, ignites short, fiery glints of pain in her face. She can't keep from grinning. Megan pulls away, holds up a hand mirror: a dark, velvety strip over Gerry's right ear. Gerry touches it and feels heat rise from her scalp. She shakes her hair and watches the strip disappear, hands back the mirror. "All of it."

"You're sure now?"

Gerry nods. As the clippers continue, Gerry studies the skin on the underside of Megan's arms, thin and delicate enough to allows wisps of veins to show through. Gerry's body warms the bathtub, and she no longer feels the need to cover herself. "Why do you like Ian?"

"Why do you like Andri?"

Gerry bows her head to keep from blushing. "That's not the same."

"He's more than twice your age and about to be a father, but other than that, you'd make a great couple."

"Shut up."

The clippers lift away. "You don't think Ian's cute? Not even a little bit?"

"Gross." Gerry plucks a tail of hair from bottom of the bathtub, winds it tightly around her fingertip, waits for the thrum of blood.

Megan shrugs. "He was always so nice to me when he delivered Clem's medicine."

"He got fired from that job."

"It's not his fault the pharmacist retired."

"Mr. McKenzie? Who got shot in the leg?" Gerry shakes her head. "Ian got fired way before that. Is that what he told you?"

The clippers graze the bottom of Gerry's neck. "He's uncomplicated. He's kind. I don't know, I felt close to him the first time we met, like family."

"Like brother and sister?" Gerry tries not to think of Megan having sex with Ian. The idea, matched with her own nakedness, starts a low, syrupy heat inside her. She wraps her arms around her knees.

"I mean, it's just easy being together. He doesn't expect anything from me."

"But why not have Andri as your boyfriend?"

Megan smiles as she guides Gerry to turn her chin and starts on the other side. "Andri's a good person, but he's old-fashioned. He expects a woman to do what he tells her. You should set your sights higher than that."

Gerry scratches at a crust of dried blood on her knee, picks to lift the edge, glimpse the rawness underneath. She wonders about letting Lark's name slip, showing Megan she knows more than she gets credit for. The urge ripples, then recedes. "Remember the first time we met?"

"Sure."

On the sidewalk in front of Ian's house, the late August sun burning a hole through her. Megan was solid and tall, not the wispy type Ian usually went for. Her voice didn't trill up. The curves of her body under a loose summer dress. Gerry watched her lips move but couldn't hear her words. When Megan said goodbye, she took up Gerry's clammy hand and held it.

Behind her, Ian stood sun-bleached, fading. "I thought you were pretty."

Megan smiles but says nothing. Her silence warms a blush through Gerry.

"Don't squirm."

"What happened with that guy last night?"

Megan rolls her eyes. "Total waste of time. But he says he knows someone."

"Did you still have sex with him?"

The clippers clack off. Gerry scoops a fistful of dead hair, rolls it between her fingers, waits, then turns, curious why Megan has stopped. Megan's face is still but tense, as if she's trying to solve a math problem in her head. "What makes you think I had sex with him?"

Gerry worries she's gotten it wrong, that she's about to look stupid. "Isn't that how you're getting the door code?" She says it quietly, hopes tentativeness will make it sound less like an insult.

The clippers clack back on. Gerry waits for Megan to speak, tries to distract herself by braiding loose strands of hair.

"If we had money, it would be different," Megan says finally. Before Gerry can nod to show her understanding, Megan tells her to hold still.

"So. I guess Ian didn't listen to you about driving me home, huh?"

"Did you listen?"

"Are you still gonna let him do the drop?"

"Don't fidget."

"Because I could do the drop." Gerry waits. The clippers' echo a drone against the tiles, insects in a Plexiglas box. "I'm the one who marked and timed the route. He was too stoned." Gerry wants to tell it in detail, how she came up with the cut-through from Robson to Alberni, how Ian fake tap-danced down the alley, shouted, "Let me in!" at the back door of the revenue building, and fell over laughing, but Megan doesn't seem interested. She turns Gerry's head, feels for uneven patches, her hands rough and impatient. She flicks the clippers off, then stands, throws Gerry a thin orange towel. "You're done."

The towel makes Gerry feel suddenly exposed. She drapes it over her chest, wipes the hair off her body as she stands, hurries into her shirt and jeans. She catches herself in the bathroom mirror. Despite the distortions of bruising and swelling, she can see the contours of her bones, the almond shape of her eyes. She would never call herself beautiful, but seeing herself this way slows her breath. Megan stands with her arms crossed. "Well?"

Gerry stuffs her hands in her pockets, tries to push down her welling confidence. "I'm good at numbers."

With her fingertips, Megan brushes errant hairs from Gerry's face, the bathroom light reflected in the feathery grey of her eyes.

"I know the route." Gerry whispers, their secret in the closed, airless room.

Megan turns back to the sink. The rush of water thins her voice. "Maybe you shouldn't come around here so much."

In the kitchen, Michelle is on her feet, clapping. "I told you, I told you!"

Gerry bows her head as her mouth pulls in untamable directions.

Andri looks up from his newspaper. "A gesture. This is more like it."

Ian leans his elbows on the kitchen table, fiddles with a toadstool saltshaker, jimmies the cap off and on, refuses to meet her gaze.

They cram together on the living-room sofa, Clem's chair angled to the side, so they can all see the TV. Megan digs through her stack of Betamax, plastic tapes cracking against one another. Ian lights a torpedo-shaped joint. A dishtowel of ice against her face, Gerry watches him, her tongue heavy with anticipation. Michelle takes short sips, then waves her hand in front of her face, "I really shouldn't." Megan draws a long drag for herself, then a second for Clem, blows the smoke into his mouth. Andri holds it like a cigarette. Gerry takes as many hits as she can before Ian pinches the joint from her fingers. She closes her eyes, lets the high untangle the pain in her face. Something jabs into her leg. She opens her eyes to a rectangle of newspaper, corners folded sharp. Andri nods for her to look. A photograph of blurred dashes across a grainy field of white. "They take that picture with satellites. Soviet warships. Look how many."

"They're like ants."

"It's coming. Didn't I tell you?"

"Do you think they'll really do it?"

"What will stop them? People? Families?"

Gerry nods.

Andri snickers. "You think like the sheep. Where I come from, the soil is the best in the world for growing and everyone knows why. Mass graves. Blood feeds the soil. Germans took a third of our people, okay, that's war. Then our own mother nation turns against us, does far worse." Gerry tries to imagine

Andri's home, endless crops, women with scarves tied under their chins. Andri waves at Clem. "He fought for families losing their land. Look what your government did to him."

Gerry wills Clem to turn his head, acknowledge Andri's words, but Clem stares at the darkened TV.

"Last month, my aunts write me to say something is wrong with the reactor across the border. The men who work there are nervous. I write back, Leave, right away, the government will do nothing to protect you. But what differences does it make. If you believe this." He taps the page. "Missiles will get them first."

Gerry traces the tiny vessels. "What do you think it will it feel like?"

He pinches his fingers together, then bursts them apart. "*Pfft.* Nothing. Life is nothing. Death is nothing."

Michelle leans in, her body contorted so that her belly juts at an odd angle under her dress. "Don't listen to him, he always gets like this when he's stoned."

"What about the baby?" The dishtowel leaks as Gerry adjusts it, sends a cold dribble down her neck.

Andri shrugs. "You will be ash. The baby will be ash. I will be ash."

"Yeah, a regular asshole." Michelle smiles. "He doesn't really believe that."

"Don't tell me what I believe!" Andri's voice hushes the room, spurs Megan and Ian to glance up from their conversation. Michelle stares at him. Gerry notices that the silver of his sideburns has slipped down into his beard.

He turns away from Michelle, points to the newspaper. "This is proof, undeniable." Behind him, Michelle stares into space. When Megan reaches up to pat her knee, Michelle shakes her head, lowers her chin, and wipes at her eyes. The bones of Gerry's head ache with cold. "I can keep it?"

"Of course. A memento." Andri leans toward her and lifts the ice-pack from her face, scowls as he examines her. She turns her chin to give him a better look. He smiles, cups her hand with his, presses the freezing pack back to her skin. "Now, who do you look like?" He raises two fists to his face, takes cartoonish punches at the air. "Rocky."

She grins into the dishtowel, leans against him to feel the pressure of his arm through his shirt.

They watch tapes of protests, die-ins in London, blockades in Austria, human chains in Germany. Gerry tries to imagine how their own protest will look on tape, tens of thousands marching for peace, a calculated burst, panic in the streets. The news will get it all wrong, call Andri a spy, because of where he comes from, a place Gerry thinks of as Beautiful Russia, even though he insists it isn't Russia at all. Megan will be a homegrown terror-ist, expertly trained by her father. Michelle and her unborn child will be the hardest to understand. Ian will be easy, a dropout and pot-head, ruined by drug-dealing hippie parents. And what will they say about her? Maybe that she came from a broken home, a phrase she hopes will lodge itself inside her father.

Andri stops the tape during the bust-up of Greenham Common, points to background, tents in flames. "That's what they should have done in the first place. Three years of peaceful protest, for what? Breastfeeding."

Michelle slaps him in the chest. He grabs her hand in his fist and kisses it, pulls her against him and whispers into her hair until her face softens. Gerry tries not to giggle, shifts away from them on the sofa, feeling too much like she's sharing their bed.

"That's why what we're doing is so perfect. The city expects another march that everyone can ignore." Megan shakes her head. "Peaceful protest is an oxymoron." Her earnest tone only makes the words seem funnier. A chuckle burbles in Gerry's throat.

"People block one base while missiles get shipped in and out of two others just down the road."

Soundless laughter peels out of her in thin, hissy strips.

"Grandmothers chain themselves to fences."

The dishtowel shifts under Gerry's hand and she keels into Michelle's lap, body racked in guffaws. A crazed bray erupts from her and she writhes in hysterics. Slowly, her energy drains, detonations settle into long sighs. She blinks through tear-filled eyes at the four of them staring down at her.

"Jesus Christ," Megan says. "Take her home."

6

THE DAMP AIR SOBERS HER, starts her teeth chattering. Ian says nothing as he loads her bike into the trunk. He drives with the windows down, blares side one of *The Wall*, helicopters and machine-gun fire. The passenger seat stiff, Gerry shifts to buffer herself from the wind, rubs at her aching jaw, counts passing streetlights. Her mind struggles to find something to say. The pot makes her nostalgic. She creeps back to the past, the cold beneath her legs turning to the chilly floor of her elementary school gym where she sits cross-legged, arranged with her class along a painted white line. At the end of each row, teachers perch like sentries on wooden chairs. They gather to watch a movie, the principal snaking the film through the open guts of the projector, volume so loud, the room's echo doubles the warbling soundtrack, so that all that reaches her is nonsense. On screen, boys drag bare feet across parched prairie, swing gophers by their tails. Women in bonnets dig at the hard ground, hail pummels wheat, snow falls. Gerry doesn't care about the movie, loses herself instead in the gym's darkness and the sensation in her back, an awareness of the older kids rows behind, Ian's class lined up against the climbing equipment. Without checking, she knows his arms are folded and he is half-sitting on one of the climbing rungs. He has found her in the crowd, traced her outline, and if she glances over her shoulder, he will nod.

When she looks at him now, his drawn, bony profile, she sees how changed he is, their friendship left behind in backyards, school fields, his parents' basement. Even the effort of talking is too much, like having to whisper across a great distance. For the first time, she thinks she will not know him for the rest of life. The truth carries an unexpected sadness.

"It's a Pinarello." She shouts it over the music, waits. "The bike."

"I saw." His usual manufactured disinterest.

"My mom will hate it." If she looks at him as a stranger, he's partway handsome, his dimpled chin, the pad of his bottom lip, the way his eyes turn down at the outer edges. "My granddad bought it for me."

"He's not your granddad."

"He's my father's father. That makes him my granddad."

"Your dad hardly even knew him. It's not the same thing."

He makes anger so easy. The heavy bass line of "Young Lust" thumps through the door, whiny guitar riffs and dirty girls. She keeps her face turned away.

They pull up to the house. Her mom stands at the living-room window, curtains behind her like a veil. A tiredness settles over Gerry. She had hoped for one more night, a chance for her face to heal.

Ian turns off the music, flips down the sun visor, then flicks it back up. "So I need to ask." He reaches for her bandaged wrist, holds it loosely between his thumb and middle finger, as if measuring her. The surprise of his touch makes it hard to breathe. She remembers imagining him as her husband, a silly, sexless fairytale that centred around her standing at a clothesline on a sunny day, hanging bright white bedsheets.

"When you were in the bathroom with Megan?" His index finger traces the veins that crawl up into her palm.

"Yeah?"

"What did you say about Lark?"

She pulls her hand away. "I need my bike."

Outside the car, her sneakers skid on muddy grass. She tugs her sleeves into fists, waits by the trunk.

He takes his time, door creaking open, steps slow. "I won't be mad." He unlocks the trunk. "I just want to know, so I can, you know, take care of it."

The pain of hoisting the bike onto her shoulder forces her to grit her teeth, tense her muscles until she feels the wheels touch ground.

"So, you didn't say anything?"

"Do you think she likes doing it with those men?" With the butt of her hand, she punches the words into his chest. "Do you?"

He grabs her arm. "Cool it. Your mom's right there."

She twists from his grip. "Why is it impossible for you to be a good person?" She hefts the bike over the curb and onto the sidewalk. Wheels click out the seconds until he slams the car door.

Gerry sinks between the couch cushions as her mom leans in to dab at her forehead and face. Wet cotton pads, bubbly and cold, leave a sour smell as they lift from her skin. The scab over Gerry's eye splits under her mom's pressure and the raw tissue beneath burns. "Ow!" Gerry jerks away.

"Well, what do you expect?" Her mom sits back on her heels,

rolls the stained cotton in her hands, and shakes her head. "Why would you hide this from me?"

Lying to her mom isn't difficult. Like racing her up a gravel hill, Gerry just needs to keep her eyes ahead. "I didn't. I thought he told you."

Randy's plaid-shirted body leans in the archway.

Her mom gives him an exasperated look. "You knew?"

He shifts his weight, rubs the back of his head. His jacket and the front door are within arm's reach and Gerry is sure he's thinking of escape. Gerry offers him an exit. "Why is he still here, anyway?"

"Gerry." Her mom points a warning finger.

"He's always here, on the couch, in the kitchen, in your room. I never get to see just you." She musters a glare in his direction. "He told me to die in my sleep."

"Christ, last night, I mean—" Randy squints, then presses his forehead against the arch.

Her mom's face is placid, immovable. "Do you think we should take her to the hospital?"

He shrugs. "Whatever you think."

"You know, he got fired and didn't even tell you." Gerry waits for him to bolt.

His hands fiddle with his pockets. "That die in your sleep thing – she's making it sound—"

"You lost your job?"

"No." He chews his lips, the edges of his beard knitting together. "Yes. But it's temporary."

"I thought Bill said six months and you'd be permanent." Her mom pushes against the couch to stand, folds her arms across her chest.

"He did. But the union reps started making—"

"Well, for crying out loud, Randy, stand your ground."

"How? How should I do that?"

"I don't know. Keep showing up."

"So I can watch someone else do my job?"

"You can't just loaf around here."

"Oh, really? Because that was my plan."

Gerry picks at a loose tag of skin on her thumb, tries to catch it in her teeth. "I was in a fight with some girls. In case anyone even cares."

Her mom turns, her expression a perfect parental cocktail of guilt, worry, and exhaustion. Gerry hopes for a moment of softness, but instead her mom advances like an overwound toy. "Was it some gang? Did they attack you? I'm calling the police."

"There was no gang. It was just something stupid about someone's boyfriend. And then it was over. No big deal." As she says the words, she wills her lie to falter, for her mom to read her bruises and guess the truth.

"No big deal? Look at your hair!"

Gerry snorts at her mom's predictable shallowness. "I did that."

"Priceless," Randy mumbles.

"Fuck you."

"Geraldine!" Her mom steps in close, reaches for Gerry's arms.

Gerry slackens, opens herself to her mom's touch.

"I mean it. This isn't some joke for your own personal amusement." Her mom's thumbnails graze her skin. "Why would you cut off your hair?"

"I'm totally laughing, can't you tell? These bruises are hilarious. That hurts, by the way."

"Answer me."

"I said it hurts." Gerry hauls herself back into the couch. Her mom's nails catch and scrape as she struggles to grip then release Gerry's arms.

Randy takes a step into the room. "Okay, maybe we should—"

"You can go." Her mom doesn't look at him.

His mouth opens as if to speak, then his face scrunches, eyes closed in thought. Finally, he shakes his head, grabs his jacket, balls it in his fist like a shopping bag. He nods at Gerry. "Are you okay?"

She blinks at him. "What do you care?"

He slams the front door. Her mom stares at the empty foyer, hands on her hips.

Gerry traces the red lines on her arms, scored skin like tiny shreds of eraser. "So, which do you think you suck at more, being a mom or being a girlfriend?"

The slap comes like a flat, hot shock. Gerry draws a breath through her teeth, tries to smile against the pain as tears spring up behind her eyes.

"Go to your room."

"Finally." She pushes off the sofa.

"And you can send that bike back where it came from."

Gerry pounds the stairs. Kicks her bedroom door closed, then kicks it again and again, until she's too dizzy to stand.

TO THE BOY, THE WOMAN IN THE SUNDRESS is no longer a woman but a girl, crying, everything between them levelled by disaster. Exhausted, they huddle on a patch of grass. Sirens wail. The noise punctures every thought. He rocks her, strokes her hair, surprised to find himself capable of offering comfort. She clings. Her fingernails dig into his arm. I'm so scared. She sobs. Even as he understands this fear, he feels above it, detached.

He presses his face into her perfumed hair. The boy has long been terrified of exactly this moment, has imagined its ghastly unfolding, and now, while his rational mind overflows, a small, secret part of him feels absolved.

It is not the present, he wants to tell her, but the future, that should frighten her. The coming illness: strangers spewing liquidous insides, loose teeth giving way to bloody gums that gnash at mouldy breadcrusts, rotten crabapples and, later, insects, dog flesh. The almost-dead pleading for food, desperate and crazed, burnt skin torn away in sheets, the blackened pits of open wounds. The tyranny of the well and capacitated. The marvel that many who survive will be without intelligence or compassion. Eternal night, invisible sun, perpetual cold. Thirst so maddening it will make people cry and foam, hysterical with the need to quench the body's heat. Girls who continue to have babies, who parade inflated bodies on swollen, blistered feet, beg for extra food and water. Those who miscarry left to bury puddles of bloody tissue in hidden corners. While those who make it to term birth mutations, babies without eyes, without arms, legs fused in flapping primordial tails. Mothers who cling to mutant children, nurse them from empty breasts, swaddle them in blankets long after they are dead.

The girl wipes her face but doesn't lift her head from his chest. Across the street, two boys stand on the front lawn of a house, stare. To them, the boy and girl must look like lovers. On the corner, a deserted gas station, the doors to the store open wide. In the middle of the road, a yellow dog cowers under an abandoned truck.

They should continue north, the boy thinks, try for the bridge. When the girl is ready, he will help her stand. Eventually, they will find people with instructions, people who have been trained for exactly this.

The boy thinks of his mother. Knows the only thing she will do is look for him. He imagines her struggling south against the fleeing crowds, against warnings, back toward their house, into dust, into fire.

I don't know your name, the girl whispers.

And suddenly, the boy is shaking. His body turns in on itself. He presses his open mouth against her scalp, squeezes his eyes shut.

7

SIDE TWO OF *Power, Corruption & Lies* skips to a close. The pain, dulled overnight by Andri's pot, returns in waves, a queasy, rolling ache through Gerry's body. She starts the record over, eases herself to the floor, and feels under her bed. Her fingers close around the box, then her book. The box is hand-carved California redwood, her father's last gift, a birthday she remembers only as a photograph, a paper crown slumped over her face as she bends to toward a fiery cake. Inside the box, her implements, Rizlas, tweezers, sewing scissors, a stainless steel lighter found at a bus stop, a dwindling baggie of faded weed. She draws a deep breath. Saliva pools at the tang of Ian's mom's hydroponic pot. Gerry pinches the scraps of buds into tiny pieces, rolls an anorexic joint. The smoke curls inside her, plummets to her belly as she opens the book, manoeuvres the small scissors around Andri's article, pastes it onto a blank page. She stares at the satellite photo, wonders if it marks a beginning. Older clippings have started to yellow and tear at the edges. Computer Initiates DEFCON 5, Olympic Boycott Suggests War, Defense to Test Nerve Gas, Strontium 90 in Bones of Newborns. Each article triggers a low drone of panic. Time stutters ahead and she blinks, unsure of how long she's been flipping pages. She closes the cover, only to pry it open again for one more glimpse of warship survey routes, armament statistics, maps of the Persian Gulf. She pushes the book back under the bed.

The carpet tickles under her feet, a sea of loose threads. She stops outside her father's study, tries the door. Her mom has it locked again. In her bedroom, she finds a ballpoint pen, twists it apart. She jabs the refill into the round doorknob until she hears the lock ping.

The air in her father's study hangs poached and warm. As she draws back the curtains, particles tumble a sandstorm in the column of light. Gerry loves the smallness of the room, how it enshrouds her, three walls of teak bookcases stacked with her father's college textbooks, the *Encyclopaedia Britannica*, paperback spy novels, and old issues of *National Geographic*. The magazines impressed her with their baby animals until a story on gorillas eating their young gave her nightmares. The textbooks confounded her with coded graphs and diagrams, jackets dusty and brittle with age. She flattens her palms on her father's desk, the varnish rough in patches, dust like fabric under her hands. She works her fingers past the lip of the drawer, wiggles it, the stiff, squeaky protest of wood on wood. The drawer opens enough for her to feel inside, roll pencils in their grooves, their ends flakey and chewed. She rubs a gritty eraser with her thumb. As always, there is the temptation to free these objects, lift them out and see them clearly, but she resists, preserves the drawer's cramped mystery, its private smell of must and sour wood.

She climbs over the desk to the sill. The sun presses a white circle through the overcast. She thumps the window's handle with her palm. The hinges creak as the window swings open over the stretch of dirt below. Inside the massive rectangular pit, a grimy, unsecured aqua liner, edges drooping towards the centre. Flushed by rain, the shallow end looks reasonably clean, but the deep end, directly beneath the window, has filled with a sewerlike slosh of mud, water, and neighbourhood debris. It reminds her of the movie *Poltergeist*, people digging unwelcome holes. Her mom blames Expo 86, too many well-paying construction jobs elsewhere in the city. "A tragic tale of men and greener pastures," her mom says each time she looks out the back door, a yielding smile, her eyes weary and defeated.

A duck glides across the surface. Gerry considers the absurdity of a swimming pool in a city that gets ten months of rain each year. An attempt to mimeograph her father's life. Margarine, saccharine, generic cola, faking it was enough for her mom. "You can invite your school friends over for pool parties!" The woman grew ecstatic over clueless possibilities. Gerry wouldn't be caught dead in a bathing suit. Maybe if she could lace people's drinks with acid, line them up at the study window to see who could leap as far as the pool, who would splatter on the concrete patio, a life-sized re-enactment of a girlhood ritual, throwing Barbie and Skipper out the window, then pitching a reluctant Ken after them. Ken always arrived too late. A funeral under the hydrangea bush, a shattered Ken weeping. She relished his climactic breakdown, the coldness she felt as he blubbered alone.

A horn blares from the street. The duck paddles a lazy circle around a potato chip bag. Gerry pulls the window shut, closes the curtains, locks the door behind her. She crosses to her bedroom to wave to Henry but instead of his Audi finds a station wagon parked across the street. A man stands on the sidewalk. From the open door of a house, two children run toward him, bags and coats jiggling in their small arms. As the man bends to greet them, the children squeal. He gathers them up, swings them toward the sky.

That evening, the old-timers take up Megan's living room. To Gerry, they look younger than Clem, even with their worn faces and shaggy grey hair. Once a month, they sit with him in front of the TV, share a mickey of Lamb's, a couple of joints. Gerry spies from the hallway, analyzes the swells of their laughter for a hint of Clem's voice.

Their visit gives Megan a night off from Clem. She drinks beer from a glass, leaves dirty dishes piled in the sink. She climbs onto the kitchen counter to grab an old Ouija board from a high cupboard and begs Ian to play it with her. Gerry abandons the old-timers in favour of the game. Andri grumbles at the sight of the lacquered board printed with calligraphied letters and numbers, images of the sun and moon.

In a fake mystic voice that makes Gerry giggle, Megan calls upon spirits to answer her questions. Michelle gasps when the pointer begins to crawl. Megan asks for a message for Andri. "Eat my shit," the board replies. Then for Ian, "Ian fucks sheep." The girls laugh.

Gerry studies the glide of the pointer, the way it hovers over each letter only an instant before darting to the next, an agility that seems beyond human. Andri watches, eyes hard. Gerry wonders if his disapproval is genuine or part of the grumpiness he puts on.

Ian pushes the pointer to *GOODBYE*, then stands up. "You were totally moving it."

"I swear, I wasn't." Megan grins. "Come on, someone else."

Gerry wants to feel the shared sensation of their fingers on the same object. "I'll go."

"Don't blame me if it gives you nightmares." Ian leans against the fridge, chugs his beer, and crumples the can before opening the door for another.

From behind his newspaper, Andri grunts. "Those things aren't for playing with."

Michelle rolls her eyes, pats Gerry's hand to urge her on.

The pointer is smooth, cool polished wood. It wobbles side to side as Gerry rests her fingers.

"Ready?" Megan rocks the pointer so Gerry will be able to tell what it feels like if she cheats. Gerry does the same, aware that the slightest pressure on her side will register against Megan's fingers.

Megan closes her eyes, calls to the spirits in a sad child's voice. Gerry forces a laugh, though the voice frightens her a little.

The pointer sits inert, and Gerry begins to wonder if it might not have been Ian moving it, his accusation a clever bluff. The pointer tilts under her fingers, begins a slow drag across the board. She has to remind herself not to be afraid, not to pull her hands away. The pointer swings through a series of figure-eights, curving so quickly Gerry has to lean in to keep up. She watches Megan's arms and hands, her powdery pale skin for signs she's leading, pushing, but Megan sits slouched back, her body moving at the whim of the pointer, even lagging behind. The expression on her face is one of mild alarm. "Crazy or what?"

"Yeah." Gerry tries to feel the energy cycling between them, senses it just at the fringes, a warmth that begins at the crown of her head and sweeps in arcs through her arms, then joins in a rush down her centre, thickens between her legs. The pointer makes an abrupt turn, slashes the board again and again in the shape of an *X*. Gerry squeals.

Michelle tucks in close. "You better ask something before it freaks out."

Gerry can't think of anything. "What's my name?" The pointer glides through *G-E-R-Y,* and she feels her back turn cold.

Michelle leans down. "Will our baby be a boy or a girl?"

The pointers spells *B-O-Y* slowly, then swirls around to spell *G-I-R-L.* Andri snickers.

"Who's going to do the drop?" Gerry avoids Megan's gaze, hopes the board holds some sway.

The pointer doesn't answer right away, meanders between *YES* and *NO,* then slowly spells *I-A-N,* rising to the *YES* after each letter.

Ian knocks her shoulder with his hip. "Loser."

The question comes as a reflex, a habit of hitting back. "Does Ian have a girlfriend?" She feels him frozen in place behind her. The pointer travels a slow circle around the outside of the board. Megan stares at her as the pointer spells out *L-A-R-K.*

"What's a lark?" Michelle turns her body to examine the letters from a different angle.

Andri shakes his newspaper. "A bird. Something you do for fun."

Megan's eyes are calm and deep, her mouth a soft line. But the way she blinks gives her away, a flicker as she digs for strength. Gerry sees it then, the strain of knowing more than a person should, the effort behind the masterful control of her face, her body for a simple party trick.

The back door closes, and Gerry knows without turning that Ian has left.

"Fun and games?" Dennis, an old-timer with a habit of jangling keys and change in his pocket, lingers in the hallway. He catches Gerry looking at him and flinches. "Nice face." As he steps into the light, his stubbly, sagging jowls and tatty sweater vest come clear. His pocketed hand continues to burrow, a muffled, frantic shaking as if he's playing dice. Gerry tries not to stare, worried she's watching something sexual without knowing it. "We're putting him to bed."

Megan nods. "Can they do his pyjamas? Once he's asleep, I can't get him undressed."

"Hey, guys? Pyjamas, okay?" Dennis calls down the hallway. When he turns back, he tosses something onto the Ouija board. A used envelope, flap torn to reveal the coloured edges of fives, tens, and twenties, a thin stack of rumpled bills. "Not as much as we'd like this month. Karl's waiting on insurance from his accident."

Megan smiles. "It all helps."

The man's lips twitch. He rubs at the doorframe. His head tips side to side like a weighing scale. Gerry can tell by the blush under his stubble, his awkward stare, the way his teeth work at his lips, he would like to sleep with Megan. "Did my guy call you? The security camera thing?"

"He did. Yes. Thank you."

"Good, good. I want to ask you so bad, you know? What's cooking, what's the big gig." Dennis sighs.

Andri folds his newspaper, raises his eyebrows at Megan.

"You never lose the taste for it." Dennis shuffles. "But I'm this close" – he pinches the air – "full pension." He turns to Gerry as if she's asked a question. "School librarian. Almost twenty-five years. Can you believe it?" His free hand is yellowed with nicotine stains, dirtier than Gerry would imagine for a librarian. She shrugs her disinterest.

"If Clem hadn't kept my name out of it, I wouldn't be here. None of us would."

"It's true. It's much better to keep out of things." Andri says it to Dennis but stares at Megan.

"Yup. One in a lifetime, that's all you get. No one's lucky enough for twice." Dennis nods but doesn't leave his post. He points at Gerry. "You're not using this one, are you? Kids are nothing but trouble."

"Tell me about it." Ian's voice carries in with a damp gust. The back door bangs shut. Gerry senses him behind her, jumps as he rests his cold hand against her neck.

"No, I'm serious." Dennis talks as if she isn't in the room. "Don't tell her anything."

Ian's fingers drum against her skin, trace the divots of muscle and cartilage. He finds his spot and begins to squeeze. His party trick: just enough pressure to black her out, something she enjoyed once, strange reveries of circuses and running animals, the magic of waking on the floor. She reaches for his hand, tries to loosen it. They grab at each other, gouge and clench.

"Thanks for coming by, Dennis." Megan sounds tired.

Dennis lolls for a moment longer, then slips back to the living room. Michelle breaks out laughing. "What a creep."

Andri returns to his newspaper.

Megan drains her beer, folds the Ouija board, then carries it to the garbage can, crushes it down with her foot. She stalks out of the kitchen and slams her bedroom door.

"What happened?" Michelle asks Andri.

Ian wrenches his hand out of Gerry's grip, cuffs her ear before he follows Megan. The pain is sharp but pulses away quickly. She rubs her head, her face burning. The ringing lingers like a bell in dream.

8

"IS IT POSSIBLE YOU LOOK WORSE than last time?" Henry ducks to stare at her through the open passenger-side window. He himself isn't looking top form, the knot of his tie loose and askew, his trousers without their finlike crease.

"Anything's possible." Gerry leans down to give him a closer look.

"Should I drop you at the airport so you can put on your peach robe and hand out flowers?"

"Where were you yesterday?"

"Are you suggesting I could have prevented your radical makeover?"

"Take a picture, it lasts longer."

Henry smiles. "It suits you. Get in."

When they reach the house, there's an open spot where Mrs. Cross's Civic should be.

"We missed her." Gerry reclines her seat, wonders how long they'll have to wait.

Henry pats the steering wheel in a rhythm she can't follow. He snaps the buckle of his seatbelt. Before she can ask where he's going, he's closed the door behind him.

She struggles to sit up, get out of the car. Henry disappears down the path at the side of the house and she jogs to catch up.

On the back porch, Henry stoops in front of a window, feels his way around its frame. She waits at the top of the stairs. The porch is small but tidy, a floral-printed welcome mat, a freshly painted garbage corral. She hops onto the porch rail, knocks her heels against the shiny garbage cans to hear them rattle.

"Shh!" Henry turns, his face a scowl.

Chastised, she hunches, feet crossed, concentrates on remaining still. Henry feeds a credit card up through the sash of the window, slides it back and forth until the latch pops from its seat. He jiggles the window, raises it slowly, then waves Gerry through.

Kids at school bragged about B&Es all the time, but her worry is Henry, his job, how it might look for his divorce. She finds a drip trail in the porch rail's finish, picks at it with her fingernail. The paint comes away in a thin brown tear. "She's probably on her way home."

"Your father would be in there like a shot."

She shakes her head at the obvious manipulation. Henry rolls his eyes. "Just go. Make sure it's clear. If she drives up, I'll knock, shave-and-a-haircut." He taps the rhythm on the windowframe.

The opening is wide but shallow. She threads her right leg through. Her hip and chest throb as she flattens herself, ducks her head, legs stretched into splits before she huddles in the kitchen sink, hops carefully down. She slips off her sneakers and does a quick circuit of the main floor. The rooms smell like cold cream and roses. Back in the kitchen, she closes and locks the window, opens the door to let Henry in. His arms spread in a flourish. "Mi casa es su casa." He leaves her to wander.

In the living room, tufted diamond-shaped cushions balance

on points across the sofa, the coffee table candy dish brims with silver- and gold-wrapped sweets, even the Kleenex box is pretty, swathed in a crocheted cover. At the centre of the mantel, a single smoked-mirror picture frame, the photograph small, scalloped around the edges, stained an amber tint: a girlish Mrs. Cross in a wedding dress, arm linked with a handsome young man in a tall hat who is obviously not Henry.

Gerry lingers over the careful details of Mrs. Cross's life, frilly lace curtains, the tapered wooden feet of the coffee table cupped by polished castors. Matching horse miniatures trot across each of the end tables. The order of the room, the effort to maintain it, fills her with calm.

She finds Henry in the den, kneeled in front of a wooden filing cabinet, a paper grocery bag under his arm. "You never told me she was married before."

"Give me a hand with this."

While she holds open the bag, Henry plucks folders from the cabinet, stuffs them in. Files tip upside down, paper sloshes free. "So, who was her first husband?"

"Some bozo."

"Did you meet him?"

"He had the good sense to die in a war."

"What are you doing with all this stuff?"

"I'm going to read it."

"And then?"

"Burn it."

His answer skitters inside her. He forces one last file into the bulging bag, grips the desk's corner to hoist himself. His hands brush at his trousers. "How about some lunch?"

———

In the tidy living room, they watch the noon news. Henry stretches in his former recliner, a bowl of soup in his lap, plate to his chest as he chews his ham sandwich. Gerry has settled her bowl and plate on top of two placemats on the coffee table, laid a tea towel laid across the carpet in case of drips. She perches on the edge of the couch, hovers over her chicken noodle soup, careful to brush the crumbs from her face into the bowl. Henry watches her. "You're missing the point of the exercise. The stains, the debris," he points to his forehead, "that's the psychological warfare."

Gerry nods but can't bring herself to make a mess.

The newscast bears out Andri's prediction. Distorted film footage of Soviet warships gathering, what the Soviets call "routine relocation."

"Look at that face." Henry waves his sandwich at the newscaster. "So smooth, it's plastic. How can you trust a man with no lines in his face?"

She tries to block out Henry's ranting, listens to a recap of the lead story, an Iraqi MIG-23 shot down over Basra in an unprecedented offensive by Iranian forces. A measled map of the Gulf flashes as the plastic newscaster nods earnestly. Superpower intervention, now inevitable, is anticipated early in the week. The newscaster smiles as he segues into a story about banning thong bikinis.

"It's that bloody CNN's fault. Have you seen their anchors? Big hair, big teeth. It's like a herd of goddamn lions reading the news. Mark my words, the David Brinkleys of the world will soon be replaced with Christie Brinkleys, twenty-four-hour titties telling you about the latest Ayatollah. Goddamn, that Barbara Walters ruined it for everybody."

The thrum of warship engines.

"It's only a matter of time before they squeeze your favourite news anchor out of a job."

She hums in agreement as she chews, imagines the stealth progress of Soviet submarines, dark hulls that surround the city, crowd the harbour, break the surface like angry whales.

"Are you paying attention? I'm talking about something important here. A man's livelihood. Something about to go terribly wrong."

"Is this still about Barbara Walters?"

"Earning potential, pay grades, bonus schedules, profit-sharing. Those are a man's domain."

His explanation only confuses her more. "My mom has a job." The fact comes out of her like a question.

"Oh sure, mad money, trinkets and furs. But let me ask you this: who's paying for that in-ground swimming pool?"

Right away, she recognizes this as one of Henry's trick questions, the kind with an answer so convoluted, any guess she makes will leave her feeling foolish. She waits him out.

He throws up his hands. "Your father."

The mention of him stills her.

"I mean, what a waste. A swimming pool in this city. It would be cheaper to just fly you down to live with your dad every summer."

Sandwich mush swells in her mouth, her lips and chin suddenly numb. "He said that?"

Henry picks up his spoon, tows it back and forth through his soup. "He said that? Well, not exactly." He stares at the TV and heaves a loud, grumbly sigh. "But it's simple economics. Obvious to anyone."

"Well, what did he say, exactly? About me seeing him in the summer?"

Henry's usual bluster sinks into a sheepish grimace. "I may have overstated the case."

She struggles to swallow. The glob of sandwich drags inside her, tunnels a pain through her throat and back. "But he talked about it?"

Henry shakes his head. "Mostly we talk about father-son type stuff, career advice, financials."

The father-son stings her, an equation into which she doesn't factor. "Does he say anything about me?"

"Well, of course." Henry's bluster comes back as irritation. "But, I mean, it's complicated, obviously. Your father and I, as you know, years of estrangement between us, a lot of dirty water under that bridge. Years we'll never get back. But look, the man's not a machine, he's not an animal. He cares about you very much, although I'm sure your mother has convinced you otherwise. He's just, and I'm not making excuses for him here, he's under a lot of pressure. He's made some bad decisions, no doubt. But he's not a bad man. And this summer, well, this summer might not be good for him, but there's always next summer, or the summer after that."

She takes a deep breath, her father's nearness a charge in the air, the sense of him moving closer.

"I'll tell you, he was more than a little jealous when I told him we were spending time together."

"He was?"

"I was far too busy for things like this when he was growing up."

"Oh." Not the jealousy she was hoping for.

"Maybe this sort of thing just skips a generation." Henry lifts his soup bowl to his chin, slurps up a heap of noodles. "The point I was trying to make." His hand feels for his napkin, brings it to his lips with a firm swipe. "Do you know what alimony is?"

She nods, eager to hear whatever he might know about her parents' divorce, about her father's true nature.

"Well, you know in theory. Let's hope you never understand in practice. Men have responsibilities, liabilities, families. You can't just pull the rug out from under them. It's neither humane nor gentlemanly. Which is why today, I marched into the station manager's office and told him point-blank."

Despite the firm grip of her attention, the topic of her father is long gone, lost down some winding back road.

"Take your fucking co-anchor idea and shove it up your A-hole." His final word hangs in the air. The two of them sit in silence. She forces a smile to show she's still having a good time.

Henry stares at the spoon in his bowl. "Well, not those exact words, but you get the drift."

Gerry rests her face against the car window, damp glass a salve for her bruises. Henry hums with the radio violins as he drives. Outside, the world looks false and two-dimensional. Buildings like facades, people like groomed extras, even the dogs trained into their roles. The real life, the real people, the real families are in Santa Clara. Every couple of months her mom speaks to a lawyer named Larry Walsh, a man whose smiling voice makes him sound plump and almost retired. He calls Gerry "Doll" whenever she answers. Not long after her parents' divorce, Gerry asked her mom if she could telephone her father, and Larry Walsh had been the one to explain things.

His kind tone soothed with words like *emotional welfare, best interest, undue stress.* Her mom held the receiver to Gerry's face with one hand and dabbed at her own tears with the other. He told Gerry she could call him anytime, and promised to relay any message she had directly to her father, but the arrangement confused her, and she saw no reason to call Larry Walsh to wish him a Happy Easter or Merry Christmas. But now, she can imagine fragile, staticky connections, her father's voice, broken and distorted, but real, not the Christopher Reeves in *Superman* voice she hears in her head. "Can you give me his phone number?"

Henry turns down the music, seems to weigh the question in his mind. "Do you think that's a good idea?"

"I won't call him or anything. I just want to have it."

His lips pinch into a bud. "Well, it's not on me. How about I bring it next time?"

"You won't forget?"

"Look, if you're going to nag me."

"Fine. Climb through your own damn windows."

Henry sighs. "Who could say no to that face?"

A block from her house, Gerry spots the chestnut fountain of Lark's hair. Her tartan skirt swishes across the backs of her thighs as she strolls along the sidewalk. "Can you drop me somewhere else?"

Henry pulls the car over. "I'm already late."

She checks over her shoulder. If she hurries, she might make it to the back gate. "Don't forget the number."

Henry raises his hand in stiff salute.

Before she's closed the car door, Lark calls out her name, signals for her to wait, but makes no effort to hurry her leisurely pace.

Lark's face is a carefully plotted painting, swipes of blush, strokes of liner and shadow, her hair banded by white lace and a bow. She wears her white T-shirt knotted at the side, cradles her books against her chest. The sun glows over her coffee-coloured arms. Everything about her is like a magazine spread, except her shoes, dark, chunky Mary Janes with thick, rubbery soles. The shoes all private school girls wear.

Gerry stuffs her hands into her pocket, conscious of her own slovenly appearance. "What are you doing here?"

"I had a spare before lunch. What happened to your hair? And your face?"

"You took the bus all the way here to eat lunch?"

"Yeah, well, we didn't exactly eat lunch, okay?" Lark squints, her expression pained, as if Gerry's questions have forced her answers, as if she isn't bragging. "I can't come after school because my dad picks me up, which totally sucks."

"Totally."

Lark raises her eyebrows, an invitation for Gerry to continue, but Gerry has run out of things to say. She knows from Ian that Lark's dad is Indian, and this reminds her of a dare in fifth grade, sneaking into a men's changing room at the community pool to try to see a grown man's parts. Except she caught an Indian man bent over, looping his long, dark hair into the white tails of his turban. She felt guilty afterward, worse than if she had seen him naked. "Hey, does your dad, like, wear a turban?"

Lark keeps her face still, unreadable. She looks down at Gerry's high-tops. Her lips twitch in disgust, the fans of her lashes hide her eyes. "My dad drives an Alpha Romeo. What does your dad drive?" She makes a show of covering her mouth, finger-nails tipped with crescent moons. "Oops, I guess you wouldn't know. Sorry."

Gerry rocks her weight to her heels, scuffs her sneakers against the pavement. "Okay, well, see ya."

"Hey. Why are you, like, saying stuff about me?" Lark smiles as she says it.

"What stuff?"

"You know, like I'm a stuck-up private school skeeze."

The sun pricks at Gerry's eyes. She raises her hand to shade her face. "I didn't say that."

Lark head tilts, her eyes hardened to points. "You're kinda weird, aren't you? He thinks you're weird too, did you know that? He said he wouldn't even be your friend except that he feels so sorry for you." Lark pushes her lips into a pout. "Isn't that sad? He said you're probably a lesbo."

The front of Gerry's face feels paralyzed, a hot, rigid mask. "No he didn't."

"Didn't he? Gerry Mouse?"

A whine in the air, a faraway siren. She tries to draw the sound closer, fill her head with it.

Lark crosses her arms as if expecting an answer, then shrugs. "Okay. Well. Gotta go."

"Wait." She reaches for Lark's elbow, but Lark steps beyond her grasp.

"I'm seriously going to scream if you touch me."

Gerry stuffs her hand back in her pocket. "Don't you want to know about Ian?"

Lark's eyes widen in mock surprise. "Oh, is this something you just made up in your ugly little head?"

Gerry takes her time. "He's got a real girlfriend." She waits, studies Larks eyes, hungry for a sign of weakness.

"God, quit staring at me like that. You're so fucking creepy." Lark turns and starts to walk.

Gerry strides behind her. "Did you hear me? Did you hear what I said? Her name's Megan. She's older and way prettier than you, and smarter too. She has her own house and they have sex there all the time."

As Lark quickens her pace, her hair bounces in the air. Gerry stays at her, the toes of her sneakers catching the rubber of Lark's heels. "When your dad's picking you up after school? That's when they really go at it. He licks her pussy for like hours."

Lark covers her ears, shuffles to get ahead. Gerry shouts. "When he comes out of her bedroom, he's all sweaty and his face is like a glazed doughnut. He can hardly keep his clothes on around her. He has this disgusting trail of hair that goes from his belly button down into his—"

Lark swings her books, empty swipes at the air. "Stop following me! Stop following me, you fucking psycho!" Around her perfect eyes, damp mascara blooms like two fresh bruises. Gerry leaves her to stalk ahead, shoes thudding the pavement.

9

WHEN IAN DOESN'T SHOW UP at Megan's that night, Gerry knows it's her fault. After the third phone call to his house, Megan slams down the receiver, stares at Gerry. "Where is he?"

Gerry picks at her hands, scrapes the raw edges of her chewed-up nails. "I don't know." The truth brings no relief. Beside her, Andri sighs and shakes his head. Canned laughter carries in from the living room.

Megan looks tired, dark stains under her eyes. Andri wears the same drawn expression, his shirt and sweaters rumpled as if he's slept in them. Only Michelle, dozing in her seat, hair in pigtails, thick ankles propped on Andri's lap, appears relaxed.

"All this fucking trouble. Maybe you shouldn't throw things at people." Andri jabs his finger in the air.

Megan ignores him, drops dishes into the sudsy sink.

He rubs Michelle's ankles, presses dents into her pink skin. "Access is settled anyway, that's something."

"You got the door code?" Gerry pushes her way into the conversation, eager to slough off her guilt.

While Megan's back is turned, Andri reaches under the V-neck of his sweater, pulls out a small, tattered notebook, holds it opens below the edge of the table, to a page with three neatly printed double-digit numbers. Gerry tries to remember them as a locker combination, an imaginary lock in her hand, the dial spinning back and forth, each number marked with a tick. Andri snaps the book shut.

"It's nothing. All the fucking work we've done, the planning, the building, the testing, the sacrifices–" Megan throws a rinsed dish onto the counter, drops a clatter of wet cutlery on top of it. "What does any of it mean if we can't execute because he decides not to show? What a fucking waste."

Gerry rises from her seat, takes a dishtowel from the oven handle, picks up the cutlery, and begins to dry.

"Thank you," Megan says quietly.

Gerry nods and tries not to smile.

"You overdramatize," Andri says. "One absence." He flaps his hand. "It means nothing. Besides." He points at Gerry. "We have the understudent."

Gerry looks to Megan. "The what?"

"He means understudy." Michelle giggles, her eyes still closed.

Megan turns to face him, the dishrag leaking over the sink's edge. Her body blocks Gerry's view of the table. "I know what he means, and he can forget it."

"Why?" Andri's voice is loud and sharp, an interrogation.

Gerry steps out from behind Megan. Andri leans forward in his seat, peeks around to her, a smile on his face. "You let nonsensical emotions cloud your judgment. She is by far a more believable innocent." He clasps his hands at his chest, bats his eyes, his voice in falsetto. "Oh, I don't know, a strange man, he gave me one hundred dollars to leave this box, he said it was a surprise."

Gerry laughs into the tea towel, flattered to hear herself mim-
icked, even though Andri's impression makes her sound like a
talking doll.

"Blah, blah, blah, you see how perfect it is." Andri leans back.

Megan shakes her head. "It's Ian or nothing."

Andri nods. "Okay. I understand. But consider. Just consider. You or I, of course, because of our age, our connections,
if we get caught, kaput, that's it, jail, for life, no question. And
even Ian, maybe, his age is against him. But a young girl, this is
much better. Even if they don't believe her cover story, which,
if we are honest, is thin. Even if they can make a connection
with us, which they won't, but if they do, conspiracy and all
of it, she is still a child. Young Offenders Act says three years
maximum for any crime. Any crime. As soon as she becomes
adult? No record."

Gerry rubs at the plate in her hand, tries to catch herself
in it, imagines herself behind a cloudy, Plexiglas screen, legs
in shackles, the shock on her father's face as he arrives to visit
her. She wonders what three years in jail would do to her, make
her meaner, harden her like the group home kids at school, or
hollow her to a husk like Clem?

Above the applause of Clem's TV, the doorbell rings. Megan
dries her hands and leaves the kitchen. Gerry leans to look down
the hall. At the front door, Megan speaks in low tones to a man
Gerry can't see.

"The snowman cometh." Andri smacks the table, wipes his
face with his hands, tugs at his hair. Michelle murmurs beside
him, rubs his back.

The front door closes and Gerry returns to her spot by the
dishes, lifts another plate. Megan pauses in the living room,

her soft voice soothing Clem, then crosses straight to the sink.

"How long will you keep doing that?" Andri says. Michelle raises herself out of her seat and shuffles to the bathroom.

"Is it any of your business?" Megan's fingers slip a tiny paper envelope into the flat front pocket of her jeans.

"What if he gets arrested for pushing? You don't think he'll talk about us?"

"No one calls it pushing anymore, Andri, and he doesn't know anything about us."

Andri points to the wall. "Not to mention that phone. Why do you keep using it? Go out and use a pay phone, for God's sake. You take too many risks." Gerry watches Andri, the way his gaze drills into Megan, as if she is to blame for everything. "Men are like dogs and you've trained Ian to fuck and fry his brains out, congratulations. Is it any wonder he's not here? Maybe, you have to ask yourself, how serious you are about this. Perhaps it doesn't come naturally to a wom–"

"Shut up, Andri!" Megan pulls the plug out of the sink. The dirty water gurgles and slurps.

Gerry holds the dinner plate against her chest, crosses her arms over it to feel its warmth.

"Shut up, Andri?" Andri laughs and taps his head. "I am the only one thinking straight."

Megan stares into the drain. "I'll take care of it." She wrings the dishrag over the sink until it's a thin, hard rope between her fists. "Why don't we just use Michelle?"

Andri glares at Megan, both of them rigid and mute. Andri sits back in his chair. "Okay. Ian," he says. "We wait for Ian."

———

Michelle shivers in the passenger seat of Andri's Chevette, the belt of her thin black trenchcoat tied but the sides gaping short of her belly. Andri swears as he thumps the heater. Gerry lies sprawled across the backseat, plays with a gash in the vinyl upholstery, a smooth slit under her thigh that feels as if it might have been cut with a knife. She slips her fingers under the edge, finds a snarl of threads, the crusty sponge of industrial foam. Unlike Ian's oversized toy, the Chevette is a streamlined capsule, a tin-can cockpit hurtling through the dark. "I think the last time I was in here was—"

Andri holds up his hand. "No need to rewind for me, thank you."

His defensiveness surprises her. No one held it against him. If anything, it had been the weather. The days too dry, disarming for February, a mouldlike silvery frost over everything, cold that made Gerry's nose bleed. Rain returned the city to normal. Oil rose up from the streets, tainted the air with the smell of engines, like a mechanic's rag over her face as she rode her bike to Megan's.

The old-timers were looking out for Clem. Megan, in one of her wall-climbing moods, insisted they drive across town, through the park, drink beer by the water, and stare at the bridge lights while waves smashed the rocks below.

They rode silent, Andri's car radio broken, Gerry squashed in the backseat between Ian and Megan. Her sneakers slipped from the carpeted hump, one, then the other. The roof's low dip, her peaked knees and the shoulders of the two bucket seats left only a porthole of windshield for her to gaze through.

At the park gates, the road rumbled through Gerry's feet as asphalt gave way to cobblestone. The car's dappled windows obscured the park lights, turned them into low-hanging stars. Gerry could just make out the lagoon, its centre marked by the fountain's candlelight flicker.

Through her porthole, the causeway curved a wide, sloped arc the Chevette rattled to follow. As the road turned, the Chevette kept straight on.

"Shit," Andri said.

Gerry could feel it beneath her, the squishy compression of air and springs as he tried to pump the brakes. From her perch, they were gliding perfectly forward, an illusion of holding steady as road and traffic spun in slow motion to the right.

They crossed into the oncoming lane, and Andri's hands lifted from the steering wheel. High beams flashed signals through the car. They stopped with a jolt. Gerry's chin hit her knees and her teeth knocked together.

She remembers trying to breathe, a gurgle in her throat as she looked past Ian's dazed face to the oncoming headlights. She wanted to close her eyes. The only sound was rain drumming the roof. One by one, cars angled and skid, halted in a squeal of brakes, formed a crooked parking lot beside them.

The passenger door of a sedan swung open, and a boy, no older than her, held on to it like a barricade, screamed obscenities at them, his words washed out by the rain.

The windows of the Chevette began to fog. Andri fiddled with the gearshift, turned the key. The engine spluttered, then caught. Hot air blasted from the vents, burned through the haze. He nosed the car in a creeping route through gaps in the stopped traffic as drivers stared bewildered or waved their arms. He drove up onto the sidewalk, then back onto the road, edged his way to the far right lane that led them to the park drive.

Megan was the first to laugh, a low chuckle Gerry felt through her arm. But soon they were all laughing. Ian said, "Jesus" again and again as he shook his head. Face split in a grin, he wrestled Gerry into his lap and kissed her hair.

On the seawall, they drank bottles of beer, threw the empties onto the rocks, and watched them explode with the waves. They howled and screamed, and Gerry went around to each of them, announcing, "I need to hug you now," savouring the folds of their bodies over hers, the clutch of their hands at her back.

THEY CROSS THE BRIDGE BY EVENING, share a bag of cookies from an abandoned corner store before lying down to sleep on a grassy patch beside the highway, the girl shivering, tucked in front of him.

A dry trail of crumbs sticks in the boy's throat. He wonders what he is ingesting, breathing, what small poisons are planting themselves in his blood stream.

The girl curls, pulls him in behind her for warmth. He holds on to her, one arm under her neck, the other against her chest, the tender weight of her breast on his forearm.

They rise early the next day, in the dark, work the stiffness from their limbs by keeping a fast pace. He cuts through groups of confused wanderers, does not slow to answer pleas or questions. The girl matches him stride for stride.

At the Quay, local residents stranded on the north side of the inlet gather, move trancelike, perplexed. He guesses it to be afternoon, but the sky remains unlit, a hazy twilight thick with drifting ash. People carry flashlights. Their beams sharpen bodies, objects, buildings in the fog. His eyes struggle to adjust. Across the harbour, the downtown skyline is invisible except for a low amber glow at the horizon.

What is that? an older woman in a cardigan asks her husband. I think it's on fire.

The air is cold. The boy's clothes are damp from the grass, the sweat of walking. The girl shudders beside him. He takes off his thin jacket and wraps it over her shoulders, tries not to shiver in his T-shirt. The crowd stands hundreds deep. Several men climb onto a construction platform and call out plans through cupped hands. One of the men, slim, ponytailed in jeans, suggests heading north, deeper into the mountains.

That's crazy, someone shouts. There's no electricity. It's already too cold.

The walk alone would kill us, another shouts.

Someone suggests heading south, back through the smouldering city, to the border, where another country's army might be more prepared. This suggestion starts a flurry of arguments about routes and tactics.

The boy knows there is nothing left to the south.

What about east, someone shouts.

The shelter of the forest, access to the inlet. The idea appeals to some but not many.

Why can't we just stay here, go back to our homes? A woman sobs out the words. What's the point of going anywhere?

Somewhere in the crowd a child shrieks.

Two men divvy the group based on the final two options. A burly man in a workman's plaid shirt will lead a group east, while another man, in glasses and a shirt and tie, will organize those who choose to stay.

Those who want to head out, go back to your homes and gather whatever supplies you can. Think survival, not comfort. The burly man's voice is strong, assured. We'll leave here in two hours.

What do you think? the boy asks the girl.

She looks around at the crowd, then stares down at the toes of her running shoes. I don't want to stay here.

People with questions surround the burly man. He tells them calmly, I have no answers. Just get supplies.

The boy leads the girl forward, offers their names. The man shakes their hands, introduces himself as Dan. The boy explains that they've come across the bridge, have no homes from which to gather goods.

Dan points down the road. Check the stores.

A middle-aged man in a white jacket and golf shirt cuts in. This is irresponsible, he says. There's an infrastructure here. You can't just take people out of the city. Food, supplies, medical expertise, it's already here. You're putting them at risk.

Dan nods to the sprawl of houses blanketing the North Shore, an outbreak of rooftops carrying up the mountain. Those people are waiting in their houses. And all of them are going to come down eventually, hungry, angry. And very soon, they'll be sick. There is no way to control that.

The man stares up at the mountain, nods his head. I haven't been able to find my wife. He wipes his eyes.

Dan pats the man's shoulder.

The boy and the girl turn away, gaze at the downtown shore. The effect is of a brilliant sunset glowing behind a thick bank of fog.

The girl slips her hand inside the boy's, guides him toward the stores.

10

THIS IS HOW IT BEGINS: strategic manoeuvre of firepower, positioning veiled as a training exercise. Uniformed officers gaze at computerized maps, rub itchy chins as radars bleep a rash of targets. A routine Soviet dispatch balloons into a full-blown naval occupation of the north Atlantic, one hundred and forty warships and submarines hulking in the waters between Greenland, Norway, and Scotland's Shetland Islands. Gerry scratches at her hands as she watches the news. The itching spreads up her arms, down her back, across the tops of her thighs. Missiles awake in their underwater chambers. On sea-soaked decks of aircraft carriers, jet engines whine, bellies full of nuclear payload. Wars are two-sided, she tells herself, nothing definitive has happened yet.

A gopher pushes a miniature lawnmower across the screen. Gerry flicks off the TV, leaves a plate of soggy toast on the coffee table, thinks only of coasting her bike, the wind scraping her skin. She opens the front door while pushing her feet into her sneakers.

A dark figure hunches on the step. Gerry trips back, clings to the door to hold herself steady.

Ian glances over his shoulder, face ruddy and unshaven, eyes pouchy and red.

"Jesus, you scared the shit out of me."

He bows his head, drags fists through his greasy hair.

"Where were you last night?"

"Megan's." His voice is clogged and wet, as if he has a cold.

"Were not. And she's pissed about it too."

"Later." He sniffles, wipes his nose with his hand. "I was there later."

Hand on the doorframe, she swings forward to get a better look at him, his jeans and jacket splotched with dark patches. Across the road, two different neighbours stand at their living-room windows, watching. The pewter sky spits rain. "Are you sick or something?"

He sniffs again, then stretches his face as if struggling to breathe. She wonders if he's too high to go home. "You want to come inside?"

"Your mom at work?"

"Yeah. But sometimes she comes home early."

"Lark and I broke up."

"Oh." Gerry suckles her bottom lip. "Well, what about Megan?"

"Fuck Megan." His head shakes. "She gets me wasted, then she totally rags on me about her precious project, starts calling me names and shit. She's fucking my head. All night I couldn't close my eyes. I mean, even now, I can't close my eyes." He squeezes his eyes shut over and over.

The twitching makes her nervous. "Maybe you should have stayed at her place."

"Just shut up about Megan." He rests his forehead on his knees.

Gerry picks at the crumbled weather stripping, flicks pieces of it onto the ground.

"I loved her, do you get that?"

She knows he means Lark and fights not to roll her eyes. "I guess that happens."

"Do you? Do you guess it happens?" His head lifts. He pushes himself up. His legs wobble enough that Gerry offers a steadying hand. He squints, his eyes bloodshot and weepy.

It hurts to look at him. "Maybe you just need some sleep."

"You aren't going to tell me, are you?"

She nudges her sneaker into a nest of spiderwebs and old leaves under the door.

"What's the matter? You can't say it to my face?" He bends to look at her.

The sour heat of his breath makes her flinch. She turns away.

"You made this happen. So now what? Huh? What's the big plan? You and me? Is that the plan?" His hand pins her shoulder to the doorframe. He leans his body, presses his hips against hers.

She knows he doesn't mean it, still she retreats as far as she can.

"'Cos that I could understand. That would make sense."

Her shoulder aches as if her arm's about to wrench from its socket.

"You couldn't leave it alone." He slams his free hand into the door and she jolts. "You couldn't let me be happy." His voice sinks into a rasp of breath. "Say something."

The lockplate bruises against her back. She tries to speak but nothing comes out, just the metallic grind of a faraway saw, the neat thud of a car door on the street.

She reaches to touch his hand, not to pry away his grip but to feel the realness of him.

"Hey!" He makes the sound without opening his mouth, his voice catching in the distance. He rears back suddenly. Gerry slumps, touches her shoulder, catches the flash of a red shirt.

Randy holds his forearm across Ian's throat, the sleeve and collar of Ian's jacket in his fists as he hoists him against the wall. "You gonna cool it?"

"Let him go!" She beats at Randy's arm. "He wasn't doing anything." She needs to see Ian's eyes, but he keeps his face turned away.

Randy releases him with a shove. "Take a hike."

Ian trips on the step, stumbles forward down the walk.

"Keep moving."

"Wait." When she calls his name, Ian doesn't look back. She pushes past Randy to get into the house. "You're a fucking Neanderthal." She pivots in the foyer when she senses him following her. "Get out."

He leans toward her. "You're welcome."

"I didn't need your help." She tries to lose him by heading for the kitchen.

"Could've fooled me."

"A beernut could fool you."

In the kitchen, she waits, then picks up the phone, dials Ian's number, lets it ring.

Randy hovers.

She slams the receiver into its cradle. "You know, it's totally creepy and possibly illegal that you're here when I'm home alone. Maybe I should call the cops."

He looks at his watch. "Go ahead. Your mom'll be home in half an hour. I got some buddies coming over to work on the pool."

"Oh, now she's paying the freeloader. Nice."

"No one's getting paid."

"It's not going to win her back."

"Well, it's a good thing we never broke up."

"You won't even see it coming." She grabs an apple from the fruit bowl, bites into it, glares at him to make her point.

"Your mom's pretty worried about you."

"I don't want you in here when I'm here."

He shrugs. "It's a big house. Go to your room."

"Go to your truck."

He doesn't move. She opens her mouth wide and grips the apple in her teeth, lowers her hands to the top of her T-shirt and begins to pull it off.

Randy's work boots clomp in the foyer. She throws the apple after him. It hits the front door with a hard, wet smack.

That evening the quiet of Megan's kitchen makes Gerry antsy. Andri studies a stack of papers, spiral-bound manuals arranged around him in a semicircle. Beside him, Michelle reads a tattered paperback, a bridge and fiery sun on the cover. Gerry opens the fridge but finds no beer, only bowls and plates covered in wrinkly cling wrap. She crosses to the sink, fills a glass with water, drinks it in hard gulps, waits for one of them to acknowledge her presence. "What are you working on?" she says, finally.

"Cameras."

"Where's Megan?"

Michelle looks up from her book, nose crinkled in a grimace. "Clem had an accident. She's cleaning him up." Gerry notices it then, above the gurgling fridge motor, a hiss of running water, the shower's patter. She wonders how Megan manages, whether she gets into the shower with Clem. Gerry stares at the stove, the swirl of the burners, crusts of spilled food, to keep an image from rooting in her head.

Andri exhales, a coarse half-growl. She takes a seat across from him, turns one of the manuals to get a closer look at an intricate diagram.

"Please." Andri stretches out his hand. "I'm trying to concentrate."

Michelle smiles an apology.

The shower stops. Pipes judder in the wall. Gerry wonders when they will ask about Ian. The bathroom door clicks open. "Can someone give me a hand?" Megan calls out.

Andri raises his chin. "She's calling you."

Gerry takes her time getting up from the table, afraid of what she might have to witness, Clem's sagging skin, knobby bone protrusions, thatches of white hair, whether she'll have to touch his washed body, hot and clammy.

A lit shaft of steam cuts into the hallway. She reaches the door and peeks inside. Clem stands bundled in a navy bathrobe, the plush terry towel foaming up around his small face. The robe pads him, triples his size, his legs like pink twigs poked into the center of plaid slippers. Megan stands up behind him. "Just take him to the bedroom, sit him down. I'll be in to finish him after I get rid of this."

Behind Clem's legs, a mound of clothes. A thin, rank whiff of shit taints the perfumed cloud of soap and talcum powder. Gerry reaches for Clem's arm, turns her body to avoid looking at the clothes, leads him to the bedroom.

Perched on the bed, Clem stares at the curtained window. Gerry chooses a framed black-and-white photograph from his bedside, places it in his hands as she sits down beside him. He gazes at it obediently. A woman, probably Megan's mother, dressed in a heavy black coat and hat, her flinty, angular features set in judgment. Gerry scans the other photos. A group of young men she recognizes as the old-timers, their cheeks and foreheads stretched smooth. In the last, a boyish Clem in a narrow suit and horn-rimmed glasses holds a little girl with a jewelled crown atop her ringlets, her tiered party dress drapes over his arm.

Megan shuffles back and forth down the hallway with rubber gloves, a black garbage bag. Beside Gerry, Clem fusses. The photo frame abandoned in his lap, he picks at the tie of his bathrobe.

"No, no," Gerry brushes his hands away. "Not yet." She offers him the photograph again and he takes it up, studies it.

When Megan asks her to help with getting Clem into bed, Gerry can't think of a way to say no. She holds his bare arm to keep him steady as Megan eases off the bathrobe. His skin is warm and silky with talc. Gerry keeps her eyes on his face and reminds herself to not look down.

Megan chats to Clem as she dresses him, hands patting and comforting. She speaks to him like a child. In response, Clem's eyes blink, his head nods as if he's listening to an important message.

"You can tell he loves you."

"Can you?" Megan gazes at his face, shakes her head slowly. "I've never been sure." She strokes his hand. "When I was a little girl, I used to daydream about him coming home. I didn't understand what he did or where he was, but I knew he was some kind of hero."

Gerry smiles at Clem, hoping to see him smile back. "I wish he knew about the march."

Megan buttons his pyjama top. "He knows." She combs his damp hair with her fingers, sweeps it to the side. "Don't you, handsome?" She lifts the framed photograph from the bed, returns it to the dresser.

Gerry helps Clem stand, while Megan turns down the blankets. "Was he sad when your mom died?"

"She's not dead. She lives in Toronto."

Her matter-of-fact tone leaves Gerry unsteady, confused by how little she understands. The sharpness of the present blurs quickly toward the past and future. Megan turns off the bedside lamp. They stand in the dark, watch Clem's eyelids sink shut. His hands clutch at the top edge of the blankets. "He went to prison for something they both believed in, then she abandoned him. How's that for loyalty?"

"Maybe she just wanted you to be safe."

Megan snorts, a terse, awkward laugh that startles Clem's eyes open. "She was mad, all the time. She used to fly into these rages, packing things, tearing things up. One time, she put everything that was mine, my clothes, my toys, my colouring books, out on the lawn, like I was supposed to just take it and leave. She said the same thing every time: you're just like your father."

When Megan realizes Ian isn't going to show, she smashes a mug in the sink. Gerry ducks into Andri's shoulder as pieces spray up over the counter, scatter across the linoleum.

"Megan." Michelle's voice is quiet.

"You talk to him." Megan points at Gerry, the sides of her mouth cut with tense lines.

"Me?" Gerry looks to Andri, who shrugs as he marks angles on a sheet of paper with a compass and protractor.

Clem moans, restless in his sleep, the sound alarmingly close.

"We're eight days away." Megan shakes her head. "We need to know what the fuck is going on. Is he in or out?"

"How am I supposed to know what's wrong with him?" Gerry shifts in her chair.

Andri nods. "And if he's out?"

Gerry can sense his gaze, firm and heated, like the sun through her clothes.

"He's not out." Michelle's insistence makes her sound unsure.

Megan gathers the shards of ceramic, tries to fit them back together. From the bedroom, sheets rustle and flap, a furious batting that makes Gerry think Clem is fighting someone in his bed.

Her mom is still up when she gets home. Light from the kitchen casts a glow in the foyer. Gerry slips off her shoes, but the chatter of spokes as her rear wheel catches the threshold telegraphs her entrance.

"I saved you some dinner." Her mom's voice trails up like a question, an invitation to a truce. Newspaper pages crackle, an attempt to appear casual, as if she hasn't been waiting for hours.

Gerry hangs up her jacket, skates her socked feet across the floor as she approaches the kitchen. "I already ate."

"Your face looks much better." Her mom's smile is hesitant, uncertain. Gerry knows not to expect an apology, her mom's makeup tactic has always been effervescent amnesia. But tonight, her usual post-fight cheerfulness seems wobbly, her face a shaky scaffold.

"Where's Randy?"

Her mom glances to the back door as if he might be in the yard. "He left early. They were working to get the liner fixed. It actually looks like it might be a pool some day." She pats the seat of the chair beside her.

Gerry obeys, inches the newspaper toward her, finds an edge and tears it back in strips. Her mom reaches out and touches Gerry's head, fingers and palm kneading. Gerry wishes she could close her eyes, let her mom hold the weight of her.

"I guess it's not so bad. It shows off your eyes." She strokes at Gerry's temples, brushes back imaginary hair. "I'm really sorry." Her hand grazes Gerry's cheek.

The words catch Gerry by surprise. She focuses on her paper fringe, careful not to blink or swallow. "It's fine." The words seep out on a thin, impatient breath.

"My mother used to hit me. She slapped me once because I spilt a glass of milk, can you believe that?" Her mom's chuckle is low and awkward. "I want you to know that I know it's not okay."

"Mm-hmm." Hearing about her mom's past makes Gerry uneasy, as if talking about it might bend time, cast her mom back into the small, helpless role of a child.

"Can I ask you something?"

"Uh-huh."

"Do you not think that Randy's a good person?"

Gerry wants to explain that Randy is not a person at all but a giant, irrevocable idea, like communism. Good or bad, she's unwilling to live under it, have her life defined by it. "I liked Stephen." She hopes conjuring the skinny lab tech whose crumpled Wallabies reeked of foot odour will derail her mom's heart to heart.

"You hated Stephen."

"I like him in hindsight." She plucks a lash of newspaper, rolls it into a ball between her fingers. "But not in hindsmell."

"Cheeky." Her mom reaches out and pinches the side of Gerry's face.

"Ow!" She tries to brush her mom's hand away, rubs at what feel like dents in her skin.

Her mom's hand slides over hers, squeezes it. "I just want to know you're okay."

"Why wouldn't I be okay?" She asks in earnest, daring her mom to label the defects of her only daughter, to declare them out loud.

Her mom's response, a doting gaze, milky with sympathy and tortured concern irritates her, hardens her into contempt. She rolls her eyes and raises her arms over her head. Her words stretch out on a yawn. "I'm fine." She kicks back from the table, chair legs scraping over tile. "Can I go to bed now?"

Her mom looks wounded, eyelids flickering with thought. Her hair is different: shorter, choppier layers around her face, new streaks, frosted tips. The lighter colour yellows the lines around her mouth.

"When did you change your hair?"

Her mom attempts but fails at another smile. "A couple of weeks ago."

Gerry pushes up and out of her chair. "I liked it better the other way."

The xylophonic tones and feathery drums of *Architecture & Morality* seal the edges of her room. Crouched against the far side of the bed, she checks the stash box again, the baggie down to roaches, nothing worth the effort of salvaging. She flicks the lighter on and off. The flame sways, then drops back into its metal hole. She tries not to feel bad for her mom and instead passes the flame under her flattened palm, braves the heat of its tongue. Still, guilt pools like a reflex, magnetic, involuntary.

The day the moving truck loaded with the last of her father's work files and clothes pulled out of their driveway, her mom took her to a pet store. In the murky hum of the store's aquatic section, Gerry stared at the ragged tails of sluggish fish, chilled by their furless, metallic bodies, frustrated at how her mom's plans paired her with things she didn't want. The greasy man in the FIFA T-shirt netted two fat goldfish against the side of the tank, and Gerry made an effort to smile, aware that her mom's happiness was now her responsibility.

At home, without pebbles or plants to fill the terrarium her mom salvaged from the basement, the fish appeared shocked and embarrassed in their watery prison. Gerry blamed her mom, argued to fitful tears that she should know, since she was the parent, how to take care of things. Her mom promised they'd go back the next day, get everything the fish needed. That night, their constant motion kept Gerry awake. She sensed their fretful bodies darting in the bowl, felt herself drowning in her sheets, the weight of their twin needs like stones on her chest.

The next morning, gummy-eyed and exhausted, she shuffled downstairs, found her mom at the kitchen table staring at the orange bodies afloat on their sides. Gerry traced the curved glass of the bowl, tried not to look into their open eyes. Her mom searched for matchboxes. They held the burial in the back garden, the two of them silent as her mom stabbed at weeds and clay soil with a hand trowel, pink housecoat dragging in the dirt. When her mom was done, she stood, pulled Gerry close. Gerry could tell from her grip she was going to cry. Disgust coiled in her stomach. She wanted to shout at her mom to cut it out. She stared at the two humps of earth, wondered whether the fish had died of loneliness or killed each other in the night.

○ ○ ○

THE GROUP ARRIVES AT A SHELTERED INLET, proceeds
past the village, and continues along Indian Arm until the road
narrows and the woods thicken. They settle off the thorough-
fare, down by the beach. The area, Deep Cove, they rename as
their own, Peace Cove.

They take houses easily. Most residents are absent, lost in the
city. Some have loaded boats and fled. A young family lies inert
in their cellar, five children and their mother blazed through the
forehead, the father shot through the chin.

The remaining residents are cautious but welcoming. Dan
organizes the group into a roster of essential duties: sterilize
water, gather and prepare food, ration firewood collected from
homes, chop green wood to cure for later. The boy survives the
first few days clinging to the structure of duty and routine,
grateful to focus his mind on immediate tasks.

Food dwindles quickly. At first, fresh, familiar items scav-
enged from fridges and pantries, then a strange, but comforting
assortment of mushy casseroles and pies rescued from dripping
freezers, then soon, rice or oats in a watery stew, slivers of meat
seared black to mask the putrid taste.

Within the group, there are two doctors. Dr. Woo, an elderly
Chinese man who confesses his profession with a bow of his head
and whispered apology: denturist; and Dr. Patak, a young Indian
woman, an intern from a cardiac ward. Despite their unease
with the magnitude of their responsibilities, they perform their
ministrations with efficiency and calm. A small group of people
volunteer to help them: a retired nurse's aid, a veterinarian's
assistant, a woman who once canvassed donations for the Heart

and Stroke Foundation. Others make sacrifices for the doctors, leave extra wood, food, blankets at the door of the house they use as a clinic.

Without electricity, houses are used like cabins, all cooking done communally, on the beach. Though some gas appliances still work, Dan forbids their use.

There's only a finite amount in the line. We'll save it for sterilizing, in case someone needs surgery.

Both doctors blanch at this pronouncement.

The boy and the girl stay together in a small beach hut on the property of a larger house. A single room with a wood-burning stove, an antique writing desk, a wire cot, and a small sofabed. They find out from the two families sharing the main house that the property belonged to a writer. Inside his desk, the boy finds glossy images of naked men curled around each other, oiled skin and muscle, sticky, handwritten notes of longing and frustration, the author, a writer of erotic science fiction serials no one in camp admits to reading.

Each night, after their meal, the boy and girl play cards or read. The girl, a hobby seamstress, takes to mending clothes for the group. They come with their fallen hems, missing buttons, torn sleeves. The boy watches as she squints in the candlelight, handles dirty, fraying fabrics as if they are silks. Once the candle has burned its allotted hour, she murmurs and swears in the shadows as her fingers feel for the needle. When she is ready to sleep, she unfolds the sofa bed. The boy lies down on the cot.

It is only in the dark that they recall their former lives. Not a conversation but a relay of monologues. Night after night, they talk each other to sleep. The boy dreams of the girl's job as a receptionist in car dealership, her voice crackling over the company loudspeaker, her fiancé, an accounts manager at the bank next door. He dreams of her wedding dress, layers of tulle and ecru taffeta she sewed herself, wrapped in clear plastic and hung in the back of her closet. He smells the ink of the full-colour honeymoon brochures she keeps in her desk, tastes the spongy sweetness of the cakes she sampled and argued over with her sisters. When he wakes to hear the girl crying in her sleep, a soft, plaintive mewling, he wonders if it is his mother she is dreaming of.

The sickness starts suddenly around the camp. First, vomiting and diarrhea. Careless food preparation, someone says, unclean water. People stagger to the woods, soil their clothes. The doctors scuttle about with worried eyes. A rigored bird washes up on the beach and everyone takes it as a bad omen.

I have a sister in California, a woman says as she stares at the bird.

A man shakes his head. Doubt there is a California.

Within days, there are lesions, sores. People complain of fever, burning throats and chests, douse themselves in the frigid waters of the inlet.

On the beach, in front of everyone, Dr. Patak starts a vicious argument with Dan. We need basic supplies, she shouts. At least IV fluids and antibiotics. These people are all going to die.

Dr. Woo stands behind her, wipes his forehead with a handkerchief.

That night, the boy and girl watch through the window of their hut as Dan gathers a group of eight men around the fire, a large equipment bag at his feet. He talks for a while, then appears to pose a question. When all the men nod, Dan stoops down and opens the bag. He hands a rifle and a box of shells to each of them. The girl draws a sharp breath. After loading their guns, the men trudge up the hill, toward the houses. The boy cranes his neck but loses them in the shadows. The girl buries her face in his shoulder. They brace for the shots.

They hear only the scuff of boots on gravel, the sound fading gradually as the men climb past the houses, to the main road.

Two days later, the men return carrying gym bags, knapsacks loaded with drugs and medical supplies. They are exhausted. Several of them look as if they've been beaten, faces bruised and bloody. Everyone gathers at the beach, pushes food at them. Most of the men decline, stagger back to their homes.

A woman and her husband approach one of the men as he rests on a tree stump by the fire, an untouched bowl of soup in his hand.

What's it like over there? the woman asks.

The man shakes his head.

We want to know, the husband says.

The girl shivers beside the boy. He wants to cover her ears so she won't hear.

They're killing people, the man says.

Who? the husband asks. Who is killing who?

The man's bowl shakes, soup spilling onto his hand. Everyone. Everyone is killing everyone.

11

GERRY SLOUCHES IN HER SEAT, marks her disappointment with a scowl. Henry aims his binoculars at the beauty salon across the road, his back a defiant sharkskin wall. She refuses to look in the same direction, focuses instead on the sidewalk's crowd of bodies.

"Don't pout, it's not ladylike."

"I don't want to be ladylike."

"You don't say."

"She's just across the street, is your eyesight that bad?"

"I like to see her face. It tells me what she's thinking." He lowers his binoculars. "After Tuesday, I'll bring it. I promise."

"Why Tuesday?"

He settles the binoculars in his lap. "Okay, now you're getting on my nerves."

She shrugs to show how little she cares.

"Tuesday? Judge Wilson Fennimore? The courthouse?"

She notices he's wearing the same suit he wore earlier in the week, a soup splash visible on the lapel. "You better wear something nice."

"Why should I?" He cocks his chin as he says it, his voice bellowy and gruff.

"Because it's like, court?"

He shakes his head. "I will not kowtow to the conventions of the establishment." The binoculars rise to his face. "Given the vulturous nature of ex-wives, a man should show up in rags, or better yet, with his entrails hanging out."

"It's a phone number, you sure you can't just remember it?"

Mrs. Cross emerges from the salon a newly minted super-hero, silver cape aflutter, hair slicked wet. Henry sinks low in his seat. Mrs. Cross feeds the parking meter, a small change purse clutched in her hands. As her chin lifts, her gaze settles on their car. "Get down!" he whispers.

"She knows it's us." Gerry relaxes her face in a welcoming smile, fans a small wave.

Mrs. Cross stares, then scoops two fingers in the air, a violent, backward V. She marches back into the salon, cape shimmering in her wake.

"What was that?"

"She's British." Henry grimaces at the steering wheel, picks at the spiral pattern of embossed leather.

Gerry waits for him to elaborate. When he doesn't, she turns on the radio, pushes the preset buttons until she finds the all-news station. The U.S. has launched a response to Soviet mobilization, a worldwide military exercise codenamed "Global Shield 84," bombers and fighter jets scrambled into international airspace, nuclear-capable subs raised for active duty. The newscaster speeds through information Gerry has already processed and filed.

"Blech." Henry switches off the radio. "It's like listening to a cheese grater read the news."

"It could be important."

He lifts his binoculars. "Newsroom's full of rumours. Missile test-fires. Something like that."

"What test-fires? Where?" Her tongue rubs at a gap in her teeth, the friction both itchy and soothing in her mouth.

"Who knows. I wasn't paying attention. She must be getting the colour done, it doesn't always take this long."

Gerry rests against her door. Her head feels cavernous. "What if something actually happens?"

"Something always happens. If not today, then tomorrow. What can we do? We get on with it. Is my camera in there?" Henry points to the glove box. "I wouldn't mind getting a photo of her when she's done."

Behind the compartment's dense nest of papers, she finds a small, black Instamatic, rubs her thumb over the nubbly plastic as she hands it to him. Outside her window, people hurry along the sidewalk. Morning sun winks off watches and eyeglasses. She imagines a flashbulb bursting over them, death shadows burned into the pavement, the overexposed world rendered down to a negative of ghosts. "I wouldn't want to survive."

"You'll have no choice. It's how we're programmed. Biological imperative. The Ruskies won't get off enough rockets to kill everyone."

"Then I'll kill myself."

"Oh, you think that's a choice? Subconscious natural selection, my friend. You sense a trait in yourself that will weaken the greater gene pool, so you weed yourself out."

"That's not true."

"Biology: two; conscious will: zero." Henry shifts in his seat, the camera tiny against his chest. He purses his lips as he thinks. "Well, okay, maybe you're just a quitter." He means it as a joke, but she can't muster a smile.

"I'd still want to die."

He gives her a wary glance, head tilted back as if to examine her from a distance. "Is this what they mean by a cry for help? Should I be calling one of those special phone numbers?"

"If the world's coming to an end, what difference does it make?"

Henry lowers his chin. The ridge of his brow sinks over his eyes like the fur of an old dog. "You're serious?"

She wonders what it would be like to put her arms around him, let the sharp collar of his dress shirt dig into her neck. She decides it would be nice, tries to imagine their faces side by side, curious to know if photos of them together would reveal similarities, her face an embryonic version of Henry's slack and weathered one. "No."

He nods. "Just for future reference, if it's a cry for help you're going for, I'd suggest a less roundabout route."

She takes the camera from his hand. "Smile," she says as she lifts it to her eye, holds him for a moment in the foggy cell of the viewfinder.

He drops her off in front of her house. The sky opens and the first pelts of a downpour hit her as she gets out. Before she's up the walk, he calls her name, waves her back. The rain drums over his voice, makes him shout. "I may have to explore some less than legal channels these next few days! Best I go it alone! We'll regroup on Wednesday, post-mortem the judge's bias!"

The words are confusing, but the message reaches her before he's finished: he'll get along better without her. She turns without saying goodbye, swings her arms, takes long, deliberate strides, as if she already has better things to do.

———

The backyard is a mess of muddy, rain-splattered men in acid-wash jeans and rock concert T-shirts. Ponytails sprout from baseball caps, muscled forearms coil with tattoos. Gerry watches through the window beside the back door as they lean on shovels around the perimeter of the pool, stare into the centre, waiting for their heavy-metal mothership to levitate from its depths.

"You're home."

She jumps at the possibility of one of them behind her.

Randy stands with rubber waders clutched in his hand, a pair of severed legs. He points over his shoulder. "I was in the john."

Gerry pokes her finger into her mouth and makes a gagging sound.

"Good to see you too." He sits down on a kitchen chair and pushes his socked feet into his boots.

Outside, the men stand frozen in place. "Where did you find these guys? Prison?"

Randy shrugs. "What if I did? You got something against second chances?"

"I've got something against being gangbanged and dismembered by your deadbeat friends."

"Nice." He stands, pulls a pair of work gloves from his back pocket. "Do you talk to everyone like that or just me?"

"I hate all psychos equally, so don't get all hot and bothered about it."

"Your mom asked me about that new bike of yours. I told her it wasn't expensive."

"Shows what you know."

"I know what that bike costs. I also know you don't give a

person, a girl, a gift like that without expecting something in return."

"Wow, is sex the only thing you think about? Child molester much?"

"Can we just cut the jokes for a sec and have a proper conversation."

"I don't speak Neanderthal."

"Fine."

She waits for him to walk out.

He pats the gloves together, peels them apart. "Gerry." He grimaces and scratches the back of his neck. "If anyone's hurting you, I mean, messing with you. A guy or whatever. I mean, if you couldn't talk to your mom about it. Obviously, because that would be the best thing. But if you couldn't. You could tell me. I would take care of it for you."

She can tell by the set of his face, his tense shoulders, he means it. The sincerity of his offer hooks inside her. She bows her head. A feeble consolation, the right words from the wrong person. She nods to recover herself, lets her voice sinks low and quiet. "Well, there is something."

"Uh-huh?" He shifts his weight from foot to foot.

"But, you have to promise, I mean, swear to God, you won't tell anyone."

He nods. "Okay."

"Say it." She holds up her hand. "I swear to God."

"Are you kidding me?"

"Say it."

He raises his palm. "I swear to God."

She makes him wait, palm open in the air, the depth of him tested and proven. She pushes off from the window ledge, slows as she passes him. "Did you get that bullshit from an afterschool special?"

She puts it off as long as she can, sits in her window watching rain flood the street, burble over clogged drain grates, wash downhill in a lapping tide. But finally the threat of facing Megan forces her to Ian's.

Under the green-and-white awning, she shivers, clothes soggy. She taps the knocker, listens for shuffling inside the house, watches through the condensation of the living-room window for shadows. The doorknob chills her palm. A twist and nudge and the door sways open. The house greets her with cloying warmth, oiled incense and cloves, a smell that reminds her of burnt maple syrup. She stamps her feet on the mat.

"Hello?" A man's voice echoes around her, detached, otherworldly. Above her, floorboards creak. She peers up. Ian's dad leans over the upstairs banister.

She wipes the rain from her forehead. "It's Gerry."

Marty blinks, his eyes set deep in a galaxy of cascading hair. He wears a patterned caftan that swings around his ankles, knitted slippers with pompoms. In his hand, a yellow telephone receiver shaped like a question mark. He points to it. "Long distance." Then ushers her along with his chin. "They're buying groceries. Make yourself at home."

The living room is an overstocked garage sale, shelves crammed with record sleeves and paperbacks, clusters of wood-handled tools, gutted electronic gadgets, laundry baskets heaped with clothes. Over every piece of furniture blankets and fabrics. Their spaniel, Lopey, stretches on the carpet, raises a furry eyebrow, grumbles at her presence. Gerry tries to sit, but the room's disorder pushes her out to the kitchen.

Rain bathes the kitchen windows. On the large farmhouse table, hunkered amidst a litter of stuffed baggies, a cake-sized Tupperware container overflows with loose weed, a sage froth of curling fronds and buds. The aroma hangs in the room, dank and herbal. Gerry draws a full, deep breath, stations herself in the seat farthest from Alice's stash. Beside the container, Alice's antique post office scale, labels, a pile of felt pens. The filled baggies appear haphazardly strewn, random pillows of plump mossy green, nothing like Ian's feeble skiffs of faded pot.

Above her, the ceiling creaks. Marty paces as he talks, his footsteps a persuasive distance from the landing. She reaches out and squeezes a bag orphaned from the rest, stranded past the centreline of the table. The plastic is smooth and taut, the buds fairy light but packed and springy under her hand. It wouldn't just be for her. Back at her house, she could divide it, some for Andri, some for Megan and Clem. She listens again, waits for Marty's faraway laugh, then closes her fingers, draws the baggie to her jacket pocket, and stuffs it deep. Her chair scrapes as she stands to move to the back door.

Voices carry in from the front of the house. She tries the door, but it's locked, an empty keyhole, a double chain. Her wet jeans make her legs feel leaden, conspicuous. She turns a confused circle, then sits down.

Ian enters first, jacket dripping, arms loaded with wet paper bags. If he's surprised to see her, he doesn't show it, his face slack and sullen. Alice follows, shakes a gypsy scarf from her mane of copper curls. An embroidered purse swings from her wrist, chequebook, pen, and grocery receipt in her hand. "Ha!" She smiles at Gerry. "They only charged me for one carton of eggs. Isn't that nice?"

Ian unpacks the groceries, opens cupboard doors, shuffles boxes and cans.

Gerry stands.

"You should have told me she was coming, I would have hurried." Alice sidles to the back window, scrunches her hands through her hair. Tiny bells on the hem of her peasant skirt tinkle as she moves. "Back to the grindstone." Alice hovers behind her chair, stares at the container, then at the table. "You know, some days I am sure I'm losing my mind. Gerry, honey, how many do you see there? Just the full ones."

Gerry's mind blazes with a number. She trails her eyes over the bags, feigns counting. "Thirty-two."

"That's what I thought." Alice looks right at Gerry, her eyes searchlights. "Don't ever get old, Gerry, your brain turns to mush." She shakes her head and calls to the hallway. "Marty, getting old is the pits!"

Marty's footsteps creak along the landing. "Dying is the alternative!"

Ian knocks Gerry between the shoulder blades. "Go."

The car reeks of wet leather, damp and inky. Cold air blows through an invisible vent at Gerry's feet. Ian's keys dangle unturned in the ignition. She rubs her hands in her lap, clenches her teeth against her jaw's quivering. "Are we going somewhere?"

He stares out the window. His lips pinch and twitch.

"Earth to Major Tom." The Bowie reference gets her nothing.

"Can you at least turn the heat on, so I don't, like, die of hypothermia?"

"Empty your pockets."

A forced giggle masks her panic. "Excuse me?"

"I mean it."

"What are you, a narc?" Her hand feels for the door handle, grips it tight.

"Do it."

Before she can move, he is on top of her, hands on her breasts, her waist, her hips. His legs vise around hers. She squirms under him, grabs at his face. His head rears back beyond her reach, belt buckle a shock against her naked stomach. The car closes in, seat and dash squeezing her sides. His weight suffocates her. She arches, struggles for breath as tears burn up behind her eyes. She screams. Her legs kick free, and with hard, bucking shove, she pushes him off.

He falls back into his seat, glances down at the baggie in his hand, then hurls it at her face. The plastic smacks her mouth, bounces from dash to floor. "What the fuck is wrong with you?" His voice spins in the car.

She covers her ears.

"You steal from my mom?" He pounds the steering wheel. "If you were a guy, I'd beat the living shit out of you!"

It seems the best solution, let him pummel her into a bloody mess on the sidewalk, a black sheet of unconsciousness creeping over her. She tugs at the sleeve of her wet jacket, uses it to wipe her eyes. "Go ahead."

"Go ahead? Jesus, I can't even talk to you." He chews at his thumbnail, spits into the air. "What horrible thing did I ever do to you?" He stares, waiting for an answer.

The question only confuses her. Petty grudges and injuries rise, then evaporate like the fine details of a dream. Even the idea of being angry leaves her.

"Just say it."

"I don't know." She mutters it into the window, rubs a smear into the fog of her breath, doesn't know how to explain how lonely he makes her feel.

"Who does then?"

His sarcasm goads her into choosing the obvious. "You can't just do shitty things, act like a shitty person, and expect your friends to be like, rah-rah-rah, oh, hooray for you."

"Are you fucking kidding me with this?"

"If I was doing it with two guys, you'd be on my case like every five seconds."

"You with a guy? Don't make me laugh."

"Go to hell."

"Look, get it into your head. Megan and me, we're not together, we're not a couple, we're never going to be goddamn king and queen of the prom, okay?"

"Just because I don't dress like a slut doesn't mean guys aren't interested."

"Yeah, okay, who cares? I'm so sick of talking to you right now."

"Plenty of guys like me."

Ian tips his head back and groans.

She can't stand looking at him, holds her eyes closed until the insides of her eyelids flash red. Thought after thought rises, sputters a momentary presence, then slips back under. Her body melds to the car door. Outside, the rain has broken. Up the block three girls run down the front steps of a house and onto the sidewalk. Two of them stretch out a skipping rope, turn it in a high arc while the third begins to jump.

Ian's leather jacket stutters as he shifts. She counts the seconds until he speaks. "Listen. This shit you're pulling, it's fucked up. Maybe you should talk to someone, you know? One of those kid shrinks."

She covers her face with her hands, her skin hot with humiliation. "Fuck. You."

"Gerry Mouse." The pity in his voice is unbearable. Lark had told the truth.

"Megan wanted me to tell you. If you don't come tonight." She holds her breath against a sob, hopes it will hurt, how dispensable he is. "You're out."

He watches her, as if he expects her to say something else, then gazes out at the street. "Fine. Tell her I'm out."

She pushes open the door. Ionized air spills over her like a wash. The stuffiness of the car falls away. With each step, the damp sidewalk reveals itself, a panel at time. Sunlight dazzles in every corner, forces her to squint or go blind.

○ ○ ○

THE BOY AND THE GIRL ESCAPE the worst of the sickness, suffer mild, sweaty fevers, dull aches and fatigue, cough up spatters of blood. Each morning they conduct timid examinations, check each other for purple spots. The boy knows from helping at the clinic that after the spots, hair and teeth loosen, fever climbs, and the bleeding begins. With kitchen tongs, the boy has changed wads of soiled rags tucked beneath the heads of listless patients, an endless trickle from the stubborn faucets of their noses and mouths. The near-dead vomit until their black intestines come up in their throats. They whisper between convulsions about fire inside.

Still, the boy carries out his daily duties without complaint. He helps bury those who succumb, reverential digging without ceremony, grateful for the end of torture, the freshly earthed forest floor that stretches under the cover of trees.

Dan sends out a group of men each week. At first, he spares the ones with children, but as illness spreads, he calls on fathers. They leave silent and sombre, return the next day with medicine, survival gear, water filters, packaged food, more guns. When a group returns with fewer men than expected, the girl huddles by the stove, covers her ears against the shrieks of wives. The boy watches the beach, tenses when Dan glances toward the hut, wonders if he will always seem too young.

Groups of people from the city follow the men back. Dan interviews them for usable skills. Some are invited to stay, the rest quarrel, rant, plead, are escorted to the road. A clean gunshot signals their departure.

The third doctor arrives this way. Dr. Joan, a middle-aged

oncologist. Drs. Woo and Patak are frantic with happiness, offer half their meals to the new doctor as incentive. She asks to see patients right away and the two doctors swoon, squeeze her hands before guiding her up the long staircase to the clinic house.

Proximity to death makes the boy sentimental. He finds himself daydreaming of the girl while he digs graves or sterilizes water. His hand grazes fire as he turns flayed rabbits on the spit. She looks different now, face unwashed, hair tied in a rag, body whittled to bones. When he thinks back to the two of them at the bus stop, he is sure she stood taller than him, a woman and a boy. Now, she is smaller, matched to his size. Other men admire her too. Married ones raise an eyebrow or throw a wink, single ones resort to crude gestures, mouthed words. The boy watches them and suffers a slippery rage, one he cannot hold in a fist. He stands close, keeps a hand on her elbow, tries to ignore them, to deny he shares their appetite.

The weather remains cold, sky a muslin blur. The first rain brings a ghastly shower that drives everyone to shelter, skin marked by hard black drops, the sting of poison. Some change their minds, slide basins and buckets outside to catch the tarry rainfall. They boil it at the fire until it separates, then slurp the clear liquid, an extravagance of unrationed water. An outbreak of purple spots amongst the drinkers frightens everyone to seal themselves inside whenever the sky opens.

In the middle of a downpour peaked by thunder and lightning, air raid sirens sound. The boy and girl cling to each other on the cot, stiffen with each clap and explosion of light, terrified by what may be left unfinished.

For days after, while women scrape sticky black residue from the beach and common areas, men argue over the meaning of the siren. A few insist it a signal, a call to gather, evidence of a governing force, an all clear. Dan and the majority disagree, deem it an accident triggered by electrical currents in the air. They warn against false hope.

A dense curtain of fog blocks visibility past the waterline. On the beach, the fire burns day and night. People claim to hear sounds from the water, boat engines, voices in conversation, but no one has the energy to investigate what Dan dismisses as the mind playing tricks.

Inside the hut, the boy and girl fill the small stove with wood before going to sleep, huddle together on the pullout bed, blankets and coats piled to trap heat. He sleeps behind her, face buried in her hair. While she dreams, she draws his arm around her, holds it to her chest.

Each morning he wakes with his hardness pressed against her backside. Eyes closed, he lingers there as his hips urge slow, hidden rhythms, the sweet friction of worn cotton transmitting her body heat. He continues until guilt or hopelessness overtake him. After his retreat, she makes a show of waking, soft yawns and murmurs as her fingers reach to rub her eyes.

She leaves the cabin before him each morning, traipses to the woods to do her bathroom business. The boy stands at the window and watches her recede, the narrow cup of her hips, bony shoulders, abuses himself to dilute the wanting.

He knows people in camp are having sex, hears them in the forest, on the beach after dark, their huffs and pants, a hard-won race, the mindless cross of a finish line. And not the husband-and-wife pairings of mealtime. Spouses take sides against each other in camp business, a wife aligns herself with the dissenting voice of someone else's husband. Jealousy fuels accusations of theft and hoarding, husband against husband, wife against wife. Dan settles these matters with unilateral justice, punishes both wrongdoer and accuser with half-rations of food.

Mrs. Lawson, five months' pregnant on the Last Day, reminds everyone of the consequences. She gives birth prematurely. Her shouts and cries carry down from the clinic house to the beach. Dr. Woo, revered for his whispery disposition, barks orders and expletives over Dr. Patak's impatient temper.

People gather around the fire throughout the day to speculate on the birth's progress, until finally, chores abandoned, they dedicate themselves to waiting. Men stand in a circle, poke at the flames, women chatter amongst themselves, some pale with worry, some pink with stories of their own labour, others ashen with the grief of lost children. Mrs. Lawson's cries swell, then subside, then swell again. The girl reaches for the boy's hand, her grip tight. The crowd holds its breath.

After a hopeful period of quiet, Dr. Patak steps out onto the sundeck, stumbles to the deck rail and everyone quiets for her pronouncement. A heave of red vomit rushes out of her, splatters steaming on the sand below. She wipes her mouth with the back of her hand and stalks back to the house. Hours later, Mr. Lawson exits by the basement door, carries a blood-soaked pillowcase. Arm rigid, he holds the article far from his trembling body. Dr. Woo follows him with a shovel.

12

G ERRY STANDS ON THE PEDALS OF HER BIKE, rides a slow, controlled slalom down the hill, forces the cars behind her to change lanes. Her muscles shudder with the effort. The horn blares make her smile. At the bottom of the hill, she tucks as the traffic light slips to amber, swerves around a car turning right.

She pants as she sprints, a buzz in her ears, a new looseness in her body, wonders if she will seem different without Ian, like girls at school who lose their virginity, bragging chatter and gossip replaced by sly smiles, their faces etched older, more knowing overnight. Perhaps she should have done that first, had sex with him, womanhood achieved and friendship dissolved in one grand gesture. Her gut sours at the thought of him seeing her naked. She hates the idea of virginity, a gift to be given to or taken by or saved for a boy, prefers to think of doing it herself, finding a boy and using him for the task. Someone inexperienced who could get it over quickly and wouldn't disgust her in the process. She would do it in the dark without making a sound. She would keep most of her clothes on.

Boys at school are out of the question. Their idea of a come-on a centrefold pinned to her locker door, an oil-slicked blonde in a torn cop's uniform, nightstick buried between her legs, the word *CUNT* scrawled across her face in red felt. The metal heads howled, paper bag lunches swinging from their fists, while the preppy girls snickered beside her, huddled in a protective cloud of Giorgio. One of them mouthed, Eat me. When Gerry reached to tear down the picture, a peeled orange exploded against her locker, splattered her face with juice.

She rides through the cemetery, the careful order of monuments, headstones nested in trimmed grass relaxes her. Along the crematorium path, a line of blossoming cherry trees. She raises her hands, bats their swelled branches, showers herself in fleshy petals.

By Megan's block, she's brushed away most of the blossoms. She coasts to a stop just before Megan's house. The toes of her sneakers drag. Sun distorts the curves and colour of metal, plays tricks with cars. She rolls forward to see past the rusty green VW camper. Ian's car hunkers behind it, chrome grill like a half-grin telling her nothing has changed.

She feeds Clem chicken à la king from a warm bowl. He nods his head to avoid her spoon, his only interest the television, Wink Martindale's lacquered hair, square teeth, and wandlike microphone.

Laughter from the kitchen. Clem chuckles along.

She wipes his chin. "Traitor." Tries not to think of the embarrassment of catching Ian halfway between Megan's bedroom and the bathroom, his body flushed and bare except for his briefs. Then Michelle and Andri coming through the back door, so that Gerry had to swivel to show she hadn't been staring, her face on fire. "The prodigal son," Andri had called out. Gerry had no idea what he meant. But Andri was in good spirits, wrestled off his parka and two cardigans, babbled about the strengths of the new device. When Megan emerged from the bathroom, Ian's Iggy Pop T-shirt tight across her bra-less chest, Gerry volunteered to feed Clem, couldn't bear listening to them get on without her.

She touches the food to Clem's lips, a signal for him to open. The television audience applauds.

"He's sure gonna miss you." Michelle smiles from the doorway.

Gerry scrapes the dribbles from his lip with the edge of her spoon. "He doesn't even know who I am."

"He knows."

"Maybe I'll visit him in the home." Gerry searches Clem's face for a flicker of agreement but finds none.

Michelle's hands settle like birds on top of her stomach. She's grown so big, it's hard to believe Andri isn't taking her home each night and inflating her with a bicycle pump. "Come back in when you're done, okay?"

Gerry takes her time, watches Clem swallow, lumps of food slipping under the fabric of his skin. She consoles herself with game show victories, hysteria over washing machines and luggage sets, imagines throwing her arms around Wink's tanned neck.

In the kitchen, Andri sits with his arm around Michelle, fiddles with drawings curled in a roll on the table. Megan stands at the ironing board, a notepad and pen beside her on the counter. At her feet, Clem's washed shirts hang over the edge of the laundry basket like wrinkled ghosts. Gerry takes the empty seat beside Michelle. Ian sprawls in his chair, head cocked to avoid her, a smirk in the corners of his mouth.

"So. Now that that's all settled." Megan smiles. Her face appears lit from the inside, cheeks high with colour, eyes like mirrors. "Andri and I have decided to make an adjustment."

Andri leans across to Gerry. "My idea."

Megan nods. "We want Gerry to do the drop."

Gerry's mind rearranges Megan's words, tries to make sense of them.

"She's smaller, so she'll have a better chance ducking the cameras. She's younger, which makes the cover story more believable. And, as Andri pointed out, the law offers her more protection."

The fluorescent bars of the ceiling light seem brighter than usual, force Gerry to blink. Heat rises in her face.

Ian tips his chair back. "Bitchin'. You guys want to make me feel like shit, go right ahead, knock yourselves out."

Andri looks up. "Who cares how you feel?"

"Oh, for fuck's sake." Ian shakes his head at Gerry. "Do not believe it."

A milky haze gums her eyelids and she worries she might cry for no reason. A hand touches her arm.

"It's okay." Michelle's voice, small and far away.

Gerry presses the table edge to ground herself, then rubs at her eyes. "I'm fine." The table tilts in front of her.

Michelle shifts closer. Her belly presses into Gerry's arm. "Put your head between your knees."

"Are you watching this? You're torturing her." Ian pushes out of his chair, posts himself beside the fridge, arms across his chest.

"She's fine," Megan says.

"I wouldn't count on it. She used to have these episodes when she was a little kid."

"Shut up!" Gerry wills herself not to look at him. "I'm okay." She feels herself nodding.

"You're changing the plan a week out?" Ian shakes his head. "I don't think so."

"A week is a long time." Andri's furry hands play with the drawings. "Do you want to go to jail, Ian?"

"Well, Andri, I know you don't." He turns to Megan. "Or you either. It's not exactly like father, like daughter, is it?"

Megan smooths a sleeve on the ironing board. "What if you don't show? What if you show, but you're too fucked up to pull it off?"

Ian laughs. "Well, what a hypocrite you turned out to be, Snow fucking White." He leans against the fridge, stares at Gerry. "How's it going over there? You getting that floaty feeling? Her mom thought it was epilepsy or something. Turns out it was just stress. A nine-year-old stress case."

"Shut! Up!" The room wavers as if the walls and cupboards are painted on fabric. Gerry focuses on the back door until the window sets in its frame, the floor hardens beneath her feet. "I'm fine."

Ian nods to Megan. "I need to talk to you in the other room." He stares, but she resists his gaze. The iron puffs steam.

Andri shakes his head. "How you do things, it's tempestuous. You'll get caught, you'll go to jail. And then, we all go to jail. This girl" – his eyebrows rise as he points to her – "she is the perfect operative. She makes our cover story make sense. She does not look suspect. I have confidence." He taps a thick finger to his jacket. Gerry feels the thud in her own chest, repeated, as if he's jump-started her heart. "Even if she gets caught, what will they do? Scratch their heads." He smiles at her and she feels flushed with gratitude. Andri sits back in his chair, tips his chin at Ian. "This is the plan. No argument. If you want out, if you want to go, now is a good time."

Ian points at Megan. "This isn't for real."

Megan shrugs. "It is."

He steps away from the fridge, pulls his keys from his pocket, jangles them in the air, nods to Gerry. "Come on."

She looks to Megan for confirmation. Megan buttons a finished shirt onto a hanger. "Do whatever you want, sweetheart."

Ian jitters in front of her.

"I'm staying."

He kicks the side of the fridge. Gerry jumps in her seat.

"Ian," Michelle murmurs.

"Oh, come off it!" His shout echoes in the small room. "There is no. Fucking. Way." He stares at Gerry. "This is never gonna happen."

She reads it in his face, the shock of all of them against him, a fracture below the surface, hobbling and permanent. His gaze drifts, lost, and she is surprised by how difficult it is to watch him flounder. "I'm responsible for her." He points at her, his eyes on Andri. He makes her sound like an animal, something tied to a fence.

"The girl wants to stay," Andri says gently.

Hands on his hips, head bowed, Ian rubs his palm over his face. He turns for the back door. Michelle takes Gerry's hand, squeezes it.

Ian pauses at the threshold. He kicks the door with his boot. The small window rattles. She watches the glass quake, waits for it to shatter. Rooted in his spot, he slams the door, opens it, slams it over and over. When he finally knocks the door closed with his boot, the quiet is a relief. He stands with his back hunched, jams his fists into his pockets, flaps his elbows like wings, stares up at the ceiling. "So now what?"

For a while, no one speaks. Gerry doesn't breathe.

"Now," Andri chuckles. "We eat crow."

Megan shakes her head. "You eat crow."

Andri rolls the drawings, taps them against the table. "Yes. Okay. I eat crow."

Gerry struggles to decipher their code. Ian turns, his face a replica of her confusion. Michelle rubs Gerry's shoulder. "Told you it was okay."

Megan starts on another shirt. "Andri had no faith."

Andri shrugs. "I'm an atheist."

"What are you talking about?" Gerry says it loud enough to hear herself.

Ian shakes his head. "Assholes. All of you."

"Take it as a warning." Andri pounds the table with his fingers. "You cannot just show up when you like."

"What are you saying?" Gerry's desperation echoes back in answer.

Megan's brow furrows. Her eyes flit to Ian. "It was a test. He passed. We need to know we can count on each other."

Gerry eases out of Michelle's grasp. Ian stares at her, his face drawn with relief. She waits for the insult, the put-down. That it doesn't come only makes the moment worse.

"It was never going to be you, Gerry Mouse."

Andri chuckles. "Don't be so sure."

Gerry slides from her chair. Their cooing attempts to keep her stop as soon as she's out the back door. Their silence follows her, airy absence as she climbs onto her bike and rides away.

$$13$$

DOWNTOWN SHE FINDS A 7-ELEVEN, buys a pack of menthol cigarettes and two fistfuls of red licorice. She locks her bike to the rack outside. Across the street, an office tower's mirrored windows reflect the setting sun. The road crackles with the slow roll of rush hour traffic as she walks to Robson Street.

"1999" pumps from a cruising car. Spring break has made a Mecca of shopping. Outside shoe stores, jewellers, hair salons, girls worship in pods, swathed in white with neon accessories, elbows dangling plastic bags blazed with labels, fingers busy with whipped drinks and frozen yogurt. Gerry gnaws at her candy, washes it down with a waterfall of minty smoke. Even though the girls are strangers, they know to stare, assess with their gaze, fall into giggles as they pass her. She tries to ignore them, imagine the storefronts dark, street cleansed of superficial consumption, filled instead with marchers carrying signs, shouting slogans, Prince's bass line replaced by the pounding of protest drums. The shops are garbage, logo after logo, uniforms for brainwashed masses. Only one window impresses her, an out-of-business tobacco shop, its half-empty display of lighters and switchblades dusty and mean.

She finishes the last of the licorice just as her stomach starts to churn, her body drunk on syrup and ash. The shade of the arched pass-through beckons, the shortcut she mapped, a route none of the others had considered. She slouches there, shadowed between the street and the alley, watches girls with crimped hair, glazed lips, and turned-up collars prance past in jelly shoes, tries not to throw up.

In the alley behind the revenue building, security lights buzz. Their frequencies harmonize over the percussive drip of a drainpipe. Crouched beside a dumpster, Gerry watches the concrete steps, her feet numb inside her sneakers, wet from walking and rewalking the route.

A clever paint job camouflages the small metal box. The security door opens and closes, raincoats, suits, umbrellas, goodbyes. The office workers pay the box no attention. A shopping cart rattles, then stops, then rattles again. The breeze turns and the fishy stench of garbage forces Gerry to shift her position, breathe through her mouth. Office workers mutter conversation, shoes scuff concrete, water burbles through a drain. In the parking lot across the alley, cars idle.

It takes time for her to build up the courage. She waits through the blue dusk, the swish and rumble of traffic. Above her, the sky between buildings darkens. A woman stops just outside the door to check for rain, shakes an umbrella at the ready. Her hesitation offers a glimpse into the hallway, a white channel, a small camera mounted near the ceiling. The woman steps aside and knocks the door closed with her hip. Gerry counts to a hundred.

She takes the stairs carefully, listens for voices, the tap of heels. The cover on the metal box is spring-loaded, stubborn against the pry of her fingers. Inside, a beige keypad with a black faceplate and white rubber buttons, the tiny display screen shows a red digital zero, beside it, two tiny, unlit bulbs, one red, one green.

The green light flashes as she begins to punch in numbers, each digit displayed in thin red outline. She pauses before the final number, then presses and waits. The red light blinks, then glows solid, the door handle tight. She tries to focus, each number formed in her mind and on her lips before she presses. The same flashing red light. Was there a trick to the sequence? Did she jumble it? She can no longer be certain the numbers in her head are the ones scrawled in Andri's notebook. She tries again quickly, gouges her frustration into the keys. As if sensing her mood, the keypad lights wink out, leave the screen a dormant black square.

Inside the building, a door opens, voices in echo. She crawls under the rail and hops down from the landing, crosses the alley and squats beside the dumpster. Businessmen slip out, raincoats flapping at their knees. Their talk is loud, assured. After they've gone, she knocks her head against the dumpster's metal wall, *stupid*, *stupid*, tells herself she's not allowed to move, must sit there all night, watch the moon pass overhead, let the stink of the alley soak through her clothes and skin, a loser's vigil.

The door bangs open against the metal rail. A man in a dark cap and jacket hovers at the keypad, then props the door with a toolbox, gives Gerry a full view of the hallway. At the far end, a green door with a small window to the lobby. The man scans the alley and notices her, squints to make her out, nods before he turns to get something from his toolbox. He's older, a heaviness nested around the edges of his body, settled in the seat of his jeans.

She stands, pushes her hands into her pockets. "Hey."

He glances at her. "Geez, I thought you were a guy sitting there."

"Is it broken?"

"Were you foolin' with it?"

"Uh, not even. Some guys just came out, though." She walks up to him, folds her arms over the safety rail, rests her chin. "You work here?"

"Why? You looking for a job?" His smile shows that he's teasing.

"I'm still in high school."

"Wow. Okay, well, this conversation's over." His hands busy with a screwdriver, six screws to remove the spring-loaded door.

She struggles to hold his interest. "I'm graduating."

Four screws loosen the faceplate that lifts to reveal a narrow screen and a single cable jack. He shakes his head. "Sure you are. Your dad doesn't work here or something, does he? 'Cause I really don't need the trouble."

"No."

"You sleeping rough?"

"What?"

"On the street?"

"No." She worries the dumpster smell might have clung to her, feels her jacket and finds a sticky patch near the shoulder. She slips out of it, rolls it into a ball, presses the wad against the rail, and leans her chest over it. "If it's not broken, why do you have to fix it?"

His eyes flit to check her out.

She pulls her shoulders back a little, something she imagines Megan would do.

"What's with the hair?"

"What hair?"

Her joke gets a chuckle. He goes back to his work. "They're only supposed to try twice on this thing. If the door doesn't open, they're supposed to go around front, check in with security. Three times and the keypad shuts down. They always try three times." He taps the screwdriver against his thigh. "Anyway, you should scram. I'm supposed to do this in private. Don't want to get you in trouble."

"I like trouble." The words trip out of her, eager, awkward.

His mouth crimps at the corners, amused but unsure. From the toolbox he lifts a black plastic console. It opens like a book to reveal another keypad, a wire he plugs into the cable jack.

"You go to school for that?"

"My brother taught me. I do installs out in the sticks, but he took his kids to Disney for spring break, so here I am in the big shitty." As he leans forward to check the connections, his T-shirt rides up, bares doughy flesh pinched by the band of his jeans. In the light, his wrists are pasty, spattered with freckles. The rim of his cap flattens a brush of rust-coloured hair, thick and wiry like the coat of a terrier.

"Does that machine make new keys?"

"Keys?" His face is flat and broad, ginger fuzz grows over his upper lip. "There are no keys, grasshopper, only numbers."

She wonders if she will have to kiss him, tries to imagine his taste, raw and creamy, meat soaked in milk. "That machine makes codes?" She presses her body against the rail, cocks her hip, rests her cheek on her arm.

He stops working and stares at her, brow tight, as if her questions make him nervous. "Did your boyfriend do that to your face?"

Something bitter and squeezing inside her makes her feel ashamed. She turns her head and stares up the alley. "I don't have a boyfriend." When she looks back at him, she forces a smile.

He fiddles with the console. "So, you're graduating."

"Not really."

"You like to party?"

She shrugs. "Depends."

For a while he works without talking, pushes buttons, digs a small notepad from his back pocket, flips through pages of numbers, scribbles new ones with a stubby pencil. "Wanna see something cool?" He gestures for her to climb the steps.

She kneels beside him, aware of his body heat in the air between them. He points to the console box, his voice bolstered with authority. "This is way state of the art. Futuristic and shit, you know? Most companies stick with a single four-digit code, but we do three double-digit numbers, harder to crack, easier to remember, year, month, day, or like, 36-24-36." He smiles.

"That's the code?" Even to her, the pretend innocence sounds moronic.

"Would I tell you the code? Do I look like a retard? Geez." The muscles in his neck harden, then relax. The light leaves half of him in shadow, and his body seems momentarily frozen in place. He shuffles back on his heels, and as he does he settles his hand on her leg, just above her knee. She fights the impulse to crawl away, wonders whether Megan enjoyed it with the man who looked like Magnum P.I., whether she took off all of her clothes.

The hand squeezes but doesn't travel. He gestures to the box. "Anyway, every few weeks, we have to update the code. But we can't just make a random change 'cause people don't want to have to memorize a whole new code every time. So we use an assigned number key for each door." He points to the panel. "3, 1, 3, right here. We add the digits of the number key to the digits of the previous code to make the new code. Takes people a while to figure it out. That's why they're always jamming up the keypads."

"So, if the old code is 10, 10, 10, then the new code is–" The security light makes it hard for her to see his eyes. "13, 11, 13?"

"I guess you're on the honour roll."

She lets her shoulder rest against his. "But, if you don't know the old code, the number key won't help you?"

"Bingo."

"I guess I can't break in then." She nudges him, tries to knock him off balance, but his body holds rigid, a reminder of his size, his strength, the fact that no one knows she's here.

"Don't know why you'd want to, anyway. Nothing but men in suits in there. You don't go for that, do you?"

She shakes her head.

"Didn't think so." His lips make a smacking sound. "What kind of music do you like?"

She guesses at what he likes. "I don't know, old stuff, Zeppelin."

He nods. "Cool. *Zeppelin IV*?"

"Sure." Another code. When a guy played *Zeppelin IV*, it meant he wanted to have sex with you. "What if the number hits 99, do you just go back to 0?"

"You're pretty smart. We get a lot of calls about that one. You good at math?" He presses the plate back onto the door, his fingers quick and skilled with the screwdriver.

"I guess."

"What are the odds of me running into you in this alley when I don't even work downtown?"

She waits for the punch-line.

"Probably," he draws the word out, pretends to think. "Sixty-nine to one."

She rolls her eyes. "Don't you mean to two?"

Grinning, his face in full light, he's not threatening at all but full of goofy humour. She sees how relieved he is, how she's done him a favour by being a good sport. He's the kind of guy who wouldn't care if she was fat or strange-looking, as long as she could laugh at a joke, have fun. "I'll be finished up in about half an hour. If you wanna wait, maybe we could do something?" The offer makes his mouth crooked.

She feels for the rail and pushes herself up, tucks her chin to look down at him. "I thought you didn't talk to high school girls?"

He stays on his knees. "So did I. But you don't look young enough for jail time."

She smiles. "Thirteen'll get you twenty."

"Look at us, a regular Cheech and Chong." He reaches for his toolbox, stands and pats the door. "So, anyway. Think about it." The door glides closed behind him, locks in place with a whir.

She considers staying. Despite his size, he seems harmless. They'd drive somewhere, maybe Lost Lagoon, find a place to park. He would have beer. Afterwards, he'd be grateful, make jokes. He'd want to drive her home, but she'd ride her bike, speed away, catalogue how she felt different.

The number key repeats in her head. She doesn't trust herself to keep the secret, what she will be part of because of him, can't be sure the details won't leak out after enough beer. She swings over the rail and jumps down from the landing, tries to stop the smile that pulls at her face. Each trotting step she takes lightens her, each rain-filled pothole pond holds the moon.

———

Through the small back door window, they look like a family sitting down to dinner. The amber globe over the table lights their faces, leaves the rest of the kitchen in shadow. Michelle giggles into her hands as Andri builds a pyramid of beer cans in front of her. Andri laughs, squinty-eyed, teeth the size of Chiclets. Hidden by the table, Ian reaches for Megan's arm, strokes it with the backs of his fingers. Their ease makes Gerry feel as if she is the bomb, a collision of particles meant to blow everything apart. She turns the doorknob.

Andri's cheeks flame red, he raises his beer can. "Behold the tiny devil! She returns to us!" Beside him, Michelle shakes her head, mouths, "He's drunk."

Megan slides away from Ian, stands beside her chair. "I thought for sure you'd figured it out and were just playing along. We didn't mean to scare you."

"No." Ian takes a swig of beer. "You meant to scare me."

Across the table, Michelle wags her finger. "You deserved it."

"Michelle, I swear to God, if you weren't pregnant." He makes a cartoon of himself, heaves out of his chair and punches into the crook of his arm. In his flailing, he knocks against the counter, then the table. The beer can pyramid topples.

Michelle laughs and sticks out her tongue. Andri's head swings back and forth between the two of them, his mouth a smeared grin.

Megan holds out her arm. "Come sit down."

Gerry wishes this moment could be a photograph, the group of them captured in black and white, suspended in a cone of light, loose smiles, Megan beckoning. Or perhaps an oil painting, like the ones she's seen on school visits to the art gallery, carved gold frames, historic people about to do historic things. "You don't have the code." She says it plainly, without malice or gloating.

Andri sighs, rests his face on the table, bats at a beer can with his fingers until the can clatters to the floor.

"Gerry." Megan shakes her head. "Ian, grab her a beer out of the fridge."

Ian leans back against the counter. "None left." He closes one eye and aims at Gerry, his fingers in the shape of a gun. "Sorry, kiddo."

"I was there with the guy who changes it."

"What is she talking about?" Andri mumbles into his arm. "*Where* were you?"

"He showed me how to figure out the new code."

The low growl of Clem's snoring drifts in from the bedroom. Megan walks toward her, tries to take her hand. Gerry curls her fingers in a fist.

"Look, I know you're mad," Megan says.

Andri sits ups, tugs a battered pack of American cigarettes from his jacket, tips one to his lips, and lights it.

The air cracks as Ian opens a fresh beer. "Let her sulk."

"I can prove it." Gerry says.

Michelle's hand waves away the smoke. "Andri, the baby."

"Forget the baby." He points his cigarette at Gerry. "What can you prove?"

Andri parks the car in an alley two blocks from the revenue building. The engine pings as it cools. He stuffs the car keys into his pocket, zips his parka. "I hope you are not wasting my time." Gerry shakes her head, prays he can't tell she's spent the drive trying to sharpen her fuzzy memory of his notebook.

On the way, they pass a tunnel that leads to a teen night-club Gerry has heard of but never been to. The tunnel is dark, shadowed with kids lined up to get in. Here and there a lighter flickers, casts a fan of hair in relief. Two girls climb out of the tunnel and lean against a concrete pillar to share a cigarette. They wear long white shirts with rolled-up sleeves over black tights, and tall, buckled boots with pointy toes. Their eyes sink between bands of black liner, both of them with a side of hair shorn. While one smokes, the other dances to the throb of bass coming from the back of the club, a military stomp that makes Gerry bob her head. She wonders how hard it would be to slip away from Andri, ask to bum a smoke, and join them in the lineup. The club's back door swings open and Frankie's "Relax" pours into the alley. A guy in a T-shirt and suspenders with a short blond Mohawk steps out and calls to the girls. Behind him, a swirl of coloured lights, a strobe's rapid-fire flash. The girls scream as they fling their arms around his neck. He ushers them through then pulls on the door so it seals them in with a thud.

Andri lags behind her, sucks on his cigarette and grumbles about the cold. To Gerry, the night is warm, heat brewing against the back of her jacket and under her arms. She doesn't mind the slow pace, uses the time to tease apart numbers that swim together and switch partners as she attempts to put them in order. Perhaps, she decides, if she tries not to think about them, they will come clear. She turns and walks backward, focuses on Andri's face. "Have you ever been to prison?"

He picks tobacco from his tongue. "One year at a labour camp. Much worse than your prison. Right after university."

"What did you do?" She imagines Andri smuggling refugees across a border, breaking into government laboratories, sabotaging missiles with computer code.

"I had some pamphlets. Political writings. I didn't agree with them, but I was handing them out for a friend. They sent us to a mine in the north. Disgusting place. They poison your food. But only now and then, so you get sick, then you're afraid to eat. No blankets, so you can never get warm. Anyway, I survived. My mother paid money for us to come here, so I could drive a forklift. Canadian dream." They reach the parking garage beside the revenue building and Andri stops at the locked-down gate. "I will watch from here." He clutches the hood of his parka up around his neck.

Gerry takes the cement stairs slowly, pauses at the door to give herself time to think. She stands with her fingers on the spring-loaded cover but knows without even opening it, there's no point. She hops off the stairs and walks back to Andri.

"What?"

Gerry shrugs. "I don't remember your numbers. I mean, I thought I did, but– You get two chances, maybe three, I'm not sure what the guy said."

"This is what we drove here for?"

"Just show me your book again."

"Forget it. Let's go."

"Without my numbers, your code is useless."

"What's useless is a girl who can't remember a simple code."

"I thought you wanted me to do this." Gerry feels the fight drain out of her. "So what? I'm supposed to give you the change code? So Ian can do it? Or maybe Michelle?"

Andri's face tightens. He digs in his pockets for his cigarettes, lights up and draws a deep drag, scowls behind a veil of smoke. "Michelle has done her part. Ian." Andri flaps his hand in the air.

Gerry waits, listens to the horns of cars cruising a few blocks away as Andri finishes his cigarette. He crushes the butt in his fingers, reaches into his jacket for his notebook, holds it open.

She jogs the stairs. The keypad triggers fresh anxiety, rubber buttons mocking her. She takes a deep breath and recites Andri's code in her head, adds her numbers, then presses the buttons slowly. A soft click inside the door signals an unlocking. She reaches for the handle. The door doesn't budge. Over her shoulder, Andri nods his head for her to hurry.

She double-checks her math, tries to see the numbers in her mind, pushes the buttons more firmly, allows for a longer pause. The same click, the same locked door.

"No luck?" Andri calls. "You tried, anyway. We go back to the car. Back to the drawing–"

She kicks at the door in frustration.

"Hey, hey, hey!" Andri waves his arm. "Get down from there, let's go." He walks toward her.

It occurs to her then that the code has been updated more than once. She pictures the code in her mind and adds her numbers to it twice, double- and triple-checks her math. The buttons offer spongy resistance as she presses. The doorframe whirs. She reaches for the handle, it drops, and the door swings open.

Andri stops at the foot of the stairs. He raises his hands and claps. She stands at the threshold, basks in his applause.

As they walk back to the car, Gerry notices the lineup for the nightclub has dwindled, everyone now inside, the tunnel empty.

She listens for music leaking out, imagines stepping away from Andri, disappearing through the club's back door, losing herself in a pit of strangers and vanilla smoke, bass pounding in her chest, eyes closed as lights spin over her face. She strains to hear, but the song has changed, the pulse now muted and distant, not a song at all but the beat of blood in her ears.

At Megan's, Andri orders Gerry to wait on the back porch. She shivers, watches their outlines through foggy glass as Andri and Megan argue and pace, Michelle and Ian silent at the kitchen table.

"You called the guy," Andri says. "You asked him what we paid for?"

"What *I* paid for." Megan's voice is sharp. "We called from a phone booth. He hung up on me. Twice."

"The girl is smart."

"That's not how this goes."

"How it goes? My dear, this is how it is. Without her we have nothing."

"How does she know the door code?"

"What does that matter? We need both codes, we only have one."

"Then make her tell us." Megan turns to look at Gerry, her expression obscured by the murky window.

"Don't you think I tried?" Andri's shout rattles the glass. "She's too stubborn."

Ian knocks over his chair as he stands, moves to the door so fast that Gerry hasn't time to step back before it flings open and Ian has her wrist gripped and torqued, pulled up between them.

"This isn't a game now," his voice cold and hard. "Tell them what they want to know."

She sucks a breath to ride out the pain of his hold, shakes her head.

○ ○ ○

THE DAY ARRIVES WITHOUT SURPRISE. Too many men have fallen ill. Dan tells the boy in front of everyone, so that he can't make a fuss. The girl runs to the hut. Wives snicker at her weakness. The boy finds her sitting cross-legged on the bed. You don't have to go, she says. They can't make you.

He doesn't explain that he wants to go. Instead, he stuffs the stove with branches, tucks her into bed, lies behind her, on top of the covers. His hand pats a soft, lulling rhythm on her hip. He worries about her, left alone through the night.

Her breath smooths to a deep tide, her body still. He knows she pretends for his sake, and if he spoke, she would reply in a clear voice. He rises from the bed at the first murmur of men on the beach, slips into his jacket. The outline of her body develops in the grey light of the cabin. He opens the door.

The men meet his presence with neither welcome nor rebuff. Each glance, eye grazing eye. All of them have been out before. Dan arrives with the same black equipment bag, doles out guns and ammunition. The rifle sits heavy in the boy's hand, metal barrel cold against his fingers. He asks how to use it, but no one answers. Dan hands a piece of paper to Roger, a firefighter, one of the few to have gone on every expedition. Roger catches the boy's stare, waves the paper before folding it. Shopping list, he says.

The men chuckle, a palpable release of tension.

The trek is long and slow. Many of the men are unwell. Terry, a librarian who has lost so much weight he ties his canvas belt in a knot, vomits repeatedly before the group is even out of the camp, ignores insistence that he turn back. Chester, an older man, complains about his weeping sores until Roger asks him to stop.

The night hangs low in the trees. One man carries a small flashlight, its dim beam shudders. The group navigates by shadows and sound. The boy trips and scuffles his way along, while others step sure and heavy. He waits for conversation to begin, mutterings to fill the long, dark minutes that stretch in front of them, but there is no small talk, only the intermittent *Shit* as a man missteps or *Goddamn* as a tree branch catches him in the face.

As the group arrives at the road, the flashlight goes off. The men take on a casual march formation with the boy near the middle. Men breathe on either side of him, but he cannot see their jackets in the dark. They walk the road for hours, far beyond the village where the empty faces of abandoned homes loom above.

Light dimples the landscape, sporadic fires perforate the mountain's surface, signal that town is close. As the road leads past gas stations and storefronts, the boy hears a distant scurrying on gravel, whispers under the scuff of men's boots.

On the ready, Roger says.

The men raise rifles, scan the empty streets. The boy does the same, though he has no idea what to look for. Four men with flashlights turn them on. As the group comes to the main street above the Quay, their flashlights flick on and off in an erratic pattern. The sounds confuse him, whistles, shouts, the dull stomp of footfalls in retreat.

The group stops at the corner of Lonsdale and Eighth. The centre of town, streets strewn with debris, shop windows shattered, storefronts charred, the shambolic work of looters. Roger separates everyone into groups of three and assigns tasks.

He lumps the boy with Marcus, a short insurance salesman, who despite camp rations and illness has managed to stay rotund, and Chuck, a bespectacled bus driver who shares a house with his dead brother's wife.

Roger hands each of them a keychain flashlight, a touristy thing decorated with a photo of a ski resort gondola.

Shops, says Roger.

Marcus groans. Jesus, there's nothing left.

Roger moves on to the next triad, tears off a piece of the shopping list.

Why don't we get a list? the boys ask Marcus.

Marcus smiles. 'Cos of you.

They do the first shop together, a ransacked outdoor adventure store. The boy mimics the other two, fills his sack with a stray water bottle, some loose bike repair tools, two granola bars he finds jammed between the cash register and wall. After that, they split up, tackle three stores at a time, meet back on the sidewalk to gauge their success.

In the appliance store, the boy finds a mess of overturned dishwashers and clothes dryers, all the microwaves missing. He wonders who took them and for what. Who thought all the greeting cards from the stationery store or the aquariums from the pet store would prove useful? He works his way through the broken glass and past the debris to backrooms, offices, culls janitor closets and inventory cupboards.

While he's in a skateboard shop, digging through cardboard boxes filled with Styrofoam packing, a rifle blasts outside. He runs into the street and finds himself alone, the other two still in their shops. Three more shots fire in the distance. The boy dashes into the Indian supermarket Marcus claimed as his territory, finds Marcus on his hands and knees, flashlight in his teeth. He sweeps a scatter of dried lentils from the floor into his palm, studies them under the flashlight, then slaps his palm to his lips.

Marcus.

Marcus turns, startled, struggles to swallow. He coughs, his face red. Yeah, what? It was less than a handful.

The boy points to the door. They're shooting.

Marcus shrugs. So what? His flashlight beam trails along the floor, hunts under the lip of the empty shelves. He looks back over his shoulder. Get lost, will ya?

The boy heads back to the skateboard store.

In the stinking, graffitied staff washroom, he finds a brick of weed meticulously wrapped in plastic, taped inside the dry toilet tank. He stands and weighs the score in his hand, marvels at its size before slipping it into his bag. A thin whistle hisses out behind him. He fumbles with his flashlight, draws back against the toilet, and shines the beam into the corner.

A man huddles against the garbage can, his clothes shredded and dirty. His face, a skinned peach, fleshy and damp, hairless, features melted into suggestions of eyes, a nose. His mouth, a raw slash, opens and closes, the wheezing sound, his breath. The boy cries out, a sickened, terrified wail that echoes around him. Underneath the man lies a woman, bloody, inanimate. The man raises his left hand, barely, but enough for the boy to notice a thick gold watch hanging obscenely from his wrist.

The boy looks to the door. Two steps, three, at most. Flashlight on the man, he inches away from the toilet. The man's hand jerks and the boy screams, runs out of the bathroom, out of the store, barrels into Chuck on the street.

Whoa. Geez. Meet your maker?

It takes the boy a second to find his voice. He babbles about the bodies.

Chuck slaps him on the arm. Don't worry about it, chum.

They scavenge until dawn. Now and then, a burst of gunfire, a rash of yelling, a scream. Chuck seems unaffected by the noise. The sounds cause Marcus to pause on the sidewalk, stare wistfully up at the house-dappled side of the mountain. The three of them make their way back to the meeting point and wait for the others as the sky lightens, black to charcoal to muddy grey. The boy and Chuck struggle with their hauls. Marcus catches the boy eyeing his empty bag.

Ain't much worth taking, am I right?

The men return slowly. Roger and his team arrive first, sacks full, one of the men with a scrape across his forehead.

How'd it go? Marcus asks.

Roger gives a single nod.

Of the next group, only two men return, and between them, only one bag. Jojo, a Slavic gas station attendant, sniffles and wipes his eyes. His partner, Brett, a long-haired musician, carries a bag in one hand, props up Jojo with the other.

Oh God, oh God, Jojo says.

Roger pats him on the back. You did good, Jojo, you did good.

The last group comes back with nervous smiles, bags full. Marcus lures one of the men aside, asks urgent, whispered questions. The man replies quickly, also in a whisper, makes a gesture with his hands, locking his thumb and fingers in an O. Both men grin.

All right, cut it out, Rogers says. Let's head back.

Men take turns with rifles ready, four at a time, while others carry the bags. The boy doesn't get a turn at rifle duty. An hour in, a rock scuttles across the road and Brett fires into the trees, three quick shots. The boy waits for Roger to reprimand him, but no one says anything.

He smells the camp before he sees it, rodent soup boiling on the fire, the perfume of civilization. Relief wells up inside him. Men break into a trot as they enter the wooded area. The boy follows, bag slamming his lower back, strap cutting into his shoulder, his neck.

He expects a cheer to erupt as he makes it to the beach. Instead, everyone falls silent. Each man drops his bag at Dan's feet. The boy does the same.

Dan shakes his hand and says, Thank you. Looks him dead in the eye.

The girl waits for him by the fire with his meal, burnt bread like gritty stone, a bowl of watery soup. He walks to her and lays his arm across her shoulder. She wraps herself against his waist, squeezes. As he eats, he's distracted by her presence, senses every shift in her body. He pushes his food toward Marcus, who accepts it with a scowl. The boy leads the girl to the cabin.

Before the cabin door is closed, she is on him. Mouth, tongue, hands, her body smashed against his. Her salty-sweet taste undoes him. She tears at his shirt, fingers cold against his skin, kisses his chest, her lips warm. His hands feel under her cardigan, to the watery softness of her shrunken breasts. He kneels in front of her, suckles at one side, then the other. Her hands grip the back of his head, pushes him down, down.

He pulls at the button of her woolly pants, lets them drop down her legs, thin, pale, goosefleshed. Her panties, grey and frayed at the elastic edges, sag off her hips. He smells her, the candied tang of her unwashed skin. With his tongue, he works the fabric against her. She gasps, opens her legs and his tongue slips deeper, fabric pushing inside, a tiny hardness against his upper lip.

She grabs his hand and pushes it to her, grips him through his jeans. She moves quickly, unbuttoning, unzipping. Her thumb and forefinger smooth down him in a fluid motion that makes his legs twitch. His fingers burrow inside her.

She draws him down onto the cot. While he untangles himself from his clothes, she raises her knees. He stares into the dark of her hair, the folds of her skin, braces the cot with one hand, guides himself slowly. She rocks her hips and whimpers, legs tight around him.

He lowers his chest to her body, so that he feels her everywhere, holds himself, her body rocking beneath him. She gazes up at him, small lines around her wide, glistening eyes, creases at the sides of her open mouth. He sees clearly how much older she is. A wave of tenderness overcomes him. His groin tightens. He grips her shoulders and thrusts, the future rushing through him.

She touches his face. Her fingers trace him, shoulder, back, hip. She kisses his forehead. He closes his eyes and, for the first time, hears the lap of water on the beach outside their hut.

14

THE MOOD AT MEGAN'S IS SOMBRE, cheerless. Gerry struggles for a deep breath, bodies closed around her at the kitchen table as she recites the route step by step. Megan stops her at every slip, when she says clockwise but means counter-clockwise, when she calls the cut-through an alley, when she gets the timing wrong. The interruptions confuse her, force her to double-back and stumble through details she's covered. "I know it in my head."

"You don't." Megan's face has sloughed its kindness, splintered into prickly impatience. "These are stupid mistakes."

Andri, too, is moody, distracted, chews on the skin around his thumb until it looks pink and shredded. "Have you noticed a van?" he asks Megan. "A white one?" He makes circles with his finger. "Driving around?"

Megan ignores him.

"There are lots of white vans. It doesn't mean anything." Michelle massages his neck, but his anxiousness infects her, causes her hands to patter and fuss until he fans them away with an annoyed grunt.

Only Ian seems unaffected, body slung like rope as he watches them, his expression amused. He outpaces Megan and Andri two beers to one. Gerry doesn't dare take a sip, her mind already too loose and unsure.

Megan rubs her eyes. "That's enough for tonight. We'll do it again tomorrow."

"When you are falling asleep tonight, go through the timing." Andri taps his finger to Gerry's temple. "Program the subconscious."

"I know the timing." Gerry tries for defiance, but it comes out as a whine.

Megan pushes away from the table.

"Wait." Andri leans down, gathers a battered gym bag into his lap. "You wanted to see how the switch works." From the bag he lifts a flat, rectangular gift-wrapped box, gold foil paper tied with a red bow. He turns it over, flicks his finger across the short edge. "Like this. A simple tab, you tear it off. The device is activated. A child could do it."

"A child is doing it." Ian stretches his legs, crosses his boots.

Gerry pulls a tight smile to show his jibe has no effect.

Megan takes the package from Andri. "You'll have to give it a good push, so that it slides. The floors are marble, but you don't want it to get caught on a seam."

"Make sure you slide it." Andri eases his arm forward in a fluid motion. "No bounce. Aim for the centre of the lobby. The charge will take out the glass, but the concrete terraces in front of the building will act as a buffer, keep the marchers on the street safe. Like we said" – he nods to Megan – "property damage only."

Megan turns the package slowly in her hands, rocks it back and forth so that the kitchen light glints off its wrapping. She holds it out to Gerry, an offer, her face expressionless, then lobs the package in the air. It tilts, falls. Gerry catches it just before it hits the table's edge. Her hands clamp in reflex, she sucks a gasp. Andri stares, eyebrows arched. Everything they do now feels like a test. She steadies her grip, stifles a frightened laugh.

The device is dense. Its inner workings shift slightly as her fingers search the edge through the wrapping for the raised bump of the tab. When she can't find it, she tries not to let on, weighs its heft once more, then decides to make a joke. "Feels like a box of chocolates."

"Ha!" Michelle's voice cracks in the air.

Ian snatches the package from her hands, rips the paper from the corner. A black box printed with a rainbow and the words *Pot of* in gold script. "Moron."

"It would be imprudent to handle the actual device." Andri breaks into a hairy grin. "But there is a delicious one called cherry bomb."

Heat rises through Gerry's neck and face. Michelle shakes her head at Andri.

Megan rolls her eyes. "Can we move on, here?"

"Okay." Andri clears his throat. "Like I said, impact is not good for the device. Extreme heat, also not good. And whatever you do, do not put it near fat people." His body shakes, a high-pitched *hee-hee-hee* leaking from him. His laughter scores into Gerry. Perhaps all men were this way, giddy for humiliation. She imagines herself in the middle of the march, trapped in a crush of bodies, the knapsack tight against her back. A rough jostle, a loose pin, a flash of light without warning, her body bursting, spraying through the crowd in a million bloody sparks. He would be sorry then.

The possibility rumbles through her as Andri winces with delight, sighs to catch his breath, wipes tears from his eyes.

———

Because Megan tells him to, Ian drives her home. Windows down, the churchlike chords of "Five Years" carry out into the dark, Bowie's voice a torture of hopelessness and despair. They pull up in front of her house, and she reaches for the door, gathers herself for a polite thank you. Ian tosses something at her. It lands in her lap.

"Happy birthday," he says.

She feels the delicate weight on her leg, not a full baggie but more than half full. "My birthday's in September."

"Yeah, well, I figured you'd need it now."

The plastic crinkles as she touches it, broadcasts her appetite. She moves her hand away. "You're an asshole, you know that."

"Fine. Give it back."

"I'm not telling you my numbers."

He shakes his head. "I don't want your stupid codes. That's your shit to deal with now. If you're feeling in over your head—"

"I know what you're doing. You're praying for me to fail, like every single second."

"No. I know you're going to fail. There's a difference. You backed them into a corner, good for you. But if you think they're going to go through with this." Ian shakes his head. "You're an idiot."

"Shut up." She folds her arms across her chest. The space around her tightens. Something has sealed her in while she wasn't paying attention, a membrane that separates her from the rest of the world. She's sure if she reaches out, she will feel it resist, waxy and supple like the skin of a balloon.

Ian stares into the street. "I've been thinking about going to community college."

Gerry sniffs at the idea, another flakey scheme he'll give up on before the week is out. "You didn't even finish high school."

"I finished, I just didn't graduate. Anyway, I still can, correspondence or whatever."

"Community college is for retards."

Ian nods. "Got to consider the future, Gerry Mouse."

She feels herself sulking but doesn't know why, something heavy and childish she wishes she could shrug off.

They sit in silence until Ian nods at the baggie. "If you don't want that, I'll take it back."

Outside, the night is a galaxy, vast and heavy. The streetlight on the corner douses the sidewalk and grass in metallic light. She stuffs the baggie into her pocket, whispers her thanks, cracks the door open so she can float away.

Her mom yawns and stretches on the couch. "Out with the boyfriend?"

Gerry hovers in the archway. On TV, a stone-faced anchor with oil-slick hair reports that the *Bulletin of Atomic Scientists* has dialled the Doomsday Clock forward. In the wake of escalating military exercises, the clock now reads 11:57 p.m., the closest to catastrophic destruction since its inception. "He's not my boyfriend."

Her mom pats the couch. "I'll bet he's your boyfriend one day."

"Mom." Gerry draws out the word in protest, flops down to feel her mother envelop her. Warships haul through rough seas, under the domes of cockpits, fighter pilots wait, tubes and masks hanging like tentacled parasites from their faces.

Her mom's chin rests a warm pressure against her forehead. "There's leftovers. Go eat something." The bossiness smothers and soothes her. She crawls off the couch, drags her socked feet, tries to stop her heart from thumping.

Randy hunkers at the kitchen table, fork in one hand, a folded newspaper in the other. His clothes, streaked in dried mud, make him look as if parts of him have turned to stone. He stares at the paper. "When your mom asked me to stay for dinner, I assumed we'd be eating together."

Gerry opens the fridge, pours a glass of milk. "Yeah, well, she probably ate dinner at dinnertime, like a normal person."

He shrugs. "I was busy." His fork stabs a hopscotch across his plate. He shoves the food into his mouth. The mechanical workings of his jaw remind her of cows chewing grass in a pasture. "Take a look." The muffled words break from his cheeks.

She sips her milk as she crosses to the back door.

Through the glass, a halo of inset lights illuminates the pool liner, a surreal aqua pit, its perimeter braced in jigsawed two-by-fours. The angle gives the illusion of water, and Gerry feels a compulsion to swing open the doors, throw herself in.

"We pour the concrete tomorrow. Start filling, and that's it."

"It's dirty."

"Filters will get that clean in a few days. It'll be cold though. I told your mom, solar panels are a pipe-dream in this city."

"She's guessing it's what my dad has."

He scrapes his plate. "Yeah, well."

Behind him, her mom leans in the doorway. "I thought you left with the rest of them." She wraps her cardigan tight.

Randy stands, carries his plate to the sink, rinses it carefully under the tap, loads it into the dishwasher. Gerry studies them,

Randy's slow measured movements, her mom's tense eyes, chin tipped away as if she can't bear to look.

He straightens, wipes his hand on his jeans, then brushes his palms together. "Maybe you want to watch a movie?"

Her mom shakes her head. "You're filthy."

He flinches, a subtle tic in the muscles of his face. "I brought a change of clothes."

Gerry leans on the counter. "I'll watch a movie."

The offer evaporates into dry silence. Randy stares at her mom.

Flustered, her mom blinks at the floor, shakes her head, kicks her foot at something unseen. "I have to be up early."

He raps a knuckle against the counter. "Okay then." Stalks to the back door, packs up his toolbox, and lets himself out.

Her mom moves to the dishwasher, opens it, begins rearranging the dishes inside.

"If you're going to dump him, just dump him already." Gerry turns her empty glass, watches the opaque film gather into a drip. "Don't make him finish the pool."

"Geraldine, why do you say such things?" She reaches for Gerry's glass, then stoops under the sink for a scoop of dishwashing powder, sprinkles the powder carefully inside the washer like she's decorating a cake. "I'm not going to dump him."

"Yes, you are. I can tell by your face. And then what? You'll be alone."

"I've got you."

"Sure, now. But what about when I'm, you know, gone. Who's going to take care of you?"

Her mom chuckles. "Geraldine, I'm your mother. I'll be, you know, gone long before you."

"That's not what I meant." But it's exactly what she means, her fingers feel the air for the weight and shape of Andri's chocolate box. "I like him. I think he's nice."

Her mom shakes her head as she straightens. "I don't think that's true." The dishwasher burbles. Water sloshes in a lazy rhythm. "But it's kind of you to say so." She wipes her hands on a dishtowel, a weary smile on her lips. "I'm going to bed. Come here and give me a kiss before I'm, you know, gone."

Gerry lets her mom kiss her, rub her shorn head, squeeze her until her ribs ache.

The grey light and chilly breeze of predawn flit under Gerry's bedroom curtains as her mom's car mutters in the driveway. Gerry falls back into inky, dreamless sleep, a buoyant blackness she clings to, even as a thin, insectlike sound pricks at her. The shudder wakes her, a vibration that rises up through the floor to her mattress, a flicker at the window. Lightning, a spring storm. Beneath the rumble of thunder, a whining electrical note, the neighbour's power saw, a lazy ambulance winding toward a nuisance emergency. She turns on her side, tries to muffle the noise with her blanket.

The siren doubles, triples, dips low and reluctant, then spirals up to single sustained note, a fever-pitch of alarm that startles her from sleep, cold with recognition. She throws off the covers and checks her clock radio. A series of faded eights, the power out. She tries the light switch, the stereo.

Downstairs, she tries the TV. Her thumbs jam the buttons of the remote control, reveal only the reflection of her bare legs in the dark screen. In the kitchen, the emergency radio's battery case is empty, the cordless phone dead. She sprints upstairs, grabs a pen from her room, prods the lock on the study door until it pings open. Her knees slide on the surface of her father's desk. As she throws open the window, sirens rush in like water, fill the room with a panicked whir. Up and down the block, neighbours stand in their yards, hands to foreheads, eyes to the sky.

Beneath the alarm, the unmistakable scrape of speed against atmosphere. She leans out the window. From beyond the fence one neighbour calls to another, "What is that? Is that something?"

She searches but sees nothing, the sky shielded by a ceiling of muddy cloud.

The black receiver shakes in her hand. Her fingers fumble with the dial, the translucent plastic wheel dragging out each laboured rotation. No answer at her mom's lab, Ian and Megan's phones both busy. Henry's extension rings back to the station receptionist. Her finger dials zero, pops free to let the tiny window skid its countdown around the face of the phone. "Is something happening?" she asks the operator.

"What do you mean, sweetheart?"

"The air raid sirens. Has something happened?" She swipes at her face, swallows to clear her voice.

"Well, I don't think so." The operator's vowels are deep, cushiony holes. "But I'm in a cubicle, so sometimes it's snowing outside and I don't even know."

Gerry slams down the phone, holds her knees in her arms. Emergency broadcast messages, civil evacuation plans, she scolds herself for being gullible enough to believe in warning systems. She tries to remember the articles she's read, how much time she has, twenty minutes, maybe less.

Cold air drops around her shoulders. Faraway, thunder buckles. She waits, stares at the sky. Through the dirty overcast, she pictures it again and again, the tip of a warhead breaking through. Her body shakes, a vessel emptying and filling with tears until an arid calm settles over her. She hugs the windowframe.

The sky darkens to a smoky dusk. Hail, a raucous clatter, pelts the yard and house, comes down on her like icy spittle. Over the roofs across the alley, lightning scores thin white veins. Hail passes to rain. The sirens wind down, a mournful retreat. She sinks back into herself, presses her palms to her eyes, half her T-shirt soaked through, her legs splattered wet.

The front door opens with a creak and brush. She rushes to the landing and finds herself hovering above a herd of workmen as they stomp their boots. They all notice her at once, crane their necks. Smiles split their faces, except Randy, who frowns. She shivers in her panties and T-shirt, covers her body with her arms.

"Go on," Randy says to the men. They shuffle through to the kitchen. Some of them arch back to keep their eyes on her. "You should get dressed," he says.

"Did you hear the sirens?" The words stutter out of her.

"Yeah." Randy lifts his arm, wipes the rain from his face. "Some big electrical storm moving east. Everything's haywire."

"Are you sure?"

He squints at her. "About what?"

"They cut the power." As if on cue, the house ticks, bristles with static, the fridge and furnace rumble, the foyer lights blink then shine, raucous voices from the TV and radios. The workmen's applause wafts in from the yard.

"That's some party trick," Randy says.

She clutches herself to stop shaking, and she's suddenly aware of her nakedness, his eyes on her, a flush of heat through her stomach.

"Are you okay?"

"I'm fine."

"All right, then." He nods and waits, as if giving her the chance to change her mind. When she doesn't, he reaches for a bundle of tarps tied up with string. "Put some clothes on."

As soon as she hears him outside, she rushes to the living room. Remote seized at her chest, she searches for any kind of news. Finds only the plastic buzzer hysteria of game shows, soap opera nurses with powdered cleavage and glossy lips.

Showered and dressed, she waits for Henry in front of the TV. The noon news covers the storm, offers a tally of lightning strikes and hail dents in cars, no mention of sirens. More worrisome is the international news: an Iraqi Exocet missile has hit a Greek tanker in the Persian Gulf. The flagrant attack by Soviet-backed forces is expected to draw U.S. retaliation. When asked if President Reagan would consider the use of nuclear weapons, a pepper-haired man with a pursed mouth reassures a room full of reporters that the president always considers the use of nuclear weapons. His accent, coarse, wheatfield America soured with a drawl, makes Gerry feel as if she's choking on dirt.

When Henry doesn't arrive by late afternoon, she pulls on her sneakers, rounds the side gate to unlock her bike. The noise from the yard is like rocks being ground through gears. A cement truck idles in the alley. Beside it, a man stands with his shovel near his shoulder, guides sludge as it funnels off. Two men flank a long, cylindrical trough, hold their paddles, urge the sludge along. Randy watches the pour spout, hands on his hips, while beside him, two men bend at the waist like dipping birds, smooth the cement as it drops into the wooden forms. Gerry glances at the sky. A shadow streaks behind the clouds. She follows the shape until it disappears. None of the men look up.

"What are you doing?" she shouts.

"What does it look like?" Randy shouts back. "You wanna help?"

"No." She stares at the men, disgusted by their greasy ponytails and stoner eyes. The men squint, as if trying to see her from a distance. "Hey!" Gerry waves her arms. "Yeah, you guys. I want to tell you something."

"Gerry." Randy's voice shimmers under the growl of machinery.

"They're starting a war. Do you get what I'm saying? Right now, while you're doing this, making a stupid hole in the ground that nobody gives a shit about. They're setting it all up, moving things into place. And maybe you think it's no big deal, because if it was, someone would tell you, right? But no one's going to tell you until it's too fucking late. We're all going to die. We're all going to be vaporized. The world is going to shit. So, you don't need to waste whatever time you have on this."

The two men at the trough look at each other. "What'd she say?" one of them yells.

Gerry clamps her elbows over her ears and screams. The sound plows inside her. When she opens her eyes, the men's bodies are still, their mindless, automatic hands, continue to work. She waits for the snickers, their jeers, but instead they're silent, captive. "I already have a swimming pool, did he tell you that?" She points an accusing finger at Randy. "I have a swimming pool at my dad's." The word crumbles in her throat.

She blinks. Through a haze of tears, she sees Randy's body lumber toward her. She reaches for her bike, pushes off and away.

The shouting carries out into Megan's backyard. In the kitchen, Michelle and Andri sit squeezed together at the far side of the table, as if there's a shortage of space in the empty room. Andri stares at his coffee mug. His parka rides up behind his head. From the bedroom, Megan's voice is shrill and incoherent, Ian's tone flat and hard.

"What's going on?"

Andri shrugs. "Lovers' quarrel."

Michelle straightens herself in her seat. "She's upset about Clem."

"Is he okay?" Gerry steps into the hall, leans around the door-frame. Clem watches *Gilligan's Island*, hands folded on his lap, feet crossed at the ankles, a smile on his face.

"He is fine. She." Andri teeters his palm in the air. "She is thinking maybe Clem will stay here, not go to the home."

"Cool." Gerry sits down across from them.

"Not cool. Imprudent. The future is too uncertain."

"For us and Megan, he means, not for you." Michelle's face is uneasy, a soft crush of skin between her eyebrows.

"Maybe for you too, now." Andri shrugs. "If Clem is in an institution, someone takes care of him no matter what."

She had only heard them call it a home before. The word *institution* jars her, as if they're sending Clem back to prison. "Where will Megan go?"

Michelle smiles. "Clem has a lot of fans. Megan can go underground. They'll take care of her."

"What are you guys gonna do?"

Andri smiles. "It's better to know nothing. In case you get arrested. We disappear, *poof*." His hand waves an invisible wand.

"And Ian?"

Michelle looks toward the bedroom door, the shouting now a push and pull of high and low murmurs. "Oh, I'm sure he'll go wherever Megan goes, right?"

Andri nods.

Pair by pair, the future forms slowly. Gerry will be left behind like Clem. "Maybe I could go with Megan, or you guys?"

"Nobody needs a kidnapping charge. We have to leave, you have to stay," an edge to Andri's voice, as if he's scolding her for a mistake she hasn't yet made. His mistrust annoys her, then makes her feel strangely guilty. Behind her, the bedroom door opens. Ian steps out. Megan sits on Clem's bed, her face spongy. She snorts loud and wet as she holds her forearm to her nose, glowers at Gerry. "What are you staring at?"

"I'd visit him all the time." Gerry offers it as a pledge, a way for Megan to feel better about her decision.

Megan kicks the door with her bare foot. The slam judders through the house.

"Cut that out!" Clem shouts from the living room.

Michelle pushes herself up to standing, shuffles to the bedroom, opens the door and slips inside.

"Well?" Andri says.

Ian lingers in the unlit hallway. "Get ready for her to call it off."

Andri sniffs in disgust.

"We'll take Clem on Friday. If she doesn't want to go through with it, we'll pick him up again." Ian glances at Gerry. "I'm gonna need help with him."

She shakes her head. "She doesn't want my help."

"For fuck's sake, Gerry, can you just grow up for five bloody minutes?" His temper catches her off guard.

"Okay already."

"Everything is bad news." Andri pats his jacket until he finds his cigarettes. "Time for some fresh air."

When Ian doesn't follow but stands rooted, staring at the bedroom door, Gerry scrambles out of her chair to join Andri on the back porch. She reaches into her pocket and slips a menthol from the pack, hopes the gesture looks like a tired habit. She holds the cigarette for Andri to light.

Andri shakes his head as he flicks a match against his thumb-nail, snaps a flame into the air, and brings it to her face. "A child shouldn't smoke."

"Why are you all being so mean to me?"

"This isn't mean, this is adult life, adult problems. You'd like to go back to play-school?"

She grinds her sneaker against a crumbling board, watches debris fall into the well of the basement stairs. She'd expected more from them, at least gratitude. "If you guys don't want me around, then fine, I'm gone. Kiss your building access goodbye."

"You know, ego is a human nuisance." Andri holds his stubby cigarette in his lips. "You and Megan have that in common." His hands feel out the wooden porch rail, shake it. The porch shifts under her feet, the stairs rattle. "Do it or don't do it. No one is going to beg you. No one is going to force you. Something like this, just imagining it brings out weakness."

"I'm not weak."

"We are all weak." He squints at the horizon, then points. Far away, an airplane glides a slow, downward trajectory, aims for the airport across the river. "You've been watching the news?"

Gerry nods, keeps her eye on the plane as it glints low in the sky, drops behind a stand of treetops.

"Those men are weak too. It's not enough to build bombs, to collect them, they are desperate to play with them." His cigarette bounces on the porch. He stamps it with his boot, kicks the butt into the yard. "Anyway, we will be counted before we are blown to dust." He rests on his elbows. "But maybe you don't want to be counted?"

Flinty smoke jabs at the corner of her eye. "I do so."

"Then why this childish nonsense?"

She slumps on the rail, her body tired, her mouth tasting like ashy toothpaste. She rubs the lit end of her cigarette into the peeling paint, leaves a charred smudge. "I just want Megan to like me."

Andri rolls his eyes. "Put your head into what we are doing. She will honour Clem and yet she must leave him behind. It's painful for her."

"So, she can stay here with him. We don't need her at the march."

"You think she wants to just sit at home and watch this on TV?" Andri shakes his head. "Show her a little respect."

"What about me?"

"What about you?" He nods at her. "What are you sacrificing?"

She imagines talking to her father through Plexiglas, his features scratched out and blurred by the battered window, his voice crackling and distorted out as she holds the sticky receiver to her ear. "I might go to jail."

Andri smiles, raises his fists in his Rocky pose, dodges back and forth to fake her out. He sends a slow-motion right to her jaw. His knuckles graze her skin. She turns her face to take it.

"Now, jail," he says. "Jail would make you my hero."

When they get back inside, Michelle is sitting at the kitchen table. "She's resting," her voice, the even hush of motherhood. Andri and Ian grab beers from the fridge. Andri points at her. "After the news, we rehearse."

Gerry wants to join them in the living room, but Michelle holds her hand. "Keep me company."

They sit across the table from each other in silence. Gerry catches herself listening for sounds from Megan's bedroom, wonders if Michelle is doing the same.

"You shouldn't be scared," Michelle says finally, a smile on her face as she braces the table to stand. "They make it sound worse than it is."

"I'm not scared." From the living room, jet engines whine, a reporter shouts over the noise. Gerry pictures him at an airfield, wind battering the sock of his microphone. The sound shifts to shutter clicks, dog-piled voices, muttered response, a press conference. Gerry smiles at Michelle.

"You can go watch, you know," Michelle says.

She feels bad for Michelle, so easygoing that she hardly seems to matter. "It's okay."

Michelle's face has become round and babyish, a projection of the life inside her. Her blue-green eyes remind Gerry of ocean water. "Do you want to see the letter?" Michelle lowers herself into the chair beside Gerry, digs in the pocket of her dress for a folded sheet of paper. Gerry opens it carefully. On the page, neat lines of typewritten words:

THIS DETONATION IS AN ACT OF RADICAL PEACE, AN ATTEMPT TO COMMUNICATE WITH THE WAR-HUNGRY IN A LANGUAGE THEY UNDERSTAND, AN EFFORT TO ILLUSTRATE, FOR THE COMPLACENT, PRIVILEGED, AND UNCONSCIOUS, WHAT DISTANT ABSTRACTIONS LIKE BOMB, MISSILE, CONFLICT, AND WAR REALLY MEAN. WE REGRET THE NECESSARY DAMAGE TO THE REVENUE BUILDING. THIS DAMAGE IS AN INFINITESIMAL FRACTION OF THE DESTRUCTION CAPABILITY OF EVEN THE SMALL-EST NUCLEAR WEAPON. TAX DOLLARS BUILD WEAPONS OF ANNIHILATION. LET THIS BOMBSITE SERVE AS A WARNING TO EVERY CITIZEN NOT ACTIVELY PRESSURING THEIR GOVERNMENT TO DISARM. YOU, THROUGH APATHY AND NON-ACTION, ARE THE WARLORDS.

The letter is anonymous, no signatures, no group name. "It goes to all the newspapers. Through the mail. Once every-thing's, you know, happened. Do you like the writing?"

Gerry nods, thinks of how the cover story will look to the media, how it transforms her into a delinquent stupid enough to take money from a stranger in exchange for breaking into a building and leaving behind a gift. "No one will know we were together."

Michelle smiles. "Cool, right?"

Andri strides past them to the fridge, bends down into its light, then stands with two beers cradled at his chest. "Stop flashing that thing around."

Michelle slips the letter back into her dress.

"It's really good writing," Gerry says in her defence.

Andri grunts. "Words, words, words. The action says all we need to say."

Michelle waits for him to leave, then leans close to Gerry. "He doesn't believe people will change. They just need a chance. That's what we're giving them, a chance to wake up. Everything will change. Decades from now, people will look back on this time and shake their heads. The Dark Ages." She smooths her hand over her pocket. Her eyes widen and she grabs Gerry's wrist. "Did you hear the sirens?"

Gerry's fingers link into Michelle's with relief.

Michelle's palm squeezes a damp pulse. "I just burst into tears. I didn't want it to happen before the baby was born, you know? Andri knew it was nothing. He kept telling me to calm down, that I was overreacting." Michelle rubs at her belly. She blinks and her eyelashes glisten.

Gerry stares at the dome of Michelle's stomach. "There was no one home at my house. The power was out. I tried to phone, but no one–" Her mind grapples with the question of where a baby would go if the world ended before it was born, a puzzle that turns her thinking inside out, panics her with a need to touch Michelle, to feel the baby alive.

Michelle seems to read her mind. "Go ahead."

Gerry presses her hand flat against the side of Michelle's belly. Through her dress, the surface is firm, but pliant, impossibly warm. Gerry's hand travels, skims patches of tightness and tensing muscle as Michelle shifts in her seat. The nub of her belly button startles Gerry, reminds her she's touching another woman's body. She thinks to pull away when something nudges her, a small lump that forces her palm into a cup. From the universe of Michelle's body, an alien creature pushes out, reaches into their world.

"It's a foot." Michelle's words whispered like the final flourish of a master magician.

Gerry giggles with delight.

(15)

W HEN HENRY FAILS TO APPEAR the next morning, Gerry calls the station. The receptionist doesn't
expect him until later in the afternoon. Gerry spends
the day in her bedroom, window open to vent the pot smoke,
scrapbook splayed on her bed, stereo loud enough to drown out
Randy's crew. At four, she rides to the station, body numb from
the waist down. The high glides her bike along cushioned roads,
bounces it over inner-tube curbs. Cars and houses soften at their
edges like plasticine. The Jell-O glow of traffic lights triggers a
rush of saliva, ignites a craving for warm, sugary batter, a tower
of pancakes. She stops at the Nuffy's Donuts, buys a half-dozen
honey dip fresh from the fryer, stuffs them into her mouth. Each
one disappears to air as she swallows.

At the station, Gerry locks her bike to the building's saggy
chain-link fence. But before she can make it into the newsroom, the receptionist jabs her pen toward the door, whispers,
"Parking lot."

In the far corner, Henry's car idles. Exhaust billows from the
tailpipe as he revs the engine. Gerry approaches the car and a
security lamp blinks on above her, casts a cone of amber light in
the building's shade.

Henry sits with his hands on the wheel, face masked in on-air makeup. A ruffle of protective Kleenex over his shirt collar, limp petals, his face a scowling flower. She taps the passenger-side window. The electric lock thumps inside the door. As she opens it, radio woodwinds pipe a depressing tune. She climbs in. "Why are you out here?"

"A man's car is his castle."

"I think that's his home."

"Premonitory. That's the word for what you just said. Look it up."

"I can guess what it means." The car's heat fogs the windshield. Her window glitters with tiny prisms of condensation. She touches a drop and draws it along, watches the beads of water race one another down the glass. "How did the court thing go?"

Henry examines his face in the rear-view, turns his chin back and forth. "The female co-anchor starts tonight, we're leading with a cat story. If that's not the end of days, I don't know what is." He clears his throat, a low, guttural roll. "I have to sell the apartment."

"She has the house."

"Mortgaged to pay the first Mrs. Cross. Mortgaged again to pay the second Mrs. Cross. The third Mrs. Cross doesn't like to share."

His black mood begins to smother her high. "Remember the alimony." She says it to cheer herself as much as him.

Henry winces. "That joke is going to bury me." He settles his head against the headrest, a corner of tissue stuck to his chin. "She looked so beautiful." He sighs. "I don't know how long I'm supposed to keep fighting. Three wives and I've got nothing left. How the heck does a man win at this thing?"

"Maybe you need a better lawyer."

"You mean, *a* lawyer."

"Oh." The security light flickers off and she blinks in shadow. "You should have asked my dad about Larry Walsh."

Henry runs a thumb over the lines in his forehead, nods. "Have you ever done something you're ashamed of?"

"I don't think I've done anything I am proud of. Does that count?" She wonders if now would be a good time to let the plan slip out, a slow, careless scatter of clues to make him curious, urge him out of his funk. "Not yet, anyway."

"You do the right thing for the wrong reasons, the wrong thing for the right reasons, who can make sense of it all." The *thunk-k-thunk* of the electric lock vibrates against her arm as Henry plays with the switch. "Which do you think is worse?"

Gerry shrugs. "I don't know."

"I am intimately acquainted with one Larry Walsh, Esquire." He opens and closes his mouth as he turns his head from side to side, the way a fish might give a slow-motion refusal. "Plugged ears. That ever happen to you?"

"I don't think so."

He frowns, chin low. "The esteemed and expensive Mr. Walsh represented my first two wives. I credit him with two-thirds of my misery. A man can't help but have enemies, and as soon as he does, that's the end of a good night's sleep."

"Maybe if you ask my dad—"

He slumps back in his seat and groans as if he's bored with the conversation. The tissues ripple with his breath. "The problem with enemies is that once you start fighting, you can never stop, even when you can't remember why you're fighting. You have to keep going, and never give in, no matter what. It's exhausting."

"What I mean is, maybe my dad knows a different lawyer."

"There's something I have to tell you. It's not good news. And yes, I should have told you sooner."

The change in his voice catches her by surprise. "Okay."

He fiddles with the turn signal, wiggles it back and forth, up and down. Headlights spray through the wire fence. "To finish life as a disappointment to oneself, that is a black hole beyond any man's reckoning. Who said that?"

"Shakespeare?"

"I did. Will you remember?"

The set of his face worries her, a stiffness in his orange cheeks. "I'll try."

His foot taps the gas pedal, *shave-and-a-haircut*, then stops. He shifts closer to her, leans in over the gearshift, dips his head, so that his face hovers slightly lower than hers. "Give me your hand."

She edges back, hopes he doesn't notice. She can smell his glazed cologne and underneath it, the sour of his skin. Her mind jumbles with plotlines from bad movies of the week, unshaven uncles and handymen who corner teenaged girls, unbuckle their belts as they whisper phony reassurances. "Why?"

"Just. Come on." He bobs his head like a horse.

She offers her hand, then hesitates, thinks to tuck it safely under her leg. Before she can withdraw, he catches her fingers, jams them into his hair. Touching his scalp makes her dizzy, queasiness rising like slippery yolk behind her eyes.

"Hard now." His earthy voice alarms her. She pulls away as he clutches her fingers together. A flap of hair comes off in her grip and she screams, flings it away, shakes her hand in disgust.

He laughs, chin tipped up, scalp shiny, the back and sides of his head rimmed by a thick hedge. The hair huddles on the dashboard, a dormant animal, an unkempt guinea pig. "Don't worry," he says. "It's human hair." He leans back to admire it, fingers laced over his suit jacket. "You can touch it."

A fresh wave of repulsion breaks over her. "No, thanks." She tries not to stare at his head. The baldness makes him look older but somehow stronger. Or maybe cleaner, though she has no idea why that would be. She decides finally that he looks more relaxed.

"Focus groups, studio execs." He points at the hair and she's sure she sees it quiver. "This is what I've become. If there's one thing I can say about Henry Cross without a hint of irony, it's that the man despises himself."

They sit in silence. The throb in Gerry's ears calms to an even tempo. "You didn't have to tell me, I mean, I don't care what you look like."

Henry snatches the hairpiece from the dashboard, turns it in his hands, gives it a shake. He nods. His lips pinch and open in a series of false starts. He looks down at the hair, strokes it as if it's a pet. "I don't actually know your father. I mean, he's my son, of course. But I haven't seen him since he was about your age. For a while, he called me every few years to remind me that I ruined his life, but eventually that stopped. I suppose I could call him, but what for? He hates me. We were having such a good time, you and I. I wanted it to be true."

Flutes trill from the radio. She presses her cheek against the window to feel its cool damp. A heady weightlessness overtakes her. In her mind, her father falls away, tumbles out of reach, while her own body rises, shrinks with altitude, until she's no more than a speck. The air feels thinner, colder. As the high creeps back, her body melts into the seat, a cottony itch around the edges of her face. She searches for the right words, syllables that will float, a sentence like a life preserver. "It doesn't matter. I'm glad I found you." She says it for him, then clings to it herself.

He nods. "I've never been good at keeping things. Wives, sons, houses. Right now, you're my only friend, kiddo."

She looks at him then. "I'm going to do something that you should know about."

He plucks a tissue from his collar, gazes at it as if he has no idea how it arrived there, drops it in his lap. "Before we go on, there's one more thing. I need to take that bike back. It's the money. Not right away. The receipt says thirty days, so, enjoy it while you can." The confession deflates him. He looks shrunken, awash in his suit.

"It's okay."

He takes a deep breath, blows the air out with puffed cheeks. "Geraldine, in the long midnight of my life, you are the one bright star," pats his hand over hers. "Now, what's this thing you're doing? Let me guess, school play? Class president?"

His sarcasm makes her feel more sorry for him, like she's looming over him from a great height. She shakes her head. "It doesn't matter." She takes the hairpiece from him, expects the hair to be coarse and rough but finds it strangely fine and fragile. She squeezes the hair, crushes it in a fist. "Tell me about the cat story."

Henry chuckles. "I have to admit, it's kind of cute. This cat works at fire station. Even rides the pole. Nestles up against the fireman when he slides down." Henry demonstrates, holds his arms as if cradling a baby, looks down into the empty space and smiles.

○ ○ ○

THE FIRST NIGHT THE BOY SPENDS naked with the girl, she holds his hand over her hulled stomach, casts a spell, makes a wish. From the beginning, the idea sickens him with worry. She corners him in the hut each day to ensure success. He is helpless to resist.

The men make jokes about dogs in heat, elbow the boy, pry for details. He smiles and shakes his head.

By the third month, the thickness in the girl's belly is noticeable to everyone. Women paw at their own wasted bodies, sneer at the girl, cut in front of her in the food line. Away from their wives, men offer the boy sympathetic words, sheepish faces.

Dan takes him aside, arm around the boy's shoulder. It's not a good thing.

I know. Even as the boy says it, he lies. He thinks of how changed the girl is. Despite the bad treatment, she smiles, radiates gentleness and calm, a state he can only vaguely remember from his own childhood. Memories have fallen away like the crumbled edge of a cliff, this new, wretched life forming a landscape that day by day stretches further from the eroded past. How can people persevere without a single happiness, a flint of hope? For this reason alone, the pregnancy seems a good thing.

She'll see the doctors, Dan says. You should go with her.

The boy nods.

The next day, he takes the girl to the clinic house. All three doctors wait, a stern tribunal behind a heavy oak dining table. Pained and feeble, the sounds of the sick carry in from other parts of the house. The doctors, though disparate in appearance are made similar by the tiredness of their faces. They lean:

— 169 —

Dr. Woo back in his chair, Dr. Patak forward onto the table, Dr. Joan to the side, as if the mere act of sitting is too much for them.

When was your last period? Dr. Woo speaks slowly.

The girl counts out loud, offers an approximation. The doctor nods and writes on a pad of coarse paper, the kind that might have once been used for sketching or painting.

How are you feeling? Dr. Joan's voice is warm and motherly. Are you having any morning sickness?

The girl shakes her head.

Dr. Joan smiles. Dr. Patak will examine you, she says.

The young doctor rises and rounds the table. The boy shifts his seat to make room for her. She gestures for the girl to lift her sweater. As she feels the girl's abdomen, her thin, brown hands look as if they are kneading dough. She finishes and nods, returns to her seat.

Dr. Woo coughs. You both understand. This is not a good situation.

Why not? The girl is confused.

Dr. Woo opens his mouth to speak, but Dr. Patak cuts in, her voice curt and stringent. With the levels of radiation poisoning we've seen, it's almost guaranteed this fetus is or will be severely damaged. There's no way to predict the extent of abnormality or deformity. And I don't just mean appearance. Radiation exposure is synonymous with undeveloped or missing vital organs. Essentially, an organism incompatible with life. Even if you don't miscarry, and the fetus is delivered alive, both of which are highly unlikely, we have no facilities to treat or help this baby in any way, and it will most likely die soon after birth.

Dr. Patak's stare is impatient. Also, the risk to you is too high. A natural birth will be full of complications. A Caesarean would be out of the question.

The girl shrugs. People have babies all the time, she says.

Not under these circumstances, they don't. Dr. Patak's disdain echoes in the room.

Dr. Woo clears his throat. Given the circumstances. We feel the safest thing. Is to terminate the pregnancy.

No! The girl covers her stomach with her arms.

This early. The procedure would be simple. Not without risk. But lower risk, anyway. Than the pregnancy itself.

The girl shakes her head.

Look, you have to be reasonable. This is no time for selfishness.

The boy sees that in their previous lives, Dr. Patak and the girl might have been friends, the girl offering advice on how to meet men, how to style her hair, how to balance career and social life.

The girl stands. I'm not doing that. You can't make me do that.

Dr. Woo looks to Dr. Joan. She shrugs.

Maybe you could both. Wait outside.

The boy leads the girl out of the dining room and into the hallway. They sit side by side on folding chairs. Dr. Woo closes the door behind them.

Dr. Patak's voice is muffled. This is unbelievable.

Dr. Joan sounds as if she's smiling. She knows what she wants.

Maybe. With a little more information, offers Dr. Woo.

I don't think she's going to budge.

There is another option. Dr. Patak's voice is quiet. We have sedatives.

Oh. I don't know. Drastic. Very drastic.

It's for her own good. The girl has no idea what she's gotten herself into. For the good of the community.

It would be hard. To justify. That sort of action. Where would we. Draw the line?

I don't think anyone else is stupid enough to let this happen.

The boy flinches and turns to the girl. She is gazing up at the hallway light, a chandelier dripping glass teardrops. If she is listening, she gives no indication.

Dr. Joan clears her throat. Regardless of what you think of these people, Dr. Patak, they are not animals, and we are not in the business of population control.

Maybe we should be.

Let us. Have a vote. Whether to terminate.

Dr. Joan votes, no.

Dr. Patak votes, yes.

I'm going to have to. Vote. No.

A hand smacks the table, a chair scrapes the floor. Dr. Joan appears in the hallway. We'll just hope for the best, shall we? I'll come around and check on you in a couple of weeks.

The girl stands and takes the boy's hand, leads him out of the house. His feet trip down the stairs. Pebbles crunch beneath his shoes as he walks the beach. His legs move separate from him, urged forward by the girl's momentum. In front of him, the girl turns, her body bobs, lightened by a sureness he cannot grasp.

16

THE LIT EDGE OF GERRY'S JOINT crawls toward her fingers. Through her window, she watches her mom bend to unlock the car door, arm piled with files, her purse and lab coat, a paper bag lunch. Gerry crouches as the car backs out, comes to a full stop on the street, then advances with tempered speed. Whitewashed nine to five, a walking coma. Gerry returns to the game of solitaire laid out on her bed, an attempt to keep her mind still. The high rolls over her tongue but does little to soothe the constant sputter of thoughts. She swipes away the lines of cards, gathers them up in her hand, shuffles them, sprays them into the air.

She arrives to find Megan's front door wide open, sunlight scalding rectangles into the old furniture. In the middle of the carpet, two grey leather suitcases, propped at attention, buckles cinched tight. She waits by the door.

Ian strides through from the kitchen, leather jacket tied around his waist. "We're ready." He hefts the suitcases without looking at her. "She needs a hand with Clem."

Clem shuffles through first, loose black coat over his suit, tweed fedora on his head, the band decorated with a small red feather. Megan follows, arm through his elbow, face grey and puffy, her colour worked away. Gerry loops her arm through Clem's other elbow, guides him across the living room and onto the porch. They take the stairs slowly, Clem pauses on each step to admire the view. He grins, face pushed up to the sun.

Ian holds open the car's back door, nods to Gerry. "You sit with him."

In the car, Clem adopts a formal posture, elbow on the arm-rest, back straight, chin up as he surveys the passing streets. Now and then he points a crooked finger and says, "That's the place." Gerry cranes her neck but can't make out anything other than a gas station, a playground, an empty lot strewn with garbage.

The care home is a low brick building with a dark canopied entrance, *Cherrywood Manor* in raised red letters above the automatic doors. As Ian parks, Gerry watches the scatter of patients out front. Wheelchairs turned away from one another, prawn-like bodies smoke, tow oxygen tanks, slouch beside metal racks decorated with fluid bags.

Sun flares in her eyes as she helps Megan hoist Clem out of the car. His arms tremble, his feet skate the pavement. Ian marches ahead with the bags.

They sit across from one another in the tiled foyer. An anti-septic sting rises from the floor as they wait for the admitting physician. Ian holds Megan's shoulders, ducks his head to check her face. Beside Gerry, Clem hums. The easiness of his mood relieves her. His eyes blink, shiny and alert, his hands still, at rest in his lap.

The doctor arrives clipboard in hand, a tall, older man with brown skin and white hair, and an accent that reminds her of

Fantasy Island. Megan stands and the doctor holds up his palm. "Just your father." The doctor lifts Clem to his feet, leads him to a room with an examination table, and closes the door.

Megan leans her face into Ian's shoulder, wipes at her eyes. Ian kisses the top of her head. Gerry looks away to give them privacy, then stands, wanders to pass the time. On the other side of the nurses' station, a carpeted expanse of living space, recliners set in rows like a geriatric movie theatre, TVs strung from the ceiling. Beyond the carpet, more tile, metal stanchions and glass cases of food, a small cafeteria.

Tucked into the recliners, fat bodies, shrunken bodies, bodies slumped into painful contortions. The men doze or sit motionless, entranced by the screens above. The women fiddle with things, rings on their fingers, the gauge of an oxygen tank, the purse wedged in at their side, some work feverishly with yarn and sticks. One TV screen offers a game show, another an old movie with cowboys, another has Merv Griffin interviewing a woman in a gold lamé dress. The sound for each channel warbles low, blends with the others into a foreign tongue. She knows this will upset Clem.

In the waiting area, she imagines leaving her own father here, a crumpled, frail package in a wheelchair. Over and over, she replays the panicked workings of his face as she wheels him in, locks him into place, and backs away slowly. She tries to think the same of Henry but can't bring herself to punish him, even in her mind.

The doctor steps from the examining room. He gestures to the nurses' station and two nurses round the corner, approach the door to help Clem as he walks. They lead him away from the intake area, toward a white hallway lined with doors.

"Wait." Megan stands and jogs toward them. She clutches Clem, her body curled over his. His bewildered face peers over her shoulder. His hands dangle loose behind her back. She lets him go, and the nurses move in to guide him away.

The doctor offers Megan a tissue. "Your father is non-responsive."

She nods, wipes her nose. "He was in prison."

"He's malnourished and dehydrated." The doctor scribbles on the clipboard. His rigid stance, the way he holds his pen, fingers straight, the angle of his chin, all of it poised in judgment. Gerry hears it in his accent, how he sees them, punks loitering in his waiting area.

"I take good care of him."

The doctor lifts a brown bottle from the pocket of his white coat. "Where are you getting this?"

"That's his medicine."

He turns the bottle back and forth. "There's no doctor's name on the prescription label."

"It's from a doctor."

"I'll need his name." He puts his pen to the clipboard.

"He's a friend of my father's."

"I still need his name."

"This is his medicine." Megan voice rises, carries down the tile hall. Gerry looks to Ian. He sits with his elbows on his knees, stares at his hands.

"This is a controlled prescription narcotic. Your father has developed a severe chemical dependency. He needs to be weaned off it."

Gerry forces authority into her voice. "That's his medicine,

I've seen him take it." The doctor glances over Megan's shoulder, winces in irritation.

Ian glares at Gerry, whispers, "Shut. Up."

Megan nods. "I just want you to know, this might not be permanent."

The doctor records another sentence, punctuates it with a tap. "Do you know what kind of place this is? It isn't a hotel. I'm admitting your father today because I have serious concerns about his health and the level of care he's been receiving. If, in the future, you decide to take him home, you will have to undergo a government-approved home-study before we agree to his release."

"Why? You can't do that." Megan grabs the doctor's sleeve. "That's not what he wants. I'll take him home right now."

Ian is beside her, loosening her grip on the doctor, pulling her away. "It's okay," he says to Megan. Then, to the doctor, "She's just upset."

"I understand," the doctor says. "It's very upsetting." He says it to the air, and Gerry feels a rush inside her, sand through her ribs, the quickness of things that can be done but not undone.

Megan sobs into Ian's chest.

The nurse behind the counter gives Gerry a sympathetic smile. Gerry looks away, refuses her fake pity. On his way down the hall, the doctor stops beside Gerry, hands the brown bottle to the nurse. "Get rid of this."

The nurse tucks the bottle behind her file tray, shuffles charts, watches as Ian manoeuvres Megan through the glass doors, the two of them swallowed by daylight.

Gerry slips back into the common room. She wastes a few minutes, wandering amongst the chairs. The alert ones stare, eyes like stones, mouths tight, dry latches, vigilant for any bad business. The lost ones shiver as she passes close, mouths agape like landed fish, eyes cloudy and frightened. She strolls back to the nurses' station, brushes her hand over the counter. The nurse looks up from her charts.

Gerry sinks her face into a grimace. "I think some guy threw up in his chair."

With an exhausted sigh, the nurse hoists herself, pushes her pencil behind her ear, rounds the corner into the living area. Gerry's hand dips behind the file tray, lifts the medicine bottle, slips it into her pocket.

In the parking lot, Ian flicks a cigarette butt in the air. "What took you so long?"

Ian trails Megan into the bedroom, closes the door. Gerry settles herself in Clem's chair, tries not to listen to Megan's crying, Ian's low, even voice. The front door hangs open, as if awaiting Clem's return. Instead, the whir of lawn mowers and a warm spring wind curl into the room.

Clem's smell rises from his chair, stale saltwater aftershave and peppery old man. The upholstered arms rest hard and flat under Gerry's elbows, two mangy patches where the heels of Clem's hands rubbed, the TV remote positioned for his fingers. She presses the remote and bright, unconcerned faces rise on the grey screen. Her hand pushes down into her pocket, traces the bottle on its side, small raised dots around its curved bottom edge, a fine lip where the label lifts away, scratches her skin.

Perhaps she could take Megan's place, care for Clem herself. With the house so close to her school, she could prepare his meals, finish her homework at the kitchen table while he watched TV. But when she thinks of the razor on the bathtub, how she would have to undress him, touch his body with a washcloth, how he yelled or cried for no reason, she knows the best she can hope for is visiting hours, kneeling beside his chair, sneaking a splash of medicine into a coffee mug and tipping it to his lips. For an instant, the image in her mind is confused, and it is her father sitting in the recliner, his young hand steadying the cup, his grateful smile. Outside, another mower grumbles to life. The perfume of fresh-cut grass trails in on the breeze and she is lolling behind her father. A flat summer sun raises dribbles of sweat around her hairline. Leather straps of sandals scrape the swollen edges of her feet. Her father walks ahead, hands in his pockets, long strides that carry him away. When she whimpers and scuffs her steps, he stops, pats his trousered thigh, a signal for her to hurry and catch up. At the summit of their walk, the smoky dome of the conservatory. She begs to go inside, but her father shakes his head, leads them to a low stone wall and a line of what look like parking meters. He jingles the change in his pocket, feeds a coin into the meter, and hoists her, his foot on the small metal platform, his knee her seat. The machine, cold against her face, revives her from sulky exhaustion. As she blinks against the eyepiece, a soft click sounds and a city reveals itself: a dark gutter of freight trains, behind them, brick warehouses, a thin stand of office buildings, farther back, the inlet, dotted with ships, all of it wavy with heat. Her father's arm snugs her waist, and she grips it like a guardrail, leans forward with the tilt of the machine to see the tops of trees, a field of rooftops, birds swooping below. She leans back and the mountains appear, steep and white-tipped. The sky unfurls around them, patterns of clouds close enough to touch. The click sounds again and two black discs close over her eyes. Her father's grip loosens.

The tears begin as he sets her down, the bottoms of her sandals dragging on the pavement. She waits for him to gather her up again, gangly as she is, as her mother still did, until their bodies sealed together. A breeze shimmers the treetops in front of them, the air around her sags. Tomorrow, her father will return to his job in California. As he stands there, waiting for her to collect herself, he lights a cigarette. He blows an exasperated breath that makes her cry harder. She hiccups into her elbow, unable to form words for her weariness, embarrassed by the babyishness of her reaction, the failure of its effect. She tries to explain herself, but what comes out burbles with incoherence, slimy nonsense scraped over tears. And though after his cigarette, he offers his hand, and they walk down through the park side by side under the shade of trees, and her father nods as she chatters desperately about school and friends and songs she's heard on the radio, she knows, from the looseness of his hand, the gentleness in his voice, the effort he puts into smiling, that he is already farther away than any machine can see.

The bedroom door opens. Gerry swipes at her eyes.

Ian appears, stripped to his jeans, his feet bare, his skin flushed pink, as if he's been dipped in hot water. He leans his forearm on the wall. "What's up with you?"

"Is she okay?"

"Yeah, she's fine." He brings his hand to his face. She notices the powder just as he rubs it away, a fine sprinkle of talc near his nostrils. Ian snorts deep, clears his throat. "That was rough today. Thanks for your help."

"What about tomorrow?"

"Tomorrow is tomorrow." Megan's voice rises behind him. He steps to the side, looks over his shoulder. Megan sways in the hallway, naked from the waist up, her eyes and nose ringed red. She blinks, sniffles into her hand. Her pupils like crystals, lit and glinting.

Her breasts are perfect, pale saucers against her chest, nipples spongy, wide and pink. Megan opens her arms to display them. Heat rushes to Gerry's face and she lowers her gaze as Megan crosses one leg over the other, reaches out to Ian to balance herself, then pushes off toward the bathroom. "Tomorrow," she says. "We all meet at the meeting place, at the meeting time." The bathroom door snaps shut.

"We're not going to practise today? What about Andri, isn't he coming?"

Ian grins. "I thought you said you were ready, hotshot." He surrenders to a spurt of frantic blinking.

Gerry envies him the escape, the buffer from thought. "What are you guys on? Do you have any more?"

Ian knocks on the wall as if knocking on a door. "You go home." He points at her. "Do something normal for a change."

17

THE PHONE RINGS AS SHE DIGS in her pocket for the house key, then stops as she wheels her bike through the door. It starts again before she has her shoes off.

"You're back." Henry huffs through the receiver, breathless.

She leans against the counter, cranes her neck to check for shadows of workmen through the back windows, but sees none. "I do have a life, you know."

"No, no." The sound is choppy, broken by rustling and thumping, as if he is moving heavy bags of groceries. "It's just. I'm going on a trip. I wanted to let you know."

"Where?"

A tinny metal crinkling. "Let's just say, out of town. I'll be gone for a while."

His generalities make her nervous. "Are you in trouble? Should I call Larry Walsh?"

Henry laughs. "Definitely not." His voice comes clear. She can tell he's standing still. "I didn't want to leave without saying goodbye."

"You're going now?" She had worked it all out in her head. He was the only person she wanted to see after the march. Maybe she would tell him, maybe not, but she needed to be with Henry, to hold her accomplishment in his presence. "You're staying for the weekend, right?" Even as she tries to force it down, a shakiness rides up in her voice.

"Would that I could."

"I don't understand. Why do you have to go right now?"

"That was a good talk we had."

"Just stay one more day."

"I've had time to think. Dark night of the soul and all that. I think there's a valuable lesson here. For you, I mean. I spent my whole life trying to be the person other people could live with, and look how I've failed. I'm batting a thousand where failure's concerned. But here's a new question: why not just be the person I could live with? What would that look like? Who would I be? Doesn't that make sense? Now that I know the right question, I can't put off finding out the answer. Can you understand that?" Scraping, rough and uneven, echoes through the phone.

"What's all that noise?"

"Implementation." The word stretches out, strained.

"What are you talking about?"

He stops with a grunt. "Before I forget. Very important. That bike is yours."

"You can't leave right now."

"I'm already gone."

"I need to talk to you."

"Impossible."

"Henry."

He sighs. "I'm at the house. But don't dally."

Blocks from Henry's former house, she hears the sirens, the winding, guttural blare of emergency vehicles as they grind through rush hour traffic. The sun slips behind a smatter of tall trees, casts only faint light, a silvery limbo. She coasts to a stop in front of the house, braces a lamppost, balances on her pedals to see above the heads of a crowd gathered on the lawn. Cartoonlike smoke, a string of black cotton balls pumps from the chimney. An overworked fireplace. Not Henry's best idea. She imagines his meaty hands tearing apart Mrs. Cross's books, photo albums, clothes, dangling them over the flames until they catch.

The firemen form a line, herd the crowd back onto the road. Flat hoses stretch across the lawn like giant tapeworms. The men shout to one another above the bang of wrenches and ladders. She rides around, hops up on the opposite sidewalk, the block crammed with red trucks. A police car coasts in behind, announces its arrival with a lazy siren whoop. Henry will appreciate the overreaction. She hopes he had the sense to leave through the back.

The crowd is a jumble of late-afternoon routines. An older woman clutches a TV remote, a housewife in a stained kitchen apron fans herself with a pair of oven mitts, men returned from work stand with raincoats slung over bent arms, briefcases wedged between their calves. A group of college-aged girls look ready to record a workout video, braided headbands, sweatshirts off their shoulders, twinkling Spandex dipped in neon legwarmers. Curvy and giggling, they pose to distract the firemen, start their own fires. Gerry drifts back and forth along the street, stretches to search the crowd, expects to find Henry camouflaged with the other suits. The men are all too tall, too thin, too young. With each pass the crowd deepens.

Through the thicket of sweaters and sports jackets, she notices a leak of smoke from the side of the house, pinched tendrils from the bottom ledge of two closed windows. She rolls her bike toward a man in a ratty T-shirt and corduroys, a video camera propped on his shoulder. "Has anyone come out yet?"

The man turns his head. "Dunno. One of the guys said there's stuff pushed up against the windows and doors. They're trying to get in through the back."

She sees now that the curtains are strangely drawn, crushed flat against the front windows. The bike tangles in her legs as she tries to throw it down. She sprints across the street. Like a slow, choreographed dance, a fireman steps in front of her, opens his arm and catches her waist, swings her off the ground. "You need to stay back."

"There's someone inside there." Her hands slip against his canvas jacket, her legs kick, hanging and useless.

He carries her in long, easy strides past the crowd to an empty patch of grass by the curb, knocks his leg under hers, plants her hard on the grass. "He's in there!" She screams it into the pocket created by their bodies. Heads turn to gawk, then swivel back, more interested in the fire.

"If anyone's in there, we're trying to get them out. What you need to do is stay put. Otherwise, you'll have to wait in the squad car." He points to the swirling lights, short slaps of red and blue. She nods. The fireman stands, gestures for another, skinnier fireman to keep an eye on her.

A glassy pop cracks the air. The crowd gasps. Flames bursts from an upstairs window, lick at the sky. Gerry hugs her knees, draws the charred taste of smoke into her lungs, waits for Henry to fall from the opening, his body lit.

The crowd is herded back once more, up onto the sidewalk beside her. Those nearest glance out of the corners of their eyes.

She covers her head with her arms to avoid their prying. A second window pops, a smaller one, off the living room. The crowd stays quiet, heads shake. Flames crawl up the outside wall, then curl back under the eaves. She thinks of the mantelpiece, the photo of the husband who wasn't Henry, how it might have hurt him, how she shouldn't have mentioned it.

Down the block, neighbours stand on their lawns, garden hoses dribbling, others with plastic buckets, clownish efforts at self-preservation. If she had a pack of matches, she'd light their houses herself. She tries to stare them down, singe them with loathing, but their nervous eyes tip her back into despair. Their outlines blur in a smoggy haze. She rocks herself, struggles to breathe. Around her people cough, wave hands in front of their faces. She buries her head in her arm until the wind changes direction. When she looks up again, more anxious neighbours have taken up posts, hose-toting sentries. Dizziness forces her to look past them, focus on a distant hedge. She tries to slow her breath. A block away, obscured by fog, a car idles on the wrong side of the road. Its brake lights blink red, flash a steady signal. She stares, mesmerized, allows her eyes to blink in rhythm. *Shave-and-a-haircut.*

She pushes the ground away. The skinny fireman calls out, but she passes him, jogs down the block. The car pulls out just as its brown back end comes clear. "Wait!" she shouts. From the driver-side window an arm reaches out. The wide hand waves, and from its fingers a piece of litter flutters toward the curb, lands in a patch of weeds.

"Wait!"

The car accelerates to the corner, signals right, and slips into traffic behind a panel van. Gerry kneels in the grass, grabs up the folded paper, picks it open, flattens it on her thigh. A scrap of heavy stationery. On one side, her name written with a flourish, on the other, the inky curves of digits, a phone number.

She walks back to the house slowly, amazed by the sensation of her feet on the ground. The need to smile strains at her mouth. She joins the crowd. People frown as she giggles into her sleeves. When two more windows blow out, she cheers, claps her hands above her head. The gawkers step aside, give her room. Some shake their heads in disgust, others in pity. Best are those who inch away, fearful her exuberance is catching. She lifts her face to feel the flat heat. Firemen aim their hoses, jets of water peak together at the roof, but the fire shows no signs of retreat. Beside her, clicks and drags, a busy chorus of hobby photographers.

The sunset creeps violet and pink across the hazy west sky, orange flames laps against the pitch of black smoke boiled on the breeze. Evening lowers a chill. While her front absorbs waves of pure and dangerous heat, the backs of her arms prickle with gooseflesh. She thinks to stay until the last embers, bed down on the grass to watch the pile smoulder as firemen trample through the charred remains of the house.

The crowd sways, shoves into her. Rooted bodies move to break a path. Mrs. Cross steps into the street, handbag slung over her shoulder, folded umbrella in her gloved hand. She looks back at the crowd, wide-eyed, her silver bob swinging at her jaw. Gerry has never seen her this close. What binoculars sharpened and smoothed into narrow cheeks and elegant bone structure appears now as the gaunt, inward collapse of age, her face pinched and wrinkled. Her stillness vibrates with a palsied tremor.

She takes a step toward the house and the skinny fireman steps in front of her, arms stretched in a gangly barricade. As she cranes to see past, her hands grab his arms. Her momentum pushes him back one step at a time. She stumbles, and the fireman struggles to support her. Gerry holds her breath. Mrs. Cross collapses to the ground, and the fireman goes down with her. Her knees splay to the side as she hunches on the wet street. He makes an attempt at comfort, tries to lift her arms and shoulders into his lap. Mrs. Cross wails. Her cry cuts through the thunder of fire and water, sucks the blare of sirens, the shouts of men into the vacuum of her misery. The wind changes direction, scatters dark flakes of ash over the crowd, people cup their hands over mouths and noses. Gerry's eyes tear with the sting of smoke.

At home, her mom hovers in the foyer, grinning. Her fingers patter the edge of the front door as Gerry pushes her bike through. The uncontained enthusiasm drains her. "What?"

"Come, come, come."

Her mom pulls her along, down the hall, through the kitchen, hand tight on her wrist. Gerry's sneakers suction across the floor.

With a flourish, her mom swings open the back door, urges her out. "Ta-da!"

The pool takes up the entire yard. Through briny water, bulbous lamps protrude along the walls, glow obscene. Tiny ripples on the surface twinkle against the amphibious haze. Vent flaps release bubbles of gaseous breath. The florescence of it all forces her to squint.

"What do you think?" Her mom bounces beside her.

Saliva gathers in the pockets of Gerry's cheeks. She fights the urge to stretch forward and christen the artificial blue with her spit. Instead, she crouches, reaches out her fingers. She expects slippery warmth, the coddle of piss-temperatured water they were made to swim in at school. The water bites her wrist. She shakes her hand dry, the pool more ridiculous now, like a tan in winter. "It's freezing."

"They said it would take a while to warm up and, you know, clear up." Her mom leans in close, sniffs at her neck. "You smell like smoke."

Gerry lifts her T-shirt to her nose, inhales the charred scent, imagines Henry driving into the sunset, unbuttoning his shirt collar, flinging his tie out the window. "There was a fire. I stopped to watch."

Her mom frowns. "That's a bit morbid.

She shrugs off the judgment, feels it slip easily from her shoulders.

"I thought I'd make a celebratory dinner."

The workmen have left no trace of themselves, every wheelbarrow and shovel gone, boot tracks raked, the path hosed clean. "Where's Randy?"

Her mom's silence confirms what Gerry already knows. The breeze blows a tide across the pool's surface. Water laps at the liner, licks away a faint line of dirt. For a moment she feels angry at not being able to say goodbye, a chill she shakes away as pathetic. What would she have said to him, anyway? She doesn't want to know the details and hopes her mom isn't in the mood to share.

Her mom sighs. "It does look good though." She sways. "As soon as the weather warms up, you can invite some girls over for a pool party."

"Wicked." Gerry squeezes her mom's arm as she steps past her into the kitchen, assured and grateful that her mom has no idea who she is.

At dinner her mom opens a bottle of red wine, lets Gerry sip a small glass. The liquid creeps musty over her tongue. She swallows, wants to like it, resists a reflex grimace. She chews a piece of steak to work away the stale taste.

"I thought we could see a movie tomorrow. A matinee. Maybe that musical one with Kevin Bacon?" Her mom was always like this after a breakup, eager for activities.

"I have plans."

"You can change them. Spring break's almost over and we haven't spent any time together. You'll be back in school on Monday."

Gerry mashes her peas with her fork, pushes them into the fluff of her potato. She hadn't thought about Monday, wonders if it will be like any other day, drowned in the rodent chatter of girls, the factory drone of teachers, the armpit and menstrual blood smell in the PE change room, the threat of yogurt flung in the cafeteria or a juice box squirted into her locker. The outside world unchanged, the only difference inside her.

"I wonder what they'll think of your hair." Her mom raises her chin as she chews, prepared to receive the answer through clairvoyant transmission. "I think they'll like it." She smiles as she reaches for her glass. "I like it."

Gerry knows exactly the type of girl her mom was in high school. Pretty enough but not mean enough to be popular. The kind who coasted on good grades and a winning personality, got along with everyone. A girl who was nice to the fat and pimple-ridden because she felt sorry for them, said things like, "You know, you'd be really pretty if you just . . ." It hurts her to think her mom sees her that way, a misfit, a project, her encouragement fuelled by pity. "I'm going to the peace march tomorrow."

"Really?" Her mom's eyebrows arch with surprise. "I had no idea you were into that. The peace thing."

Gerry makes a peace sign with her fingers.

"Well, this is good. We can go together. You father and I went to a few peace rallies in our time."

Gerry pictures a sea of hippies. Braids and headbands, bell-bottoms and megaphones, signs and talking sticks bouncing in the air, and at the centre of the crowd, her father, stiff in a suit and tie, briefcase in hand, her mom in her lab coat, stoic prisoners of a cannibal tribe. "I'm going with Ian." She takes another sip of wine, this one refreshes, slakes a hidden thirst.

"Oh. It's a date."

"God, Mom."

"What? I don't understand why you have to be so secretive about these things. I mean, what's the big deal?" Her mother's eyes are circles of glass, her cheeks bruised with wine. Gerry contemplates the smugness of her open-lipped smile and for a second considers telling her everything, grabbing her hands and whispering the details into her mouth, watching her mom's oblivious delight fold, collapse in on itself with news of the terrorizing thing her daughter has become.

Her mom's eyes narrow. "Are you having sex with him?"

"Mom!"

"I mean, he is older than you, is he expecting sex? Is he pressuring you for sex?"

"Please stop saying *sex*?" She pushes her knife flat against a bulge in her steak, watches the blood seep from the cut meat. "We're friends. That's it."

Her mom sighs, rests her cutlery on her plate, and folds her hands. "I just want you to be able to talk to me, Geraldine. I don't want it to be the way it was with my mother. I want you to feel free to ask questions. About anything."

Gerry overheard talk at school of moms who demonstrated for their daughters how to insert a tampon, who chattily answered questions over graphic drawings in *The Joy of Sex*, who celebrated with shopping and a lavish lunch after taking their daughters to the clinic for the pill. She can imagine nothing more horrifying. The prospect squelches inside her, triggers an oozing distress. Her mom's face is hopeful, bright with anticipation.

"What's wrong with us?" Gerry pushes her steak back and forth.

Her mom's brows pinch together. "That's a question?"

"Why are we the reject family?"

Her mom plays with the edge of her placemat, fingers flattening a stubborn curl in the corner. She looks up. "I've told you a thousand times. He went to work in California, and he met someone, who, I guess, he loved more than me, and he decided that he wanted to stay there and have a family with her. It's got nothing to do with you."

Gerry's face burns. "See, you say that because it's supposed to make me feel better, but it doesn't, it just makes me feel like I don't even exist." She tips the wineglass to her lips, prays for a heavy, wet mouthful, feels instead a trickle on her tongue.

"I'm sorry. I didn't know."

"It's like we're these ghosts or something, wandering around this house, like we're supposed to be ashamed of something, and I don't even know what we're supposed to be ashamed of. What we said, or what we did—" Her voice thickens, retreats to the back of her throat. She closes her eyes, feels her mom's hand on her arm.

"He's the one who should be ashamed, not you."

Her jaw aches with the effort of stillness. She sniffs and clears her throat.

"I know we don't talk about your dad a lot. But we can. Whenever you want. Maybe if we talked about him more, it wouldn't hurt so much."

She keeps her eyes closed, her body like an overfull water balloon. She imagines water draining out of her feet, flooding the kitchen floor.

"For instance, I could tell you a funny story about your dad. Would you like that?"

"Sure." The word takes effort, comes out wind-thinned and small.

"We were on our honeymoon—"

"No, thanks."

"There's no sex in this story." Her mom shifts on her seat, holds Gerry's hand, her grip warm and powdery. "So. We were in the Rockies, in Banff. Your dad and I were walking together down the main street, looking in the shop windows, enjoying all the touristy stuff, and along comes this grizzly bear. Not a real bear, mind you, but a man dressed in a bear suit." She releases Gerry's hand and raises her arm, mimes the bear's lumbering gait with a scrunched, bearlike expression on her face. Gerry smiles.

"Okay, so huge, right? And he grabs hold of your dad and starts dancing with him, waltzing him around the sidewalk.

Well, your dad is mortified but trying to look like he's enjoying it. And I'm laughing and clapping and wishing we owned
a camera so I could take a picture because no one would believe
this was happening, especially to your father. But we didn't
have a camera until much later, so I just laughed and clapped.
Then all of a sudden the bear stops and just wanders off down
the street, I guess to look for some other tourists to entertain. A
few blocks later, your dad realizes his wallet is gone, all of our
wedding money. And wouldn't you know it, we couldn't find
that goddamn bear anywhere." Her mom goes quiet, stares at
her plate. Gerry has a sudden image of her, lost on a mountain,
digging herself out of an avalanche. Her mom shakes her head.
"Well, I thought that would be a funny story, but I guess not."

While they're clearing the dishes, her mom clasps her hands
together, remembers Randy's VCR still hooked up in the living
room. "We'll get our movie after all." She carries soupy bowls
of strawberry ice cream into the darkened room, settles on the
couch, licks ice cream from the back of her spoon while Gerry
flips through the rented tapes, chooses *Alien*, Sigourney Weaver
battling a brood of orphaned monsters, a horror movie about
motherhood.

Her mom watches with one hand over her eyes, the other a
pressured cuff around Gerry's ankle, squeezing, releasing. The
strobelike flicker of the TV in the dark room reminds Gerry of
those first weeks without her father. After being put to bed, she
would creep back downstairs in her pyjamas, bundled in a blanket, sway in the archway until her mom noticed her. Her mom
would give her a stern look, then make room on the couch,

catch her up on the show she was watching. After the eleven o'clock news, they did rounds of the house, checked every door and window. This was their new job, to finger latches and locks, secure themselves against whatever darkness might try to get in. They climbed the stairs reassured by deadbolts and brass levers. Until one night, alone in her bed, Gerry figured out that a gang of men who wanted to break in had only to smash a window, a thin, shivery pane of glass. And what could they do to defend themselves, a woman and a child? Her mother offered no real protection. The realization made her sleepless with worry. She began to pay closer attention to the news, reports of murders, kidnappings, escaped prisoners, regimes threatening war, anxious to familiarize herself with the dangers of the world, hopeful that familiarity would, if not protect her from, then at least prepare her for attack.

Her mom squirms into the couch, presses her face into Gerry's shoulder. When the carnage becomes too much, she covers Gerry's eyes, a warm, yeasty palm on her face. Her other hand cradles Gerry's shoulder. "Don't watch, Ger-Bear," her mom whispers. "You'll have nightmares." The sound of her concern makes it hard for Gerry to resist falling into her, burrowing in her arms.

After the movie, as her mom settles in to watch the news, Gerry sneaks the upstairs phone into her room. The long cord loops on the carpet as she locks her bedroom door. She hides under the covers, fabric cool against her arms and ankles, Henry's folded paper in her hand. Her fingers circle the telephone, first tracing its faded numbers, then tripping as she pulls on the dial. It takes two tries to get the number right. The ring drones low and long, the receiver a cold cup against her ear. The voice that answers is a child's, then two. Hello? Let me talk. Who's calling please? Let me. No one's there. Dad, he won't let me! No one's there, okay? It's probably a wrong number, just hang up the phone. The man's voice, distant and watered down by background noise, floats through her without catching.

She waits, then listens to the receiver clatter in its cradle, the hollow of the dead line, the stir of breath in and out of her body. She wonders if it was even him.

○ ○ ○

FROM THE OUTSIDE, THE PREGNANCY appears normal. The girl's stomach grows, a bubble of skin that strains against her clothes. The women try to remain remote and disapproving but find themselves lured by her awkward gait, the thinness of her face and wrists despite her expanding middle. Anonymous gifts arrive outside the cabin door: portions of food, warm blankets. Someone leaves a perfectly knitted baby hat and booties, bright yellow, the wool impossibly clean and soft. The boy and the girl lay them on the bed, speechless.

Dr. Joan visits, supply bag in hand. She takes the girl's blood pressure, feels her stomach, nods and smiles at her progress, laughs a squealing, tearful laugh when the baby pushes out against its flesh-walled home, a surreal triangle jutting from the girl's stomach. The boy stares in amazement.

But despite the doctor's assurances, something is not right. At night, the girl cries and whimpers in her sleep. The boy wakes and massages her knotted back, her hips' cinched muscles. During the day, she winces with pain.

Something sharp and prickly, she says, this baby's covered in spikes.

The boy fears what lives inside her, a thorn-covered, squid-tailed beast. His dreams are ripe with the doctors' warnings, bloody births of giant writhing larvae, shrivelled infants with faces of old men, a baby that appears perfect from the birth canal, until its torso ends in a mess of squirming entrails. After these visions, he lies in the dark, restless and drenched with worry.

In her pocket, the girl keeps a square of paper, a list of names: Samuel, Tobias, Alistair, Harold, Richard, Niall, Wallace,

Constance, Beatrice, Penelope, Moira, Beryl, Jeannette, Grace. When she shows the boy the list, he laughs, teases her.

These are old people's names.

Her face blazes with anger, then tears. These are the names of her family, parents, grandparents, aunts, uncles. He apologizes, but she is inconsolable, grief hauled up from her belly.

The boy wraps her in a blanket, rocks her until she quiets, settles her at the woodstove. In the desk, he finds a clean sheet of paper, a worn pencil, its eraser chewed. He goes out to the beach, past the fire, follows the water's edge until he's alone.

Paper balanced on his leg, he writes carefully, in tiny block print, the pencil awkward in his hand. He begins with his parents, Caroline and James. Then Caroline's parents, James's parents, their brothers and sisters, their children. It takes time to remember. Some names cue memories that play like slow, elaborate films, others a hurried montage, the corner of a photograph, a mitten's frayed cuff, the curl of pipe smoke.

He prints the girl's name beside his, draws a line to join them, then marks a space below.

The boy walks back to the cabin and shows the girl his list. She smiles, eyes swollen and dark, reaches for his hand and places it on her belly.

He's awake.

A shift and bump under the boy's hand. He wants to pull away but forces himself to stay for her sake. You should choose the name, he tells her. He strokes the smooth stretch of her skin, tries not to feel what turns inside.

18

GERRY DREAMS SHE'S AN ESKIMO standing on an ice floe in the Arctic night. Above her, dozens of stars arc across the heavens. She tips back her head to admire their trails, then sees that they are manmade stars, missiles that grind as they pass overhead. Her body, wrapped and bound in layers of animal pelts, braces against a cold wind, the tickle of fur at her chin. Under her feet, ice cracks, glassy fractures she cannot see. The pelts are bound too tight for her to run. The ice buckles, seesaws beneath her feet. She waits to fall through.

She wakes with a jolt, blankets wound around her clothes. Cracks echo in her mind, faint and intermittent. A metallic splatter against glass. She shuffles out of bed, to the window, opens it wide.

The night air is humid and still. Ian stands in the driveway. She holds up a warning hand, leans out to check her mom's window, finds it dark.

"I'm going to a party." His whisper scrambles up from a deep pit.

She remains lost in the world of half-dreams, her feet glued to ice. "So, go."

He hucks his handful of gravel into the street. Gerry hears it skittle and ping. Ian brushes his palms on his legs. "Come on. Could be our last night."

Together. The word surfaces without him saying it, a bottled message set adrift. From above, he looks shrunken, diminished. His uncertain posture reminds her of how she once liked him best, all nervous kindness and pink, unwhiskered skin. "Wait in the car." She eases the window closed, careful to hold the latch to keep it from banging. In the dark, she searches her floor for a change of clothes, chooses a tighter pair of jeans, an oversized T-shirt with the word VICIOUS emblazoned across the front, a baggy black cardigan. In her dresser drawer, buried under a mess of useless hair ties and barrettes, behind the bottle of Clem's medicine, she finds a tube of lipstick, brushes the colour quickly over her lips, pushes the tube into her pocket. She opens her bedroom door and listens, the house deep in its night breathing, the refrigerator's low purr as the furnace begins a shuddery exhale. Before the breath is through, she is down the stairs, through the foyer, jacket and high-tops in hand, out the front door.

Ian's stereo blares *Young Americans*, signals high spirits, his face slack and easy as he sings along. He's dressed up, white shirt and a thin, black leather tie under his leather jacket, his hair combed back. Gerry wants to say something but doesn't want to ruin his mood, risk a failed compliment coming across as an insult. "So, Megan's okay?" She shouts it above the music.

He nods to the beat. "She just needed some rest."

"We're on for tomorrow?"

He doesn't answer right away, and she finds herself hoping for complication, an obstacle or setback to carry the struggle of plotting and solving through the night and into morning.

"So she says."

She nods, tries to ignore the burr of disappointment that things aren't harder. "Whose party is this, anyway?"

He turns to look at her, and his head jerks back in surprise. "Holy shit, Gerry Mouse!" He laughs. "Are you wearing lipstick?"

"Fuck you." She swipes her mouth with the back of her hand, drags the slick from her lips, closes her eyes, and tries to enjoy the speed of the car, the wind against her face. The sticky perfume of honeyed flowers blows back at her. She slips her hand down beside her seat, smears the waxy evidence on his leather upholstery.

Def Leppard pumps from the small house. On the stairs, lanky headbangers press beer cans to their lips, make moves on Pat Benatar clones in leather miniskirts. Gerry follows Ian, steps over arms roped together, feather plumes of hair, toward the living room and its pounding bass, purple glow of black light. Inside, bodies speckled with fluorescent dust, radioactive grins. She follows Ian into the easier light of the kitchen. He slaps his case of beer onto the counter, tears open a corner of the box, and passes her a bottle. The fridge door peels open, sucks shut. The back door rattles each entrance and exit. She picks at the label, rears back against the tide of strangers until the counter jabs at her spine. Ian stretches to scope the crowd.

"Who do you know here?"

"No one."

"How did you hear about this party?"

"I just heard."

Gerry has her answer when Lark, decked out in a tiered mini-skirt and fingerless lace gloves, materializes from the haze of cigarette smoke, all eyeliner and lashes. She flutters her fingers over Ian's wrists, her nail polish neon green. As she kisses him, her hair, teased high in jagged tentacles, fuels an illusion of her face as a giant spider moving in for the kill.

Gerry bangs her sneaker against a cupboard door in an increasingly frantic rhythm until Lark steps back, tosses her a glance. "I see you brought your brother."

"Easy now." Ian strokes her chin, his mouth sloppy and lopsided.

Gerry makes a retching sound in her throat.

"Well." Lark hops on the spot. Gerry half expects her to break into a dance routine, the crowd behind her falling mechanically into step, lifting their jazz hands. "Find me later." She sashays through the bodies.

Gerry groans in disgust.

"Keep it to yourself." Ian takes a swig of his beer.

"Thanks for letting her trash me."

"Oh, for Christ's sakes, lighten the fuck up, will ya?" He reaches into the case and offers her another bottle. "Pick up the pace."

She stands with a bottle in each hand. Her gut twinges as she watches him play a ridiculous game, track and pinpoint Lark, turn his head when she looks. The beer settles like ditchwater, sends brackish gas up into her throat. "Hey," she says finally, her decisiveness firmed with a kick to Ian's boot.

"What?" He speaks without looking at her.

"Since this might be our last night, maybe we should go somewhere. Just the two of us." She tugs at his leather tie.

He nods in rhythm. "Done. We're here."

"I mean alone."

"Do you get what this is?" He waves his bottle at the room. "We're soldiers before the fucking war. So get the hell out of here. Blow off some steam, catch a thrill, live a little for once in your short and meaningless life. And for crying out loud, don't let me catch you mopin' in some corner." He clinks his beer against each of hers and drains his bottle, slams it on the counter. "I'm gonna find Lark."

She reaches for his hand, threads her fingers through his, rubs her thumb against his palm to push her offer into him. "What about me?"

He squeezes her hand tight, stretches over her until the top of his head rests against the cupboard above, his body like a blanket between her and the room. "You. Gerry Mouse. Will have to get your own damn girl." He steps away, picks up his case of beer and pushes into the crowd, his departure a slow, quiet landslide inside her. She leans back against the counter, tries to wait it out, finishes one beer, then guzzles the second. The kitchen flattens like a Polaroid, the ceiling's sharp white corners, blurry faces. She shuffles along the counter, opens the fridge, and grabs without looking, a cold metal can she camouflages with shrugged shoulders.

The music in the living room has mellowed to viscous Floyd, the room glazed with smoke. Bodies clog every pathway, every seat. She leans against the closest wall. Beside her, a row of guys stares blankly forward like suspects in a police lineup. Across the room, Lark and Ian take up most of a couch. He stretches on top of her, kisses her as if trying to pulverize her face. Her arms and legs writhe around him, the limbs of a trapped insect. Gerry shivers. The beer can chills her hands.

Lark's skirt rises high over her hip, exposes the bright white of her panties. Gerry watches the guys down the wall, serious eyes, open-mouthed concentration.

"Young love." The guy beside her leans in as he says it but doesn't look at her. His shoulder touches hers. He offers his cigarette, his hand slim, the hair of his forearm peeking out over his wrist. Gerry shakes her head. Smoke tendrils over his lips up into his nose. He smiles. He wears a tattered blazer over a faded Who T-shirt, a grey fedora pushed back on his head, his chin and neck dark with stubble. "I don't want to watch, but I can't look away. It's like one of those Warhol film loops. I bet if we went up to the 89 Inn, ate a pizza, and came back, they'd still be going at it."

"I know them," she says.

He thumps the guy beside him with the back of his hand. "She knows them."

The friend, a Robert Plant wannabe in a denim jacket, hair like an unwashed poodle, gives her a toothy smile and a thumbs-up.

Farther down the wall someone hoots as Lark's tanned leg rises over Ian's hip.

Gerry rolls her eyes.

"I know." The guys beside her nods. "Disgraceful, right?"

She can't place his age, whether he's long out of high school or just looks that way. He reaches into his blazer and pulls out a plastic medicine bottle half-full of orange liquid. Without breaking his gaze, he unscrews the cap, tips the bottle to his lips. He grimaces as he swallows. "Want some?"

"What is it?"

"Bronchitis last week." He points at his neck. Mousey hairs curl up over the edge of his T-shirt. He smells like stale smoke and sweat. "The doctor gave me this stuff with codeine. It tastes like shit, but, man, it makes you feel like a fucking cloud." He rotates his palms to the ceiling and tilts his head back in a pose that reminds her of Jesus on the cross.

She takes the bottle from him, tips it without touching it to her lips. The taste makes her gag. A ball of muscle rolls up in her throat. She worries for a second she'll spray it all over him, then manages to swallow. The vile chemical sting jitters through her.

"Gross, right?"

She nods.

"Just wait."

She drains her beer, lets it wash her mouth clean. Her tongue feels softer, padded, a small animal napping in the cave of her head. A lightness circles her eyes, hidden muscles in her face fall slack and untethered. She stares at Ian and Lark but can't remember what's wrong about watching them. Their bodies churn, a slow and perfect machine.

"Good stuff, right?"

Her head floats as she nods.

"Do you want to find a bedroom?"

She recognizes the words but not their meaning. "What?"

He cups his hand against her head and speaks right into her. His voice crinkles, a paper bag inside her ear.

The sound is what she understands. "Okay," she says.

He leads her by the hand, grips and regrips, tight, but tentative. As he walks ahead, he removes his hat, shrinks in front of her. She wonders if by the time they reach the room, he will have disappeared to nothing.

The bedroom is a single bed cramped against a wall with a barred window. An ironing board leans beside the closet door. A thin bedspread drapes the narrow mattress, skims the floor with worn chenille flowers. She can't imagine how they will manage it all in this tiny space, small talk, kissing, awkward increments of touch, her hands conducting and controlling like traffic signals, stop, stop, stop, go. And nakedness. For that, she is sure they need a bigger room. She steadies herself, hand on the edge of the bed, the bedspread strangely dry and crisp, the mattress boxy, hard, searches for the best place to sit.

Near the foot of the bed, he takes off his clothes. Before she can tell him to stop, she's staring at the brush of hair across his chest, the shadowed thatch between his legs, and the pink, wrinkled tube that sways as he moves. He wrestles the covers over himself, then holds them open for her.

"Come on, before this shit wears off." He says it with mock command, a smile on his face, but she senses something folded into the corners of his mouth, an impatience that could make him mean. She undresses with her back to him. Her clothes lift away, then drip from her fingertips, her body weightless, blended with the air. The codeine floods her with warmth. She slips between the cover and a pilly flannel sheet, startles at the bristly touch of his skin.

"Whoa," he says. His smile spreads as he climbs on top of her. His hipbones pry her legs open, side to side. He pauses to cough into his hand, murmurs an apology. She closes her eyes, tries not to focus on each dry, rubbery prod. Tries to think only of the high, the sparkle in her face, the marshmellowy hump of pillow beneath her neck. She feels grateful to the owners of the room, whoever they are, as the faded scent of their lemon detergent rises from the sheets, brightens the stale cigarette funk of the room. Even the cough syrup's backwash distracts her. She rolls her tongue in her mouth to call up its bitterness.

Repetition wears her down, the chafe and drag of skin on skin. With each thrust, his moans loosen, and raw pain makes her think of meat in a butcher shop being thumped by a mallet. His body smell, musky with nerves and unwashed parts, wafts up through gaps in the bedding, clouds her face. The rhythm unhinges her, its regularity an irritation to her muscles, her teeth, her cells. He vibrates and whimpers on top of her. His wetness burns. She winces and rolls away from him, stuffs the sheet between her legs, and presses back the sting. Everything inside her pulses, flayed.

"Are you okay?" he says.

She wipes herself with the sheet, afraid to look down at the mess she might be leaving. "I'm gonna get dressed." Her clothes bind, as if she got into the bed one size and came out another. The elastic of her panties nicks at her thighs, her T-shirt tangles, the legs of her jeans twist.

"You want a cigarette?"

She opens the door, relieved to fall into the noise of the party, calmed by the faces, the smoke, the light.

ZZ Top at full volume, the living room has become a dance floor, guys with beer bottle hands. Feet planted, their shoulders wing to no particular beat. The girls are the show. They wiggle their hips, lips pursed as they shake their hair. Two girls jump on the couch as if it's a trampoline. Ian's nowhere in sight. She checks the kitchen, then takes her place alone against the living-room wall. After a few minutes, the guy shuffles in beside her, fedora crushed low on his head. "So, hey, I need to find my friend and get out of here." His eyes flit from a blank space on the one side of her to a blank space on the other. "There's this other party." He shrugs. "I'd invite you, but it's kind of a private thing."

She nods, afraid to look him, to see and possibly remember his face. "I'll take that cigarette."

He feels inside his jacket. His hand comes out empty. "I don't have that many left. Like I said, I've got this other party."

"Forget it." She pushes away from the wall, lurches for the kitchen, the back door, beer and cough syrup in a crawling race up her throat.

His voice trails behind her. "Aw, come on, don't be like that."

The back steps are empty except for a girl crying into another girl's shoulder. Gerry gulps the cold air, steals past them to a cement path that leads to a garage and a long stretch of yard. A tire swing dangles from a low tree branch, plastic trucks crouch in the unmown lawn. She staggers to the back. A sickly fence separates grass from alley, torn, splintered pickets, gaps like blackened teeth. Pickets at her head, she lies down, searches for stars. Dark, woolly clouds hide the night, keep the moon from view. Each time she closes her eyes, the earth spins like a turntable. She claws at the grass, pulls up mounds of turf, cold clay soil. The damp ground cools her back as she waits for the change, to feel newly emboldened, empowered, brimming with the cocky nerve that marked experienced girls on TV. The only sensations she can pinpoint are a thick, wet swell between her legs, a rash along her jaw from the scuff of his stubble, and her high dropping off into a pit. If anything, she feels hulled, as if there is less of her.

She gives it a good twenty minutes, waits through two episodes of Ian calling her name from the back porch, before deciding her experiment is a failure. A nagging, embarrassed heat plays up behind her eyes and she tries to fill herself with dewy air, swallow the ground's loamy smell to keep from crying.

———

Instead of driving home, Ian takes a meandering zigzag through empty streets, the road washed in tungsten light. They drive with the stereo off, the engine's stutter a one-way conversation, Ian's mood grey and pensive. The silence unnerves Gerry, amplifies the clamminess of her clothes, the soreness between her legs. "So. What happened to Lark?"

"Curfew. I took her home. What happened to you?" Ian's voice is flat with disapproval.

"Nothing." Mistrustful of her own face, she stares out the window as they slow for a light.

"I heard you were with some guy."

"I was outside. By myself." The car's idling jostles her stomach. She grips the door, in case she needs to swing it open and puke. "Thanks for ditching me, by the way."

"It was a party."

"That I didn't want to go to."

"Excuse me for living. I thought you'd have a good time."

"Well, I didn't." Her face feels stiff and hot. She knows if she says one more word, she will bawl.

"So, you met someone."

Her eyes close to block him out.

"Hello?"

She rolls down her window and loses him in the blast of wind.

He punches the radio, drowns her in a cold wave of heavy metal, then shouts over it: "You're fucking impossible, you know that?"

They park at English Bay, walk away from the streetlights toward rows of shadowed logs on the beach. Sand pulls at her sneakers, twists her in a crooked stumble. The bay hulks low in front of her, black without the moon. Freight lights glint in the distance, a sparsely starred sky at her feet.

Ian settles against an oversized log, pats his pockets. As he strikes a match, a dark shape scurries near their feet. The sound slips out of Gerry, a frightened, girlish squeal. Ian looks down, kicks at the sand. Something thumps as it lands a few feet away.

"Relax, it's rats." Smoke curls from his lips.

She sits back on the log, lifts her feet, thinks of scuttling claws, and keeps her hands clenched in her lap until Ian offers her the joint. The smoke tastes sweet and green, mixes with the sea air in her mouth. A perfect lift rolls up over her eyes, laps at her brain.

"So, I guess you're ready for tomorrow." He sips the words as he tokes.

"Yeah." A day without practice and already the details dull in her mind.

Ian shrugs. "I'm thinking of not going."

She can tell by the forced easiness of his voice, he's baiting her. The back of her throat prickles with smoke. She holds her breath to keep from coughing. "So don't. Andri and I are the only ones who have to be there."

"What would we lose if we didn't go through with it?"

"We already put Clem in an old folks' home."

"He should have been there all along."

She raises her palms to her eyes, tries to scrub away the annoyance, worries her high will spoil, sink her into a dark place she can't get out of. "Why do you do that? Why do you have to pretend you're better than everyone else? God, you're such an asshole."

He shakes his head. "I'm just saying, if you're not up for it, if you don't think you can handle it, you don't have to show up."

"It's like you think you're smart or something. And you're totally not. You're like the dumbest person I know." She watches the words hit, small detonations beneath the surface of his skin. He looks away, stares at the lit windows of apartment buildings near the park. The breeze off the water buffs cold against her scalp. She squints into the wind, surprised by her own meanness. Up on the road, a raccoon lumbers, humped over in a slow, rocking gait. "Look." She points to draw Ian back.

He ignores her, blows a thick stream of smoke. "Your mom's all alone." His voice is quiet. "Maybe this isn't the right time. Maybe you should just focus on school. There's nothing wrong with that. Some things, you do them, even for the right reasons, and other people get hurt, people who are already suffering enough. Do you get what I'm saying?"

The raccoon struggles at the curb, edges along until it finds a way to climb up. She pictures her mother as an old woman, stooped back, hands like shaking leaves.

"I wish I'd never taken you to Megan's."

His guilt repeats inside her. "You didn't make me do anything." She shivers with fatigue, rubs at her arms. "It's what I want."

"You're too young to know what you want." His condescension ignites a thin, quick arc of anger. But the night has left her drained, and it would take too many words to catalogue the ways he doesn't understand her. She drags her heel in the sand, watches the raccoon's silver eyes blink as it hides under a bush.

"Anyway." He squishes the roach in his fingers. "Nothing's carved in stone."

She picks up a pebble, throws it hard toward the water. It hits the sand. "What would you do, if you were me?"

"Kill myself." The joke pricks, a well-aimed dart. He knocks against her to show he's teasing. She forces a giggle, pushes back against his weight. For a second, he stares at her face, his eyes worried, then turns his gaze back to the water, drapes his arm over her shoulder. "What would I do?" The inside of his jacket is warm. She lets herself rest against him. "I'd stay home tomorrow. I'd try harder at school. I'd go to university, and fall in love, and have tons of kids and teach them how to do great stuff. I'd stop listening to that crappy new wave music. I'd live a hundred years, maybe more. I'd–" He stops himself. From across the water, the long moan of a ship's horn fills the silence.

"What?" she asks.

He squeezes her, whispers, "Gerry Mouse." Her body rises and falls with his breath. When he finally lets go, she stands, feels the night slip between them as she steps away. She searches for another rock on the sand, hurls it with all her strength, counts the seconds of its freefall before it hits water.

It's only after Ian's car rumbles away, turns into the alley behind his house, that she notices Randy's truck parked across the street, Randy hunched in the cab. His head bobs an uneven rhythm. She hopscotches her way over, jumps up on his running board, drops her elbows over the open window. "Kinda psycho sitting out here, no?"

"I see you're still mixing with the riffraff."

"Don't be jealous, he's not my boyfriend."

Randy snickers. An open case of beer takes up the passenger side of the bench seat, crushed empties pile on the floor. Even without the evidence, the grainy reek of booze rises off him.

"Throw in a dead dog and you'll have a country song."

Randy points to her house. "Run on home or I'll rat you out to the warden."

"You must be drunk if you think I'll be the one in trouble."

He smiles a closed-mouth smile. His lips disappear into his beard, then reappear as he nods. Alcohol has softened him, brought a youthful sadness to his face. The gather of curls near his neck, his sunken chest, creases pinched around his eyes, his weakness pulls at her. She makes her move slowly, bends into the cab to press her mouth to his. Her lips open against the prickle of his beard, her tongue flicks and pokes as she guesses it should. Randy sits rigid, motionless. She stops, leans back, tries to read his expression, but he stares straight ahead, an unblinking trance.

"I'm drunk," he says finally.

She grabs the doorframe and stretches her body. "I don't mind."

He shakes his head.

This time she reaches in as she kisses him, strokes his neck, his shirt. His lips remains a stubborn lock, a tight, impenetrable nub. She releases him and sighs.

"You should go."

"I have experience, if that makes any difference."

His face scrunches in pain. "I don't even want to know what that means."

"It's no big deal." She rests her elbow on the window edge.

"It's illegal."

"So is drinking and driving."

"I didn't start drinking until I got here."

"Come on. Seriously. Just, you know, be a man and do it already."

"Fuck you."

She leans in again, grazes her mouth over his, and waits for a response. Nothing. Her hands cup his face as she tries soft brushes and pecks. His breath buffets her skin, a long, disinterested exhale that whistles through his nose. She crushes her mouth hard on his, tries to hurt him, bruise him with her teeth. His lips open suddenly, and his tongue is in her mouth, hot and thick. She sucks on it, and it grows, forces her mouth wider. He grips the back of her head. His fingers squeeze her scalp, a pain that startles, then warms her. Runny heat melts from her head to her neck, spreads through her stomach. She holds his shirt in a fist, her tongue wrestles with his. His moan in her mouth hums through her chin. The feeling in her body reminds her of a corkscrew her mother uses, a slow spiral to drill down into the tight bottle, thin, metal arms that fly helplessly up. A low ache urges her to clench hidden muscles as her hips press hard against the metal door handle. A fizzy shock snaps between her legs, bubbles a gasp in her throat.

Randy yanks himself away, sags over the case of beer, his face red, his mouth a cavern. "I didn't mean to do that." He shakes his head. "I'm too drunk." He covers his face with his hands.

She rolls her tongue, mines the sweet smoky taste of him. When he starts to shudder, she guesses it's over. "Don't spaz. It was like, ten seconds. You won't even remember tomorrow."

He nods, but she can tell he isn't listening. She considers crawling into the cab to sit beside him but decides that would only scare him more. "I'm not going to tell anyone. You don't have to worry."

He raises his head. Tears cling to the fur of his beard. "One second she was fine, the next thing we're breaking up."

"She gets crazy about these things. She doesn't think straight."

"I don't even know why she dumped me. Maybe sometimes I'm an asshole. Maybe. But not with her. I mean, why bother being the good guy?"

"She dumps everyone. It's not personal."

He wipes his face with his palms. With each swipe, the familiar, stoic Randy rises to the surface. "That's the stupidest fucking excuse I've ever heard." His voice settles back, hardened and sour.

"You don't know what's she's been through."

"Yeah, well, I should have just treated her like every other asshole."

His self-pity grates on her. "She can't help how she is. No one can."

"Who are you, Dr. Joyce-fucking-Brothers?"

"Just cut her some slack, okay? She's got a lot to deal with."

He snorts. "She's got you. That's a nightmare. I should blame this whole thing on you."

She likes his sarcasm best, the blade of his humour cutting her with small, delicious nicks. "It's not my fault you show up in those filthy work clothes."

"Fine, I'm no Prince-fucking-Charming."

"Would it kill you to take a shower?"

"Enough already." Randy groans and massages his temples as if she's woken him from a bad sleep. His grogginess makes her yawn, the night heavy on her eyes. Still, she wants to ask him about sex, whether it makes a man feel the same way, wishing he could climb out of his body and throw it in the laundry. Randy's jaw hangs slack. The beginnings of a snore gurgle up from his throat.

She tips back her head and swings in an arc. "So." She says it loud enough to startle him awake. "I think a hundred bucks should keep me quiet."

He rubs his face and straightens himself in the seat, lets out a long, tired sigh. "Go fuck yourself."

She can't help smiling. "Fifty?"

He digs into his back pocket for his wallet and pulls out a single bill. "Here's ten. Get lost."

She leans into the cab and snatches the bill from his fingers, her cheeks warm with a grin.

Lolled back on the headrest, he turns to look at her, his face sunken, fatigued. "Gerry," her name heavy in his mouth, as if she's not a person but a decision.

"Yeah?"

"Don't ever, ever do this shit for money."

She sticks her tongue out as she backs away from the truck.

"I'm serious."

She opens her hand in a slow, low wave.

"You're not that kind of girl, Gerry."

His certainty cushions her against the empty dark.

In her room, she rolls a joint, plays side two of *Ocean Rain*, volume down, music a whisper over the turntable's whir. She sits in her window, watches Randy's truck until it pulls away, creeps down the block, headlights off. On her bed, she stretches to feel the blood-rush in her tired limbs. She knows she should focus on tomorrow, get everything clear in her head. Instead, she thinks back to the phone call to her father, the amorphous sound of him. She had expected to feel more, the magnet of shared biology drawing them together. To hear in his clogged, choked tones, guilt rising in his throat. She tries to decide if he even sounded like a man who would rush to get on an airplane.

Time pass in fits and jerks, her eyes open and close, a thin tap of drums, the needle scrape at the record's end. She wakes to the sound of the TV downstairs and stumbles to her bedroom door. When she opens it, the unlit house is silent.

She climbs back onto her bed, feels the air around her chill to an icy cocoon.

o o o

FOR MONTHS DAN DOESN'T SEND HIM on another expedition. At first the boy worries one of the men reported him timid or lazy. Then he notices how Dan dotes on the girl, assigns other women to her chores, urges her to rest. The exemption fills the boy with guilt, though none of the others seem to mind. The girl's swollen belly and wide gait command quiet reverence. Eager to share her happiness, she guides hands across her stretched skin. Even the most reticent, the most disapproving, line up for a turn.

The girl loses herself easily in sleep, the hut filled with the wheeze and growl of her snores. But for the boy, nights are torture. He imagines the thing as it churns in its liquid den, presses its scaled, stumpy limbs against the walls of her stomach. As the birth approaches, nightmares grow worse, and the boy forces himself to stay awake until the subtle shift in darkness, the first hint of dawn, when he can close his eyes for a fitful few hours.

Fear of sleep drives the boy to approach Dan one evening by the fire. At first Dan pretends not to hear him, turns his head to the water. Finally, he sighs and nods. Two nights later, Dan taps on their door.

The girl doesn't make a fuss, stands mute and angry in the centre of the hut, arms cradling her belly as he puts on his jacket. He tries to kiss her forehead. She turns away, refuses his touch.

Around the fire, men offer warm greetings, smiles, cheers, claps on his arm. The boy's relief wells up as gratitude as he shakes their hands.

The walk from camp passes quickly, and in no time they are on the road. The boy's rifle feels lighter, natural in the crook of his arm. Though the men don't speak, the mood is optimistic, the air full of pine and the salty perfume of the sea, so that he can almost believe this is pleasurable: silent company, the expansive night. But when he looks up to the sky, the dark canopy confuses him. He has grown used to perpetual dusk, the sun's faint circle a distant flashlight behind layers of fabric, has adapted to see a full spectrum in the constant grey, the same way, as a child, he saw colours in his neighbour's black-and-white television. But the dearth of stars always disturbs him, and tonight, he is jarred by the blank heavens, the moon's absence.

As they approach the city, the men grow tense, raise their rifles. The boy carries his low at his hip. Muffled shouts or maybe barks sound in the distance. Two men take aim, but no one fires.

At the divvy, Roger teams the boy with the investment banker, Michael, and Bruno, the bald handyman he chums around with. Michael kicks the heel of the boy's boot.

Hope you can keep up. He says it with a wink.

Roger gives Michael a list. Michael glances at it, nods as he presses it into his pocket. He motions with his head for the three of them to get started.

Instead of following the avenue to the water, they walk up, into the winding streets of neighbourhoods. Bruno leads, zigzags a seemingly arbitrary path. Michael follows like a man who trusts the instincts of his dog. After an hour of walking, Bruno stops at a corner, points to a small bungalow in front of them.

Here. He cocks his rifle.

Michael turns to the boy. Just stay back. If no one's home, you can join in.

Bruno and Michael approach the front door. Their knees rise in unison to kick it open. The boy stays on the sidewalk, rifle against his chest, as they shout their arrival and step inside.

A minute later, Bruno waves a thick arm. Michael instructs the boy to find and bag anything useful. Bruno starts in the basement. Michael moves purposefully from room to room, digs through closets and drawers, searches for specific items on the list.

Portraits adorn the living-room wall. A large Asian family, several generations. The boy wonders where they have gone. The glass verandah door has been smashed through, the kitchen ransacked. In the back corner of one of the cupboards, the boy finds two packages of dried noodles caught behind a shelf, a box of bouillon cubes. The meaty smell makes him salivate. Even the cartoon chicken on the front looks appetizing. He could open the box, peel back the foil, and taste one of the cubes. His fingers pick at the packaging. He drops the box into his bag, afraid the men will smell it on him.

Michael comes out of the bathroom, vials of prescription pills clutched in his hands. He pinches the lid off one bottle and shakes two pills into his mouth.

What are those? the boys asks.

Do I care? Michael says. He offers the open bottle.

The boy shakes his head, wishes he had eaten the bouillon cube. Bruno comes up from the basement, eyes the pill bottle between them. The boy knows how it looks.

Those are for the hospital, Bruno says.

Michael pushes the lid onto the bottle and throws it into his bag.

Though he's done nothing wrong, the boys feels guilty. He waits with Michael by the front door while Bruno finishes the bedrooms.

The next two houses are the same, cleaned out. Michael grows impatient, paces the front hall while the boy and Bruno do all the work.

On the steps of the fourth house, Michael puts his finger to his lips, leans over to peek through a narrow pane of glass beside the door. He nods to Bruno and readies his flashlight. Bruno kicks the door in. The house is dark, but immediately the boy hears movement, whispering.

Hold it! Michael shouts. His flashlight beam catches two men trying to scuttle out of the living room. The men freeze, their backs to the door.

I got 'em, Bruno says, rifle cocked.

Turn around! The sharpness of Michael's voice makes the boy want to run.

The two men turn slowly. One of them covers his face with his hands, Jesus, oh please.

Do it, Michael says.

Bruno fires and the boy jumps, shrieks in the doorway. Neither Michael nor Bruno look at him. The man with his face covered buckles forward on his knees as if in prayer. The second holds up his hands, stares down at his fallen friend.

Bruno fires again. The second man topples, pitches to the side, lands neatly on top of the first.

Okay, quickly, Michael says.

The boy stands dumb in the entryway as Bruno and Michael scour the house for the other men's stash. They crisscross in front of him with bags of food, knives, bandages, extra flashlights. Bruno passes with a water purifier tucked under his arm. When they join the boy back at the front door, their bags bulge.

Michael stands with his hands on his hips. You see what we do here?

Unable to speak, the boy nods, eyes the two bodies.

Michael follows his gaze. Don't feel bad for them. They did a lot worse to get this stuff.

To the boy's relief, the next few houses are empty.

This block is sucking big-time, Michael says when they're back on the sidewalk. Let's try that one. He points farther into the trees.

Bruno shrugs, lopes in the direction of Michael's finger, toward a bungalow built into the hill.

As they mount the stoop, the boy hears voices. Women. Instead of kicking the door in, Bruno shoulders it with a forceful but easy step.

Four women huddle on the living-room floor in a spill of blankets. Michael's flashlight skims their faces. One in the middle, older with thin, grey hair, is clearly the mother. The other three, teenagers, the boy's age and older, emaciated, like wires in soiled pyjamas, hair knotted away from bony faces. The woman raises a gun with a thick, stubby muzzle.

Get out of our house, she says. She stares the men down. Her girls have the same fierce eyes.

The boy takes a step back.

Michael steps forward, shines his flashlight on her gun. It's a fucking flare gun, he says. Put it down. Or we'll blow your head off.

The boy prays for her to put it down.

The woman's hand trembles. One of the girls grabs for the gun, not to stop the mother, he can tell by the lunge, but to end her stalling. The gun goes off with a screech that tears at the boy's ears. A sear through the air, then a whistle pop as the flare hits the ceiling in a burst of sparks, falls to the carpet where it sizzles and flames.

With a hand over his mouth and nose, Bruno stamps out the small fire. The boy tries to blink away the neon squiggle burned into the centre of his vision, cough out toxic smoke.

He prays the girls have scattered, sprinted for secret exits in the back. As the fog clears, he sees they've clung closer together on the floor.

Michael drops his bag. He and Bruno approach the girls, their huddle of crying. The men each grab a girl and pull to separate them, a tangle of limbs and kicks and screams.

Michael looks at the boy, then points to the older woman, who holds the remaining girl in her arms. Watch them, he says.

The men drag the two girls out of the room and down the hall.

On the floor near the door, the boy sits, unable to look at the woman and her daughter. He rests his rifle across his lap and tells himself that if they try to escape, he won't stop them. They make no move.

From another room, shouts and pleas, the slap of a hand, and a duller series of thuds, like bone hitting bone.

Bruno growls, Hold her, hold her. Then Michael's impish laugh, Yeah, yeah, yeah. The sounds get quieter. This scares the boy more. He breathes as loud as he can, tries not to listen. For a while, there is silence, and he thinks it must be over. The woman and her girl lean against each another, eyes closed.

A gun fires.

The boy leaps to his feet.

The woman wails into the girl's neck. Beside her, the girl stares down at the puddle of blankets.

Jesus, Michael cries. What the fuck?

When Michael and Bruno come out of the room, Michael's shirt and face are splattered with blood. Bruno picks up his bag and stalks out the front door. Michael wipes his face with his hand, reaches for his bag, then shakes his head as he passes the boy.

From the other room, low, guttural moans. The woman stands and tows the girl along with her toward the sound. The boy stands alone in the entrance.

Are you coming or what? Michael shouts from the sidewalk.

The boy stumbles out of the house and pulls the door closed. His hand comes away greased with something warm and sticky. He tries to rub it off on the bag.

Bruno stalks ahead on the street, guides them back to the meeting point.

Michael walks beside the boy. He shines his flashlight on his shirt and groans. As he shakes the shirt, flecks of red grit spray into the air around him. The boy steps away.

Fucking freak, Michael says.

The boy hesitates before speaking, gathers strength for his voice. We have to tell Dan.

Fuck Dan. That holier than thou man-cunt. I don't see him out here in the trenches, do you?

The boy shakes his head to feign agreement, tries to keep the shock from his face.

Michael wipes his cheek on his sleeve. Dan has no sense of the future. I mean, how long do we keep going on like this? There's nothing fucking left.

The boy realizes he has spent the past months thinking only

minute to minute, hour to hour, to gaze ahead days or even weeks sways him with vertigo.

Now you, my friend. Michael stops and points his finger. He makes two fists and pumps his hips back and forth. Repopulation. He laughs as he says it, smacks the boy's arm.

The boy smiles to get along.

That's what I'm about. Others too. Following your lead. Michael taps his finger to his forehead. The future in mind. He turns and continues down the hill. The boy struggles to keep up with the brisk pace.

They approach a wooded yard. The boy mutters about needing a piss and veers off to the right. Buffered by a stand of trees, he covers his face with his jacket and cries, pounds his fist into ragged bark until it feels raw and torn. He opens his jacket and wipes his face, blows his nose. His hand quivers, stings with pain. He runs down the block to catch up.

Close to the meeting point, voices whoop and howl. Bruno and Michael holler, Yeeoow! The catcalls boomerang back.

It's clear from everyone's bags, they've done well. Roger looks pleased. No one questions the state of Michael's shirt.

On the walk back, weighted with their secret, the boy keeps his hand ready on his rifle, convinced they would sooner shoot the truth out of him than trust him with it. It is no longer the rustle of roadside trees or the skitter of pebbles that makes him nervous but the throaty breath of these men, the stomp of their boots, the twitch of their trigger fingers. He worries that at any moment one of them will set their gun on him, press its barrel to his temple, and smile a polite goodbye. Every sigh, every throat clearing warns.

They make it back to camp as the sky lightens at the horizon. He enters the hut and with his clothes still on climbs into bed beside the girl. Men's voices carry down from the campfire, laughter crackling with conquest. The boy wraps his arm around the girl, closes his eyes, and waits for their baby to be born.

19

SHE WAKES IN A PANIC IN THE DARK, chest tight, acid and beer souring her throat. The bed rocks as she turns, a pulse thumps behind her eyes. She crawls to the floor, rolls the last of her stash, smokes at the window until the day whittles itself into mechanical details: the route, the times. Her fingers count, press out codes, flick the device switch. Morning arrives with orange light across the neighbours' lawn. Nerves simmer low in her gut. She scrubs her hands over her face, gives up on waiting to feel ready.

The ache in her head marks each moment as distinct. In the bathroom, she counts the strokes of her toothbrush, wets the nap of her hair to raise the flattened back and sides, roughs a dry towel over her arms and face until her skin tingles. Panties, jeans, bra, T-shirt, socks, jacket, she examines each piece of clothing before putting it on. For what, she isn't sure.

Downstairs, she shakes a heap of puffed cereal into a bowl, drowns it in milk, feels as if she is playing the role of a girl eating cereal, the workings of her body out of sync, unconvincing. She settles in front of the TV to scan the news.

Henry's face takes up every channel, a stiff station promo photo airbrushed to give him kinder eyes, fewer wrinkles. She leaves her bowl on the coffee table, moves to the television, kneels in front of it. In video footage of the fire, neighbours shake their heads in disbelief. She glimpses herself in some of the shots, body cut in half, shoulder, hip, the point of her elbow, a Mobius of time that drags her from her living room to Henry's street and back again. Near the bottom corner of the screen, Henry's brake lights wink in the distance. They disappear and reappear, a vanishing trick that makes her smile. On camera, the blazing house threatens, menace amplified by the troubled eyebrows of the field reporter. She counts six replays of Mrs. Cross's collapse. When they show the house again, Gerry traces the outline of her half-self, wonders if Henry is watching the same broadcast.

The newscaster's mouth sets in a grim line. A helicopter captures Henry's car partially obscured by brush, angled nose down in a ditch beside the I-5, just south of the Oregon border. An apparent heart attack, the newscaster's voice drones over the grainy film, Henry's body found slumped over the steering wheel. From the air, tan dots of uniformed patrolmen flank the site, tails of yellow police tape flap in the wind.

She can only blink and breathe, squeeze her arms against the shift of the room. On TV, a man Krazy Glues his hard hat to a steel girder, clings to the hat as he pretends to dangle above a construction site, knees tucked up to his waist. The dizziness spins her, a toppling sensation she has to close her eyes to fight. When she opens her eyes, she is gazing down from the ceiling at a shape on the carpet, a thin figure she can't quite recognize. She hears soft, wet sobs and wishes she could bring comfort, sad for the suffering she can hear but not place. Solidness returns, first in her panting breath, then the heat in her face, her boiled-up tears, the rough carpet beneath her cheek, the pulse in her head.

She lies on the carpet and stares at the room. The unexpected angle makes her feel as if she has woken in someone else's house, in someone else's body. Stretched out in front of her, her own arm and hand are unfamiliar. She stares at her fingers, watches them curl and uncurl. She tells herself to do each thing before she does it: find her shoes, find her jacket, open the front door, close the front door, walk to the bus stop, wait for the bus, count out the fare when the bus crests the hill, get ready to pay.

In the park, signs bob like the sails of invisible ships: *Your Arms Are Killing Me, Anything War Can Do Peace Can Do Better, My Dad Went to Washington and All He Brought Back Was This Shitty Apocalypse.* Gerry crisscrosses to avoid crouched bodies unfurling banners: Lesbian Mothers Against Annihilation, the Fascist Coalition, Retired Dentists for Disarmament, the Atheist League. Believers push their pamphlets at her, folk music, meditation, steelworkers' rights, communism in schools, veganism, urine therapy. The hivelike urgency of agitators and instigators buzzes against her, makes her aware of the heaviness in her limbs, the focused effort of every step.

She wades through a swarm of hippies: Kitsilano throwbacks with grey ponytails and new converts, girls her age in batik dresses and sandals, thin braids around their faces, all smiles and bralessness. Past them, the union groups, muscled working class, the brainier ones in pinstriped shirts and glasses, mouths welded into scowls. She had expected a gathering of families, young mothers and fathers marching for a better world for their children, a picnic atmosphere, ladies in straw hats, babies in strollers. Instead, the park is alive with cast-offs, axe-grinders.

Bound in leathers and spikes, the punk-rock contingent is small but loud. Mohawks lacquered, they scream and crash into one another around an overturned garbage can. Black lips and charred cheekbones, faces painted with tears of blood, they wear their darkness on the outside, something she wishes she could do. She searches the crowd for a calming presence, school-children, pastors, but finds only a group of frat boys dressed as nuns playing freeze-tag while shotgunning beer.

She catches herself looking for Henry, in groups of men, in the shaded trees, a glimpse of his posture, a man with binoculars, another with grey hair. Something about the oddball, griping atmosphere makes it seem the perfect place for him.

"Gerry!" Andri waves from the far end of the planetarium parking lot. He looks ready for a funeral: dark suit jacket, white-collared shirt, his hair slick with gel. Ian slouches on the bumper of Andri's car. Gerry blinks the wetness from her eyes, slows her walk, doesn't speak until she's sure her voice won't shake. She nods at Andri. "You look different."

"I dress for success." Andri grins, walks around to the back of the car.

She follows. "Where's Megan?"

"Powdering her nose." He presses a finger to his nostril and sniffs.

Gerry isn't sure what he means. Behind the shield of the open trunk, he shows her the knapsack. The plain brown nylon exterior makes it look harmless, unremarkable. He reaches down for it. She stops him with her hand. "Here?"

Andri scans the crowded parking lot, then looks at her, frowns

as he studies her face. "Don't worry. We look like everyone else."
He holds the bag out to her. "It won't bite."

Ian leans on the car beside them, watches with his arms folded
across his chest.

The bag hangs on Andri's curled fingers.

Gerry nods. "The switch?"

Andri pulls back the zipper. Hidden under a mess of spray
paint cans, a baseball cap, the package looks identical to the
wrapped box of chocolates. Andri eases it up, turns the package
on end, and points to an inch-long strip of wired black plastic
joined in two places. "Tear the tab, the timer starts."

She grazes the tab with her finger, feels its resistance, stiff but
brittle. "What if it comes off?" A tragedy of timing only Henry
would appreciate.

"Then you're dead," Ian says.

Andri's face is serious. "It won't. You have to pull hard to
break the wire. Break it on both sides. Once that's done, you
have twelve minutes. Plenty of time." He pushes the package to
the bottom of the bag. "Now, look." He unsnaps the knapsack's
front panel. "Money is here." A torn white envelope, razor-blade
edges of green bills.

"Two hundred. Don't forget to say that first. It makes the
story more believable. A man offered you money to leave the
package." His eyes fix on her, unblinking, as if waiting for an
answer. A pale line of skin trails over his ear.

"You got a haircut."

Andri stares. His nostrils flare as he breathes. "Do you want
to run through it one last time?"

"No."

He lifts the bag onto her shoulders, tightens the straps until it clings to her. The weight is less than she expected.

Hands rub over Gerry's head. She turns to find Megan there, eyes blinking and bloodshot, mouth a crumpled smile.

Megan sniffles, pinches absently at the tip of her nose. "I was worried you wouldn't show." Her face twitches, her hands fiddle, tug at the buttons and collar of Gerry's jacket, the hem of her T-shirt. "Just do what we told you. Don't think about it too much."

They hug, and Gerry presses her face into Megan's neck, her skin damp with sweat. Megan's body jitters, and Gerry feels her own nervousness boiling up, the morning's shock threatening to shake loose. She hopes Megan can feel it, the way loss has twinned them, made them the same.

"Good luck." Megan says.

Andri pats Gerry's cheek. "Twelve minutes, don't forget." He winks as he slips into the crowd of strangers. Megan strides in the opposite direction.

"It's not too late." Ian kicks the back of her foot.

"No one's asking you to hang around." She grips the shoulder straps. The corners of the package nudge into the small of her back. From far away, a girl's voice calls Ian's name. Gerry swivels to look. Over a park bench, girls in familiar tartan skirts and knee socks prop their private school banner as if preparing for homecoming. "Did you know she was going to be here?"

Ian ignores her question, slides his hand between the knapsack and her back. The unexpected touch soothes her. He bounces the bag twice, weighs it with his hand. "Feels heavy."

She steps away. "It's not." In the distance, Lark ducks under a bridge of arms, head bobbing as she approaches. For the first time, Gerry wonders if Ian has told Lark everything, if they will all go to jail because of him.

He offers his hand. His fingers rake the air. "Why don't you let me take it for a while."

"Why don't you go stick it in your girlfriend."

Ian smirks. "Suit yourself." He turns and jogs to meet Lark halfway. Together, they stroll to the other side of the parking lot, his hands jammed into his pockets.

The knapsack pinches under her arms, warms her back. She opens her jacket, walks to get comfortable. People mill, anxious, bump as they pass. Drums, guitars, and, impossibly, a tuba play haltingly through the crowd, the brass instrument duct-taped to the body of a short, shaggy man in saffron pants. Signs rise and fall. Hands pass food, drink, joints, some play Hacky Sack, Frisbee, while eyes flit, everyone distracted as they work at killing time, wait for a signal.

She finds her way back through the crowd to spy on Ian and Lark, finds them at the far edge of the parking lot. Lark stands with her hip cocked. Her hand slices the air as she talks. Ian shakes his head. Lark's mouth flaps open and closed like a puppet's. Ian shouts, and the arc of his voice carries back to Gerry. She waits for a rise of pleasure, the satisfaction of seeing them unhappy. When it doesn't come, she squints, tries to soften their rigid postures and sharpened words. Lark grabs Ian's arm, and he peels her hand away, throws it down. She calls out after him, pleading. He doesn't turn around.

Gerry blinks as Ian stalks toward her. "What was that?"

He shrugs, feels for his cigarettes. "I dumped her."

"Why?"

"Who cares?" He lights up. The cigarette hangs from his bottom lip. "Let me carry that thing, will ya?" His voice is forlorn, as if carrying the bag might console him.

"No way."

Jets of smoke stream from his nostrils, his head a rocketship about to blast off. In front of them, the crowd shifts. A cluster swells, then begins to funnel out of the park in a slow shuffle step. Without warning or fanfare, the march is under way. He winces as he smokes. "I'm gonna find Megan. Stay here. Don't go anywhere without me."

She watches him walk away. When he's far enough, she sprints the short stretch of vacant grass to join the crowd.

The procession has a wake of its own, an undertow that sucks her deep into its centre and bobs her along. The air thickens with the murmur of slogans. On the bridge, the crowd loosens and sprawls to fill the span. The knapsack holds snug against her. Above the inlet, clouds break to frame a swath of sky; in the harbour below, sailboats and power boats, perfect as toys, toot horns as their passengers wave. Strangers smile at one another, at her. She feels separate from them, the bodies around her like bodies in a dream.

As the march crests the centre of the bridge, the skyline rises, apartments, office towers, sharpened rectangles of steel and glass. Cheers erupt. Despite his disdain for peaceniks and hippies, Henry might have enjoyed the view, storming the city. She tries to conjure him beside her, hairpiece thrust aloft, throat open in a battlecry, but he comes to her in mismatched pieces, the whir of his car window, the smell of his shoe polish, his disappointed grumble. A sudden gust of wind blows dust into the crowd. She closes her eyes, then forces herself to open them, blink, the grit like needles. The wind streaks her face with tears; the idea of never seeing him again so large, it fills her to overflowing.

A lip of sidewalk snags her foot and she trips into the man in front of her. She sniffles as she apologizes, struggles to find her legs. Someone shoves her from behind, a hard thud that crushes the knapsack into her. She lurches toward the bridge rail, collects herself, eases the bag from her back, and unzips it. Inside, the package has upended, a corner of the wrapping torn back to reveal a mess of multicoloured wire. Air shudders out of her. Carefully, she smooths the paper, lifts a tab of sticky tape to hold it down. She rights the package and waits, hears only the rush of wind. A steady current of bodies drifts past her. Far below, waves batter the cement footings of the bridge. She zips the knapsack and slips it on. The bag exerts a tacky pressure, rubs her damp T-shirt into her skin. She joins the crowd in a quickened step, an automatic rhythm.

Two blocks past Davie Street, in front of the hospital, the march stalls. The Nelson Street hill makes it impossible to see the hold up. When they are able to walk a few more steps, the crowd applauds. The pace is haphazard, a step, then a pause, long seconds before the next shuffle forward.

She ends up beside a group of musicians, bearded men who strum sad, melancholic folk songs. People join in to sing, eyes closed. Their voices carry her along.

The block and a half to Nelson Street takes almost fifteen minutes. The hill's apex reveals the delay: Burrard Street stretches six lanes wide, but Robson, narrow and shop-lined, cuts its flow to a two-lane trickle.

The intersection thunders with protesters. Many stream off to flank the march, cheer the procession as it passes the glass-walled library. Library patrons, distracted by the commotion, fill the building's ground-floor windows and second-floor balcony. On the street, squad cars flash red and blue lights, reinforce the intersection barricades. Policemen stand at the open doors of their cars, faces obscured by sunglasses, some with walkie-talkies in gloved hands, others with batons, noses to the air. She waits for them to sniff her out, beat her to the ground with their sticks. The noise of Robson Street cushions her, megaphones and drums, the mob roar of the crowd. As she passes the officers, she challenges their mirrored eyes, dares them to notice her. She drifts by unseen.

Thousands cram the narrow Robson Street channel, some push to inch forward, most rest still against other bodies. Chanting becomes screaming, hoarse and incomprehensible. Groups lean together, arms around one another. Signs jump in rhythm, swing like weapons. Gerry threads her body through small breaks in the crowd, advances toward the middle of the block where shop windows no longer reflect flashes of red and blue.

A rash of punks carves an aimless, chaotic path, elbow, spit, and kick their way through. Groups shout their disgust, push back with collective force. Bizarre confrontations erupt, two shorn and pierced girls scream in the face of a bookish man, a Mohawked boy snatches an elderly woman's cane after she pokes him with it.

A new faction penetrates the crowd, faces masked in white balaclavas, each one painted with the crude black hollows of a skull. They scuttle over newspapers boxes and fire hydrants, spray cans clipped to holsters around their waists. Squat legs and curled arms, they remind Gerry of monkeys as they hop from surface to surface. Storefronts advertise their handiwork, red anarchy symbols, bright yellow radiation signs. Across the street, two policemen on horseback sport white helmets with face shields, swing batons to corral the marchers. Their animals, dark and mammoth, sway with the movement of the crowd. Juice boxes and pop cans fly at the uniformed men. The officers remain stoic in their saddles.

Gerry eyes the crush of bodies in the street. She could cut north, cross the road for a better chance at the laneway. Groups link arms to create human chains, others heave as a mass, their force rolling through the crowd like a riptide. Even if she squeezes through with the knapsack, a policeman on horseback stands between her and the laneway entrance.

She searches for a new route, but police hover at every exit path, seal in the crowd. Behind her, masked skeletons spray neon skulls and crossbones onto shop windows, shimmy up lampposts to escape the police, who ease their horses forward in tentative steps. Above the street, skeletons hang from the curved necks of street-lights, jeer and shake their fists. Charged and inspired, others split from the crowd, climb anything they can, garbage cans, parking meters, fire hydrants, spindly trees planted at intervals on the sidewalk. They trample the hoods and trunks of cars parked on the march route. The police steer their horses at a lethargic pace, wheedle delinquents from their perches, pry at them with batons. A half-block away, she spots Ian and Megan waving to get her attention as they struggle to push past bodies. Ian points for Gerry to stay put. Gerry nods to show she's understood.

From high above, voices holler. A skater boy with a shaved head dangles by his knees and hands from the lamppost beside her. His sway and the crane of Gerry's neck make her woozy.

Bodies part a narrow path as a policeman wades his horse through the crowd. The animal glides, nostrils shiny with mucus. The officer points his baton at Gerry. She waits, readies herself to turn and run. He stops beneath the swinging boy, snatches at him with a gloved hand. The boy torques his body beyond the policeman's grasp, his mouth wide open and crooked with mock fear. She smells smoke, charred salt air. Across the street a garbage can has been set on fire. The policeman smells it too, wrenches around in his saddle, shouts to the crowd, his commands disintegrating just past his lips. On the sidewalk, Ian and Megan have stopped moving, their eyes on the policeman.

Above him, the boy frees something from his pocket, a frayed, dark string. Gerry has to squint to see it, Christmas lights or a rope to lash himself in place. For a terrifying second, the boy hangs only by the cross of his legs, flicks a lighter in the cup of his palms. She imagines him slipping, the watery thump of his skull on the road. A spark sizzles in the boy's hand. He tosses the string out over the crowd and it bounces across heads and shoulders. People try to bat away the fizzing wick. Gerry plugs her ears.

Clatter rings out like gunfire. The crowd shrieks and screams. Those beneath the exploding string scramble. Startled by the noise, the policeman's horse rears, forelegs scraping the air. Its hooves smash down through the windshield of a parked MG. The horse rears again, bares its teeth as it brays, one leg torn and bloody. The noise of the crowd is a rolling vibration that echoes in Gerry's chest. Invisible drums beat faster, manic rhythms. Across the street the fire simmers, the second floors of shops obscured by a steady stream of smoke. The policeman fights to control his horse. It shakes its head, stumbles backward into the crowd, lopes a drunken figure-eight. Gerry covers her mouth against the ammonia stench of its piss. Linked chains of bodies break and scatter to give the animal room. Those forced too close cover their heads and faces with their arms, clamour to move as the animal knocks them off their feet.

Ian and Megan stand mesmerized by the horse.

The skater boy begins to slide down the post. His body stutters as he tries to control his descent. Gerry steps away, pushes back toward the shops. Another policeman on horseback intercepts the boy, yanks a small canister from his belt, and sprays the boy in the face. The boy screams and claws at his eyes. He lands hard on the glass-strewn hood of the MG, writhes like a swatted insect.

The smell, like burning nail polish, then vomit stabs at Gerry's nostrils, stings her eyes, sends her back to the acrid smell of Henry's house in flames, her cheers and applause. Shame burns up in her cheeks. She holds her jacket sleeve over her face, and the knapsack shifts against her back. The hard corners of the package dig through the canvas.

A man in glasses and a torn plaid shirt lunges for the policeman, grips his saddle, and hangs from the horse. The officer aims his canister, but a girl with bead-woven braids swings her straw bag and knocks it out of the policeman's hand. She seizes the officer's arm and tries to hoist herself onto his horse. His uniform sleeve tears and she falls back. Hands reach up from the crowd and grip what they can of the officer, boot, belt, pockets. A small group chants, "Down! Down! Down! Down!" The policeman swipes at them with his baton, his horse backsteps a small, nervous circle. Policemen on foot try to move into the street; the dense crowd fights to hold them back. Gerry stares at the unguarded laneway but can't will her legs to move.

Protestors pull the policeman from his horse, hit him with fists and bags, kick him where he lays. The beaded-haired girl stands up from the crush, raises the officer's helmet in the air. As she lowers it over her face, the crowd cheers.

Gerry steps down into the street. A hard pull on the knapsack tips her backward. A hand catches her shoulder, steadies her. "Don't bother!" Ian shouts over the noise.

She twists away from him, tries to quell the relief his presence triggers.

"They've blocked it off at Bute." He nods to a cluster of policemen.

Megan scans the street, her face lit with excitement. Back by the library, police tear down barricades, open the area for people to turn and filter away. A few straggle through, but most stay. Gerry waits for Megan to say something, but Megan only claps her hands, distracted by the movement of the crowd. She cheers as marchers unify their voices into a single roar. Police megaphones squawk with feedback, garble instructions lost under the crowd's swell. Human chains reconnect and brace. Row after row, protesters secure the street as their own. Megan rubs at her face, the skin blotched around her mouth and nose. Her eyes leak tears.

"Are you okay?" Gerry says.

Megan shakes her head. "Isn't this amazing!"

"Do not advance." An amplified voice announces. "The march is over. Disperse immediately." Near Bute Street, police handcuff protesters, haul struggling bodies to the empty space beyond the barricade.

"We need to get out of here." Ian says.

"It's just getting started." Megan's voice carries on a laugh.

Gerry watches an old woman fight being handcuffed. As she's dragged away, her shoes come loose and roll in the street. Closer by, skeletons overturn newspaper boxes, uproot the saplings planted along the sidewalk.

Megan grins. "Clem would have loved this. Fucking anarchy."

Amidst the noise and chaos, Gerry can't imagine Clem feeling anything but terrified. Megan steps toward her, squeezes her shoulders. "You're doing so great." Gerry closes her eyes, lets her hand drift to Megan's waist, trace the curve to her ribs. The closeness leaves Gerry pulpy, liquefied, her mouth slack. She opens her eyes, afraid already of Megan's disappointment. She points to the blocked laneway. "I don't think I can make it through."

Megan nods.

"The cops are too close." Ian holds out his hand. "Give me the bag."

Gerry looks to Megan.

"He's right. We're going to run out of time." Megan surveys the block, huffs as if trying to catch her breath. "We have to do it here."

A flush of red rises in Ian's face. "Are you crazy?"

Megan clenches and twists her own fingers in a way that looks painful to Gerry.

"That's not the plan." Gerry says it gently, to remind her.

"Come on." Ian puts his hands over Megan's to still them. "Your head's not straight."

She pushes him back. "There's nothing wrong with my head. Look around. This is better than we ever thought." Her fingers gouge into Gerry's arm. Gerry tries to shrug her off but feels herself turned as Megan angles her toward the north side of the

street. The storefront is floor-to-ceiling glass, headless manne-
quins dressed in pastel shirts and white shorts, on either side,
navy banners embossed with the label's emblem. "A polo player.
Do you know what that means?" Megan's breath is hot on her
neck. "Capitalist fucks stoking the arms race. It's their icon."

Behind the white backing panels of the window display,
shadows of shoppers drift. "It's full of people."

"We'll get them out first."

Gerry draws the knapsack snug against her. "Andri did cal-
culations, there has to be a distance between the building and
the march. Look at the sidewalk."

"Ian and I will clear it."

"No way, " Ian says.

Megan shakes her head. "Don't listen to him. It's smoke and
glass, just like we talked about."

Police move slowly through the crowd, open bags and knapsacks, confiscate spray cans, empty out bottles of booze.

"We need to get out of here and dump that thing," Ian says.

"What's wrong with you?" Megan stares at him. "When did
you become such a coward?"

Ian stands silent, a muscle twitching in his jaw.

She turns to Gerry. "We can't just let them get away with
it. You understand that, right? They expect us to do nothing."

Gerry bows her head, can't meet Megan's gaze. She waits for
Megan's tenderness to harden.

"Megan." Ian tries to put his arm around her.

She throws him off, grabs at Gerry, presses their foreheads
together, the soreness of bone on bone aching through Gerry's
skull as Megan rolls her head side to side. "It's okay. I know
you're scared. You don't think I was scared too? Fuck, those

men? Putting Clem in that place? It's okay to be scared of what you want."

Gerry lifts her hand, tries to twine her finger with Megan's, hold on to her. "It's not what I want."

Megan jerks away, grinds fists into her eyes. Behind her another string of firecrackers erupts, muffled by the low roll of drums, the thickening smoke. Up the block, skeletons kick at storefront windows, bash them with pipes and bats. Megan clutches at her head as she looks around. "Give me the bag."

Gerry squeezes the straps tight to her chest.

"Give it to her," Ian says. "We can get out of here."

Gerry shakes her head.

She sees Megan's hand before it hits her, manages to turn her face. The smack catches her lip against her teeth, starts a warm, metallic ooze in her mouth. She blinks, tastes her own blood, waits for Megan to apologize. Instead, Megan seizes the bag straps, grapples to get them loose. Gerry pries at Megan's fingers, pushes at her chest.

She feels Ian at her back, pulling on her elbows, his voice urgent. "Let go. Let go." She understands him then, deadens her arms behind her, and lets the bag slip down. "Keep up!" he shouts to her as he steps into the street.

Megan lunges to follow him. Gerry grabs her by the belt, hauls her down, and holds her as she counts on Ian's quick pace, the knapsack changing, becoming just an ordinary bag as he moves farther away from the crowd. Megan bucks underneath her, squirms until her hands batter at Gerry's head and face.

"I'm sorry." Gerry clutches her, curls to protect herself.

The light dims. A forest of legs surrounds them. "Hey! Hey! Hey!" Someone hauls Megan off. Gerry watches her thrash. A burly man loops his arms over Megan's, braces his hands together behind her head. "You stupid fucking cunt!" Megan shouts.

"Easy now," the man says. Her arms and legs flail against him.

Someone helps Gerry to her feet. She hears herself sobbing but feels nothing of it in her body. "Here, sit down," a woman's voice says, but Gerry resists, searches the street for Ian. She spots him at Bute, striding far past the dispersing crowd. He turns and walks backward, the knapsack on his shoulders. He scans the crowd and she knows he's looking for her, waiting for her to catch up. She shouts his name, pushes through the mob.

For a second, her ears plug with air as if she's slipped underwater. Then a crush of noise, immense and metallic, acres of glass shattering. A force plows into her chest, knocks her off her feet, and for what feels like minutes, she is flying.

20

A CHILD'S WHINING CRY, the stench of burning plastic. A dirty cloud hovers over the road, obscures everything above knee level. Gerry thinks to move, but the idea circles useless in her head. Eyes at the sidewalk, she watches bodies rise and stagger. Her chest burns. She sucks for oxygen until her lungs release and draw a breath that singes like bleach. She chokes, battles to inhale and expel at once. Her eyes and nose water as she coughs. The crying, she can tell now, is the wail of sirens. She curls onto her side, lifts herself just enough to see the shattered shop front around her, a gravel of broken glass, an unmarred rainbow display of dried fruit to her right, a halo of blood where her head has lain.

She pats her shoulders and back for the knapsack, searches the ground for it. Seconds pass before she remembers Ian. Beyond the stretch of her arms, nothing is visible. Pain rivets through her hip as she stands. Her legs quake. A few cautious steps forward and she's hit from all sides. People shout and push. She tangles in their arms, gasps as she pulls herself free, crouches to the pavement. When she tries again, the hard flank of a horse knocks her to her knees. Down here, the air is clearer. She draws deep, deliberate breaths, thinks to wait it out. A few feet away, a young woman lies flat on her stomach, face bloody, eyes open.

Her hand reaches out to Gerry as people trip and stumble over her body. Gerry scrambles to stand.

The able-bodied move haltingly through the crowd, call names, ask questions. Others stand rooted and dazed. Beyond the sirens and cries is a sound she cannot place, a roar like air blasting overhead.

She finds the edge of the curb with her foot, thrusts out her hands. Step by step, the white smoke opens in front of her, seals behind her as she drifts through worsening vignettes: bodies on their feet, bodies on their knees, bodies on their backs. When the bodies thin to nothing, she wonders if she's turned herself around, sidetracked down an empty alley. Above her head, a stoplight swings from a severed wire, pendulums through the intersection. Splinters of wooden barricade litter the road.

Beyond the barricade, the buildings are torn hulls. Gutted foyers drip with girders and wires. Entrances peel back on themselves, window casings flayed. She struggles to remember what detail she saw last as she looked at Ian, a marquee, an awning, a storefront sign marking his location. Voices in the sky call down for help. She turns a circle, waits for him to stumble out of a doorway, face blackened by soot, debris falling around him. As if on cue, an apparition dashes from the pitted opening of a building, a streak of light, a body on fire. Two bloodied and injured men grab it and drag it to the ground, roll and pat it frantically. A pane of glass crashes to the sidewalk beside them. The body screams out: a woman. She writhes across a border of blackened cement. The pattern reveals itself then, the sidewalk powdered in a sunburst, Gerry at its centre. The ground is strangely bare, a black circle without debris. Gerry tries not to look at the litter that lies beyond, knows there's nothing left to find.

She covers her mouth with her jacket and pushes back through the smoke.

Near the intersection at Burrard, the smoke breaks to coloured lights, all three arteries jammed with police, firetrucks, ambulances. Under storefront awnings, a sombre triage line. She checks the faces, once, twice. Uniformed staff spill from the hotel across the street. Desk clerks, bellhops, doormen sprint toward the intersection, arms loaded with towels and blankets. Firemen unfurl hoses, jog them into the smoke; paramedics spread their arms like birds, catch people as they emerge and point them into groups. She veers to avoid all of them.

The viaduct is a frozen river of traffic. By Main Street, drivers have left their cars, cluster on the sidewalk with folded arms to stare at the haze that rises between the downtown buildings. She pushes past them, keeps her head down. Some try to stop her, find out what's happened, offer help, but she ignores them, tips her shoulder away as they reach for her.

A lumbering reflection in a storefront window shocks her, her gait stilted and mechanical, clothes white with ash. A stab of pain through her neck keeps her head from turning to the left, a twinge in her knee startles every few steps. She wipes at the dribble of blood that seems to leak from her forehead, a wound without pain. Time snaps against her, jars her with the sensation of waking. The blocks double endlessly, then slip past in a blink.

Halfway home, the streets are quiet. People consumed with daily business, unconcerned, unaware. Through the window of a storefront office, she sees a couple nodding as a man behind a desk gestures to the papers in front of them. Outside a bakery, women cluck amongst themselves, wait to be served. She approaches a bus stop where a toddler fusses. His mother gives his padded behind a spank. Onlookers chuckle at the boy's misfortune. The boy's sobs bring tears to Gerry's eyes. As she passes the bystanders, they stare, faces grave. Exhausted, she alters course, turns off Main and follows a maze of empty neighbourhood streets home.

The TV is on, but no one is watching. She shuffles cautiously from room to room, alert for sounds. When she's certain her mom isn't home, she makes her own sound, a whimper of pain and gratitude.

She turns off the TV, draws the living-room curtains, the house like a cave, dark and silent. She climbs the stairs to her room and closes the door. As she sits on her bed, the stink of her clothes overwhelms her, the acidy stench of chemical burn, beneath it, rank sweat. She eases out of her jacket and T-shirt, layers that peel like cling film. Her skin feels raw and damp, prickles and itches as it's exposed to the air. She rubs at her arms, tugs at the straps of her cotton bra, lies back on her bed. Above, dead ash swirls in the New Mexico sky. She struggles to stand up on the mattress, legs quivering, rips the poster, shreds it, crushes it in her fists. Her mind is full of Ian, the bony rectangle of his shoulders, the smell of his shaving cream, sea water and astringent, his smile when he teased, the way his voice got wistful and gravelly late at night. The swarm of him, so real and immediate, forces her to her hands and knees. Her jaw aches as her mouth stretches wide. She clutches her head and howls.

The fury passes, leaves her crying into her hands, body shuddering with cold. When she has strength enough to rise from the bed, she steadies herself at the dresser, opens the drawer, feels for the glass bottle.

The door to her father's study is unlocked. It bumps behind her, closes with a click, the room's cool must soothing against her face. She climbs into his swivel chair and lets it rock her, then crawls up onto the desk and opens the curtains, stares out at the neighbourhood framed in the window, the east sky clear and untroubled as mid-afternoon sun glazes decks and rooftops. For a moment, she is afraid. She glances back at the door, then presses her face to the window.

She unscrews the cap from the bottle, stares at the medicine's faint amber stain, then tips the bottle to her lips, leans her head back. The liquid pours thick and bitter, flares in her throat, tendrils through her chest. She coughs, then drinks again. Her throat begins to numb. Her limbs lighten, foamy and inflated. Her hand floats in front of the window, unhooks the latch.

The living world rushes over her, children playing, radios, the laughter of men. She smells the trail of gasoline from a lawnmower. Below, ripples creep across the pool's surface.

She sits on the ledge and waits for a signal, a glint in the sky, an engine turning over, a dog's bark. From her perch, she can just make out Ian's yard. She pictures Alice at the kitchen table, hair a frizzy aura, Marty at the landing, the hem of his caftan swirling at his feet. The clueless tragedy of being a parent. Her own mom saddled with a daughter who has brought her only sadness.

Gerry mashes the tears from her eyes, then forces herself to look down. The height doesn't alarm her. It will be quick. A flashbulb, a somersault.

Clem's medicine raises a swell inside her. The pain in her muscles eases. Her head glitters and she blinks at the feeling: joy. She wipes her nose and streaming mucus comes away in a clear strand that catches the light. She admires it before scraping it across her jeans. The burr of denim hums under her hand. Her arms braced against the windowframe, she closes her eyes. With a push, the house slips away.

Her body hangs weightless, as if only her troubles have fallen. For an instant, all questions are answers, all problems dissolved. She tumbles. Water breaks against her skull, her ears. She thrashes, but her limbs connect with no surface. The bottom surprises her, knocks against her feet. Her legs, drugged and dull refuse to straighten. Her head grazes the floor. Water burns in her throat, her chest. She sees a park on a hill, a shady path through the trees, hears the sound of her breath, the pad of footfalls behind her, wind through the leaves. She closes her eyes to sleep.

The tide tugs at her, gently first, then insistent. She pulls free of its grasp and clings to the jelly cradle of darkness. Until she is squeezed, pushed, her heart pumping hard outside her. A woman's voice speaks her into being. She is lips, a mouth. She is waiting for a kiss. It comes wet and ferocious. A sweet spearmint taste, the smell of laundry soap.

She retches, racked with watery convulsions. Air sears into her. The weight of her head is enormous. She blinks the water out of her eyes and sees her mother's face, dripping and pink, gaping in shock, smiling and crying at the same time, over her shoulder, the hazy silhouette of a man.

IN THE HUT, THE GIRL DROPS TO HER KNEES. Face grey, hand gripped to a chair back, she emits a low, savage moan. The boy takes her arm over his shoulder, holds her firm, guides her across the beach, up the snaking stairs to the clinic.

Dr. Patak leads them both to the dining room, where a long table has been covered with sheets and towels. The doctor grumbles about ruined mattresses.

The boy helps the girl undress from the waist down, boosts her onto the table.

Dr. Woo and Dr. Joan enter wearing kitchen aprons: Dr. Joan's, a homey red-and-white check, Dr. Woo's, a psychedelic pattern of giant strawberries. Dr. Joan snaps on rubber gloves and opens the girl's legs, inserts her fingers, then pushes. Pink-tinged liquid dribbles out over her wrist. She smiles.

We're on our way.

While Dr. Joan coaches, the other doctors fetch pillows for the girl, help her change positions. At first, the girl endures the contractions with gritted teeth, her hand seizing the boy's, but as the baby descends, the girl shrieks, releases the boy, slips away from him into the world of her suffering. Her sobs between contractions leave him feeling useless. He whispers words she cannot hear, dabs at her face with a damp tea towel, clutches her swollen fingers.

You're doing great. Dr. Joan's voice remains emphatic, unwilling to indulge the girl's misery.

For an agonizing time, the birth stalls; the girl pushes, but the baby is stuck. Dr. Joan looks to the other two, their faces blank with fear. Dr. Patak and Dr. Woo each shoulder one of the girl's legs as Dr. Joan forces her hands inside in an attempt to turn the baby. The girl howls and bucks. Dr. Woo struggles to keep hold of her slippery thigh. Dr. Joan's hands emerge streaked with blood.

The boy holds his breath, waits for the next contraction. The girl's screams are shrill and terrifying. Dr. Joan yells, It's good, it's good.

Dr. Woo hurries across the room and returns with a turkey baster. The gummy crown of the baby's head stretches the girl, a circle of rippled flesh yawning back. In a queasy, light-headed moment, the boy thinks the girl must be turning herself inside out. Another strained contraction and her body pushes a child into the world. A head with eyes, a nose and mouth, the relief of arms, torso, legs, everything smudged in waxy white film, but perfect in its right place. A girl. The baby makes no sound.

Gently, Dr. Woo guides the tip of the turkey baster into the baby's mouth, releases the bulb slowly, until suction draws a viscous slurp. He does the same for the baby's nose, while Dr. Joan flicks her finger at the baby's palms and feet. The baby's body terrifies the boy, limp and grey. The girl sits up to see, her face a grimace of tears. The boy wants to cover her eyes, but knows if he tries to touch her, she will push him away. Dr. Joan takes the baby by its ankles and gives it one hard shake. The baby gasps, shakes, mewls like a forlorn cat. A flush spreads over its body. Everyone laughs.

Dr. Joan lays the baby on the girl's chest, then turns to hug Dr. Woo, who wipes the tears from under his glasses.

The boy kneels beside the girl, presses his face into her shoulder and sobs. She sniffles, coos to their child, while her hand strokes the boy's hair. He stands to let the doctors embrace him. Dr. Patak offers her hand and he shakes it, unable to meet her gaze. When they ask about a name, the girl kisses the baby's head and says, Caroline. The mention of his mother forces the boy from the room, away from baby's delicate breathing, its soft skull and gauzy skin. In the kitchen he finds an empty pantry, shuts himself inside. He crouches in the dark, feels the hard wooden panels with his hands, breathes the damp rot, prays to whatever god is left for strength.

The baby refuses to feed, only wails, fussy and unwilling to latch. The girl is despondent, beyond the boy's comfort. They remain at the clinic so Dr. Joan can persist with her awkward positions, whispered instructions, while the other two doctors chew their fingers, exchange worried looks. Finally, in the middle of a crying fit, the baby suckles. Dr. Woo jumps to his feet and claps. Dr. Patak shakes her head. The cupboards are bare, she says. Day and night, the doctors advise, feed, always feed. As the girl sleeps, the boy curls against her back, clings to her, pretends they are still just two.

The doctors send them home. The boy helps the girl down the steep wooden stairs, Dr. Woo, with his shy grin, follows them with the baby. Dr. Joan and Dr. Patak bring up the rear. On the beach, the crowd cheers their slow procession.

The baby's arrival draws even the sick from their beds. At the bottom of the stairs, a diseased, malnourished receiving line of women manic with happiness. Their smiles betray weeping gums, absent teeth. They press rough, cankered lips against the baby's pink, powdery skin, reach out sore-covered hands to stroke its cheek. They rub the baby's blanket between their fingers, make wishes, pronouncements, leave behind their grimy prints.

The men gather at the fire, swagger backlit by dusk. Guilty smiles, anxious hands, pockets full of secrets. They clap their dirty palms together, growl and hoot their approval like patrons at a strip bar.

She's gonna be a looker! one of them shouts.

I saw her first! another replies.

They all laugh.

The boy's rage simmers in his face. He nods it away as embarrassment.

Settled in the cabin, the boy waits. He watches the baby feed, tiny fingers that curl at the girl's flat breast, his child's eager snuffle as it works for its dinner. The girl changes the handmade diaper, then rocks back and forth, sings the child to sleep, a familiar love song about vampires and the hooded claw. Outside, the beach is deserted.

Returned to the comfort of her bed, the girl sleeps heavy, the cabin thick with her grateful snore. The boy stays awake, holds the baby when she cries, drifts like a ghost, swaddle brimming over his arms. When the baby's lips suck at the air, he offers his pinkie. Her small legs flex, her back arches, hungry, always hungry. He kisses her forehead and whispers her name. He wakes the girl to feed her.

Nights later, he lies stiff on the cot until the girl's breath lapses into heavy, guttural waves. He counts to two hundred just to be sure, then rises carefully. He is surprised to find the baby awake in her padded drawer, eyes open, mouth pursed, small limbs waving. As he lifts her, she makes no sound but kicks to launch herself into his hands. He cradles her against his body, head warm in the crook of his arm.

As the boy crosses the beach, sand pulls at his steps. The boy's eyes struggle to adjust to the sooty night. The baby smacks her lips. He bounces her to keep her quiet. In the woods, he staggers over deadfall and vines, darkness thick and mystifying. Afraid to draw attention from the camp, he uses the small flashlight sparingly, presses it on and off, memorizes the instant picture. Once or twice, jarred by his stumbling, the baby cries out. The boy lifts his shirt, tucks the baby inside. The baby tries to suckle his rib.

The boy comes to a place that seems far enough away, the lap of tide receding in the distance, the flicker of campfire no longer visible. He sits down on the damp forest floor, rests the baby in the cross of his legs, its shape reduced to lines in the blackness. The baby kicks it feet against the boy's empty stomach. He takes this as a sign that the baby understands. One day there will be no mother's milk. One day there will be no one to protect her.

The boy's hand searches the ground, gathers up loose twigs, tree sheddings, a rock, a branch. He feels the baby with his hands, its tiny toes, pinching fingers, small, jittery arms and legs, the wonder of its torso full of calibrated organs, the curves of its face, a clever, overlaid hologram of himself and the girl, a perfect double-print of their families. He rubs his left hand along the downy border of the baby's hairline, then with his right hand raises the rock.

The baby does not cry. The only sound is the boy's own whimper as he waits for the right moment, for certainty.

He sits until dawn, rock gripped in his aching hand, his arm slipping inch by inch, until it drags on the forest floor. The baby sleeps, eyelids twitching against the dim grey light. Nearby, branches rustle with the brush of returning men, urgent foot-falls, hungry breath. From the beach, new wood crackles on the fire, women's voices murmur, the camp rises.

$$21$$

I N THE HOSPITAL, CROUCHED AT Gerry's bedside, her mom recites the story over and over, like a prayer: she hears about the explosion on TV, breaking news without images, calls Randy to drive her downtown, to help her search. Gridlocked traffic forces them back home. As they climb out of the truck, she hears the splash, sprints for the yard. "I knew it was you. It didn't make any sense, but I just knew," she whispers, as if keeping a secret from the doctors and nurses who glide in and out.

One of the nurses tells Gerry she's the only girl in history to be born to the same woman twice, her own mother pumping her chest, breathing her back from the other side.

It is her mom, though, who seems reborn, her anxiousness replaced with bottomless strength. Her hands in constant motion to change bandages, adjust pillows, bend plastic straws to Gerry's mouth, massage her feet through the blankets. Gerry waits it out in silence, braces for the morning her mom wakes as her old self, begins to demand answers.

The elderly woman in the next bed draws back her curtain so that Gerry can sit in a visitor's chair and watch the news on the woman's TV. Grainy video captured by a hotel security camera shows Ian walking backward, a flash of light before the screen turns to snow. Witnesses come forward and describe the anonymous figure as sinister, erratic, deranged. Gerry is stunned by how quickly and falsely the story forms: homemade bomb, disturbed young man.

By the time she is discharged, tucked into the bed her mom has made of the living-room sofa, police have confirmed his name. The television flashes old school photos: Ian with thick glasses, feathered hair, posed with a soccer team he never played for. Watching them, she feels as if a child has died, a gouging horror that leaves her silent. At night, she fills her sleepless hours listening for his car in the street. She finds everything he's ever given her, old 45s and cassettes, a peeled Rubik's cube, a tattered Heinlein novel, his broken Coleco Quarterback, gathers all of it under the covers to feel it against her skin. In the dark, she tries to remember his voice, the things he said, cries as she mouths her own cruel words.

Gerry sleeps her days away. Her mom, on leave from the lab, sits beside her on the couch, hypnotized by the news each time she watches it, face still in disbelief. She pats the blankets, brushes the backs of her fingers across Gerry's forehead. "He didn't tell you anything?"

Speaking has become difficult, the threat of careless words. Monosyllables crawl over a rickety barricade. "No."

"Maybe something you didn't realize at the time? Something that could help the police now?"

She shakes her head, sinks low into the couch.

"His poor parents. The house is all padlocked. I went to see them, but the neighbour said the day before the police came, Alice and Marty put everything into a moving truck and drove away. He said Marty was in a daze and Alice's hands wouldn't stop shaking. They must have recognized him in that security video. Can you imagine? What a horrible way to find out." Her mom leans down, presses her face to Gerry's, nuzzles back and forth, whispers, "I don't know what I'd do."

Her body begins to heal. Stitches in her scalp harden, scabs crust her arms and legs. Her mom helps with the stairs when she needs the bathroom or goes up to bed. Each day passes in a blur of *Password Plus* and *Donahue*, reruns of *Hart to Hart*. Her hand shapes to the fat rectangle of the remote. Speech is useless. What can she describe, anyway, except a catalogue of Ian, his words spliced in an endless tape that winds her back to that night at the beach, his body close. He would have stayed home. He only went to the march because of her. The possibility cinches inside her like metal wire; the slightest tug and she feels herself cut.

Gerry ignores her mom's questions, becomes skilled at formless sounds, infantlike murmurs. Her mom tries with sporadic success to coax words out of her. "I won't make it until you say it."

"Macaroni," she says, finally, her jaw sore with the effort.

Randy comes over, her mom's idea of reinforcement. He spends an afternoon beside her on the sofa. "Are you in pain?"

"No."

"Is it because of Ian?"

"No."

"Are you angry at us for pulling you out?"

"No."

"Are you still thinking about hurting yourself?"

"No."

She wastes days of words on him. He leaves, stops to murmur to her mom in the foyer, fatigue and frustration etched in his face. Exhausted by the effort, she sleeps through suppertime to the next morning.

Her mom's hushed voice filters through with a sting of daylight. Beneath Gerry's shoulder, her mattress dips, threatens to roll her away. Her mom's hand strokes her hip through the blanket. "I invited her in, but she wanted to wait outside by the pool."

Half-sleep slips away, leaves her mind scoured. Her first clear thought is police, but her mom is too calm for that. "Who?"

"I don't know. Come down and see."

Without opening her eyes, Gerry can picture her mom's face, restraint drawn tight over expectation.

"Do you need help?"

"No." She waits for her mom's retreat, then pushes back the covers, begins the slow ceremony of getting dressed. She prepares for it not to be Megan. A return would be too risky. Maybe Michelle. Or a stranger carrying a cryptic message of condolence, apology. She decides to play it stubborn and cold, withhold her forgiveness. Unless it is Megan.

She takes the stairs one at a time, shuffles past her mom, who stands in the kitchen, knife tip picking at a cellophaned package of meat as she pretends not to watch Gerry.

Beside the pool, a woman's back, curved as she stoops, reaches toward the water, her head low. The door sticks and squeaks as Gerry works it open. The figure stands and turns.

Gerry hides in the shadow of the roof's overhang. She barely recognizes Lark, legs saggy with sweatpants, an oversized bomber wrapped tight across her chest. Hair in a ragged ponytail, skin splotchy without makeup, her eyes are pin dots. She drags her deck shoe in an arc across the cement, a move that betrays her grace. "I heard you were hurt." Her proximity to the pool's mirrored light makes Gerry nervous.

"Not really."

Arms closed around her body, Lark tightropes along the pool's edge, swings her foot over the water. "Can you believe what they're saying about him? Have you seen it on the news?"

Gerry nods. The motion of her head sends a dizziness through her. She crouches to sit, holds the concrete step, roughness solid under hands.

"You know he didn't do it, right?" The sky's glare breaks around Lark.

Gerry blinks but can't see her face, can't work out how much she knows.

"He wasn't that kind of person."

"What kind of person?"

"I don't know." Lark shrugs. "Insane?" She shifts her weight, hip cocked to the side. "He wouldn't know anything about that kind of stuff. I mean, bombs?" Lark's urgency makes Gerry tired. "Don't you even care what they're saying?"

Gerry wonders how long Lark will stay.

"Do you have any idea what it's like having a boyfriend who's always thinking about someone else?"

"The girl I told you about, she wasn't really–"

"Jesus. You're not exactly sharp, you know?" Lark shakes her head.

Gerry lets the insult pass, relieved that Lark hasn't come to pry about Megan.

"He was worried about *you*, like all the time. It wasn't even normal."

The air fills with the mechanical beat of a passing chopper. Gerry pushes at the stairs to stand, leans against the chalky brick of the house, scans the sky until she finds the glint of white, tracks it moving south.

"My dad recognized him right away, isn't that weird? He went through my stuff, found a letter from Ian. He gave it to the police."

Gerry shields her eyes, squints to see Lark more clearly. "Why? What did it say?"

"Nothing. It was a dumb breakup letter. He didn't want to hurt anyone, he felt so confused, he was so sorry, blah, blah, blah. The police told my dad it might be a suicide note, that it could show something premeditated." Her face is stiff with accusation. "But you know that's not true, right?" She steps closer.

Gerry feels for the back door, the curve of the handle and latch, wishes for the dark of her bedroom.

"It might not even be him on the video." Lark's jacket falls open to reveal a loose tanktop, lines of ribs visible above the small swells of her breasts.

"I guess."

"Well, you have to stand up for him. You have to go to the police and tell them it's just a breakup letter. You knew him better than anyone. You can't let them make him out to be this person. If you know something—" Her hands paw at Gerry's wrist.

"I don't." Gerry tries to step back. Lark begins to cry. She slides her arms around Gerry neck, rests against her. Gerry pats Lark's back, listens to her touch echo through Lark's jacket, smells her unwashed hair.

Lark pulls away, tips her head to the sky and sniffs, wipes at her eyes with stiff middle fingers. She nods at the pool. "It's nice," she says as she crosses back to its edge and swirls her hand in the water. "Ian and I used to sit on his garage roof and look at your mud pit."

Gerry tries not to listen to the watery sounds.

"I know he was confused about a lot of stuff." Lark stands, her feet slipping like a child's in her loose shoes.

"He didn't want to break up with you."

Lark stops. The corners of her mouth twitch. She stares at the ground, then up at Gerry. "You never really say the right thing, you know that?" She pulls her jacket tight around her, glides away. As she reaches the gate, she turns. "The police didn't ask about you. But I could still tell them."

Her mom plays at superhero, bottomless energy, steady reassurances, smiles that show just a hint of teeth. But Gerry can read her face, the slackness that comes with exhaustion, thin lines cutting down through her cheeks, fine red veins in the whites of her eyes. At night she hears her mom coughing in her bedroom.

She wakes at night to mewling, a frightened cat at the window. Drunk with sleep and sedatives, she eases herself out of bed, feels her way to the window and opens it, but finds nothing, just the black sheet of night. The cool air sharpens her but muffles the sound. She closes the window. The mewling rises from the floor, accompanied by an urgent musical rhythm. She limps to her bedroom door and opens it. Downstairs the television blares chase music, gunfire. Tire squeals carry up to the landing. Her mom's voice, ragged, unhinged by emotion, hides beneath the noise. "I've never asked you for anything. For anything. If she could just see you—" Her voice dissolves into sobs.

"Well, when then? What does that even mean? Later, when? No, wait. Please. Just listen. I need your help. I'm begging you. I am begging–" The words stretch and catch, shredded and wet. Her mom slams down the receiver; a startled bell echoes from the phone. The channel changes, volume rises, the frail pitch of her crying lost in jeering laughter and applause. Gerry closes her bedroom door, climbs into the muddled covers of her bed, squeezes a pillow over her face.

22

THE NURSE AT THE CARE HOME is young and tan, blond hair in cornrows, white beads rattling at her neck. She stands to keep Gerry from passing. "You're here to see someone." A friendly declaration accompanied by a wave that guides her back to the desk. "Resident?"

Gerry says his name, the syllable a soft trap in her mouth.

The nurse scans a list, makes a mark with her pencil. "He's just in his room. I'll have someone bring him down." Her smile is gummy and sincere.

Gerry waits in the hall, beside a stack of coverless magazines. The floor is clean but streaked with dark scuffmarks that make Gerry think of a person being dragged against their will.

A different nurse wheels Clem over. He wears stripped pyjamas and a hunter green robe. He sits stiff in his seat, larger, rounder at the edges. His tremor has worsened. His lips work as if he is trying to loosen something from his teeth.

Gerry follows them into the lounge. Except for a few residents up front, the room is empty. She asks about other visitors. The nurse shrugs. "I'm not here every day. Besides, honestly? He wouldn't remember." Gerry nods, feels herself blush, embarrassed that what she is really asking about is Megan. The nurse parks the wheelchair, kicks at the brake with her white clog. "There you go."

Gerry kneels beside the chair. The nurse has left Clem turned away from the TVs, and he cranes awkwardly over his shoulder, strains to see the screens. His face is fleshier, softened to curves.

"Clem." She watches his eyes for a glint of recognition, his name, her voice. He rocks against the resisting chair. She strokes his hand, the skin cool and dry. He grabs at her fingers, clutches them hard, quivering with the effort. The pain skips her flesh and goes straight to the bone, his fingers like wooden clamps. Tired of contorting, his body sinks. As his head turns, he glimpses her, flinches. She worries her bruises will upset him and thinks about turning away.

His hand rises, hovers in front of her. His fingers graze the stitches in her forehead. "Did I do that?"

"No." She settles his hand in his lap. His thigh's loose muscle shakes beneath the thin fabric of his pyjamas. The nurses have brushed his hair forward, and she tries to fix it with her fingers, back, the way he likes it.

He grips her arm tight, his eyes rimmed in red. His cheeks and lips shiver, like a child about to cry. "Forgive me," he says, his voice a desperate order.

She searches his face for a flicker of awareness. His eyes water, vacant and worried, his offence either long forgotten or falsely imagined. She could torture him, goad with a few words to make him cower or cry, punish him for the wrongs of every father. Her own wounds driving her to hurt. The reflex fills her with shame. "I forgive you."

He stares at her for a while, until a phone ringing on one of the TVs spurs him to swivel in his seat. She stands and pops the wheel break with her sneaker. Turns him so he can watch the screens as she combs his hair.

———

Outside, a clump of wheelchairs blocks the door, residents in robes and gowns, a bald woman with tubes up her nose. A man in street clothes leans against a pillar, smokes with his back to the entrance, wavy grey hair tangled and dirty-looking. As Gerry passes him, a sound catches her, a jingle of coins. She circles around and checks his face, then steps in front of him. He looks up, shakes his head, waggles his cigarette. "Last one."

"Dennis, right?"

The coins clatter faster.

"I was at Clem's."

His gaze rests on something beyond her, smoke curls up into his nostrils. The door swooshes open behind them, and he nods with recognition. "You're the kid."

"Have you seen her?"

He grins, tiny yellow teeth darkened around the edges, points his cigarette. "Why? She forget to leave you your allowance?"

"I have to talk to her. About Ian." She waits for the name to register with him, for a shadow of respect to pass over his face.

Dennis sways on his heels, stares past her as if he hasn't heard.

"She'll be wanting to see me. To explain things."

"Is that right?"

"Where is she?"

"Who knows? She's long gone." He shakes his head. "Probably getting the hero's treatment. That was one helluva fireworks display."

"It was an accident."

"These things never go as planned."

"A person died."

Dennis shrugs. "Whatever happened had to happen."

"I need to talk to her."

Lazy eyelids droop over his gaze. "She doesn't need to talk to you. A thing like that, it gives you troubles to wrestle. Lifelong troubles. Her battle's just beginning. Not that you'd understand."

"You weren't even there."

The coins stop. She expects him to get angry. Instead, his face softens and opens. He draws his hand out of his pocket.

Because of its constant jittering, the hand appears, at first, to be a fist bound in strips of brown tape. Until she makes out the crude thumb and pinky poking out at each end, burnt skin binding the knuckles in folds and puckers in between.

"Homemade." His cheeks puff as he blows the sound of an explosion through his teeth, widens his eyes and mouth in mock amazement, then arcs back in a mime of trying to shield himself. He laughs at his own performance. "The thing about self-sacrifice is, you have to have the stomach for it." He nudges the twitching limb toward her face. Gerry rears back, turns her head so she doesn't have to look.

Dennis laughs, flicks his cigarette into the air, shoves his hand into his pocket as he heads for the entrance.

23

W HEN HER MOM DISCOVERS the notice for Henry's funeral in the newspaper, she stares at Gerry, mouth open, a piece of half-buttered toast in her hand. "Henry," is all she says as she slides the newspaper over. The photo shows a younger Henry, tan, with thick sideburns and darker hair, below his picture, details of a service arranged by the station. Gerry skims her bare feet over the cold tile floor, stares at Henry's name until her eyes refuse to focus. Her mom shakes her head and pulls Gerry close. "It might help to talk about it," she says. Gerry can only poke at her cornflakes and shrug.

Someone at her mom's work recommends a doctor, an expensive trauma specialist. In the car, Gerry's mind feels blank as glass. The city pummelled with spring rain. Despite the day's gloom, her mom is giddy with hope. Gerry can't bear to look at her, turns to face the window, breathes its dank smell.

"I think the doctor will have some answers."

Gerry tries to block out her voice, lets the drag of the wipers whine in her ears. On the streets, drains flood up into long, mucky lakes, bus tires spray waves onto the sidewalk. The car drifts, loses traction on skiffs of water as they stop and start, sloshed by the downpour. Even inside the car, she feels as if she's drowning, an undertow in her stomach. "Pull over." She fiddles with the door lock.

"What is it?" The car's turn signal clacks, her mom erect with instant alarm. The tires skid as Gerry swings open her door. "Do you need to be sick?"

Gerry leans down, stares at the muddy stream beside the curb, a sludge of garbage and dead blossoms. Her stomach seizes, but nothing moves. She waits, listens to the rain patter the car, then closes the door.

"Are you okay?"

Beside them, a fire station, a school field strewn with litter. Red trucks sleep behind the panelled glass door, excused from emergencies. She stares at her hands.

The words come slowly at first. Each phrase plugged with tears releases the truth a fragment at a time. She tells the story backward, begins with the pool, the walk home, then the rally. When she says Ian's name, her body stops her completely, a soundless sob. The telling brings no relief.

She watches her mom's face, the crease of her forehead, the squint in her eyes, searches for signs of her closing off, proof that when they arrive home, she will vacate herself, her heart, be polite and efficient, and beyond reach.

Her mom blinks. Tears spill over the rims of her eyes. She breathes through open lips. "I don't know what to say." Her face crumples, but quickly she collects herself. "You know, I feel like some stupid, useless child." She laughs as she brushes the tears from her chin. "All this time, I was supposed to be taking care of you. What was I doing? What was I doing?" Her hands smack her face. "What kind of mother are you!" She hits herself again and again.

Gerry tries to reach for her. Her mom folds over the steering wheel. Gerry can only wait, slip her arm under her mom's, feel for a sign of closeness between them.

Her mom stops beside a phone booth, stares at it through the rain. "I don't think you understand how serious this is. What they could do to you."

If Gerry closes her eyes, she can feel Ian behind her, the tug as she let the knapsack slip from her arms. She wonders if it happened then, while she was struggling with Megan, the plastic tab cracking, tearing away. Or whether it was earlier, her carelessness in the crowd. "I understand."

"I know he was your friend. But this won't bring him back. He was trying to keep you out of trouble."

"I'll go on my own if you're not going to take me."

"Gerry." Her mom's face is tight with defeat.

She watches as her mom stands in the phone booth, digs through her wallet for a business card, then punches the number in, plugs her ear to speak, nods as she listens, quickly, then slowly, the person on the other end carrying the conversation. Her mom gets back into the car, her clothes splotched with rain. "He agrees with me. You don't have to do this. We could just wait and see what happens."

Gerry shakes her head.

"Okay." Her mom sighs. "He'll meet us there in two hours."

Gerry starts to shiver, her body prickling with cold. She pulls her jacket tight.

"Here." Her mom slides her seat back. Her hands guide Gerry to crawl over the console, the gearshift. Gerry settles in her mom's lap, wedged by the steering wheel. Her mom strokes her face, rocks her, shields her from window's harsh light.

They park outside the police station. Her mom fills the time with worried glances, questions about whether Gerry is hungry or thirsty or cold. Policemen walk to and from the building, guns in holsters, batons dangling. Gerry waits for one to approach their car, to ask her to step out and turn around, and handcuff her. When someone does finally approach, it's a shadow on her mom's side, a tap at her window. "You stay here, okay?" She nods as if she herself isn't sure, then unlocks the door, steps out with her purse clutched in her hand. Gerry turns in her seat as they round the back of the car and stand on the sidewalk. A man in a suit carries a briefcase. They talk for a few minutes under his umbrella, her mom gripping the strap of her purse. Gerry hears the man say, "Okay," and her mom approaches Gerry's door, opens it. "Sweetheart, you remember Larry? You've spoken to him on the phone?"

She always imagined Larry Walsh Esquire as a cartoon, a heavy man with porklike wrists and bright pink skin. He stands before her tall and slim with tidy grey hair and a warm, narrow smile. Fear bubbles up as panicked laughter she has to bite her cheeks to fight. As he squats in front of her, the hem of his raincoat drags on the pavement. "They'll just want to talk to you today, get your statement. Probably a few police officers, a lawyer for the Crown, they'll have a video camera in the room."

The mention of a video camera makes Gerry start to cry. The shock of actions recorded and preserved.

"It's okay, it's okay."

She feels like an animal he's trying to calm. It isn't a bad feeling.

"I'll be sitting right beside you. Your mother will be watching from outside the room."

Larry Walsh steps back and her mom leans down into the car. "I'm not going home without you."

The police station begins like a dream. Even as she answers their questions, her voice is not her own. The descriptions she gives them, of Megan, of Andri and Michelle, are like descriptions of strangers. When she tells them about testing the device and Michelle's family farm, two men hurry out of the room.

As the questions go on, she feels as if she's suffocating, has to remind herself to breathe. She worries about feeling dizzy, about the floor tipping under her feet. Larry asks them to bring her a soda, and she sips it slowly, a syrupy trickle in her mouth.

Details are what break the spell: the small red light of the video camera, the dusty rows of venetian blinds, the wire grid embedded in the room's windows, the way the other lawyer's chewed-up Bic looks like a tube of crushed glass. Her voice settles in her body, a vessel of shame and guilt. They ask her to repeat her answers, her voice too distorted by emotion to be heard clearly on the tape. When she talks about Ian, the words come out a mess and everyone clambers for her to slow down, forget about elementary school and summer holidays, focus on the group, the march. Their questions about Ian are pointed and sneering. By the way they say his name, lean into each other, she can tell they have no interest in accidents, in Ian's attempts to keep her safe. No one believes she was the one making the drop. The more she talks, the further the truth is buried.

At the end of the interview, Larry Walsh uses words Gerry doesn't understand: *coercion, duress, diminished capacity*. He makes the men an offer, her testimony against the others for a lesser charge as a minor. She remembers Andri's talk of prison and feels like she might be sick. A bitter worm of acid pushes up in her throat. She holds her arm against her stomach. The policemen shake their heads. One of them says, "Not on the floor" and slides a metal garbage can beside her chair. The other lawyer nods, cleans his glasses with a wrinkled handkerchief, says he'll take it all under consideration.

Outside the police station, her mom and Larry talk under his umbrella while Gerry waits in the car. Distance makes her mom a stranger, an elegant woman with wavy hair, a straight back, elbow hard over her purse as she talks to a handsome man, and Gerry wonders at the life her mom might have had without her father, without her.

"He's hopeful," her mom says as she gets into the car. "He said we should stay positive." Washed by tears and rain, her face looks girlish and delicate, the ribbon-fold edges of her mouth, freckle dust over her cheeks. Gerry imagines her mom before she was married, gentle and optimistic, smart enough to study chemistry, certain and secure. She touches her mom's fingers, traces the divot left by her wedding ring.

"I always wore that thing too tight."

Gerry rubs to smooth the dented skin. "Do you ever wish you didn't have me?"

Her mom's face pinches, concerned. "Never."

"It's okay for you to say so."

"Why would you think such a thing? Is that how I make you feel?"

"You got stuck with me. It wasn't exactly fair."

"I didn't get stuck with you, I fought for you. I wanted you. Even before I met him, I wanted you."

"You wanted a family."

Her mom's eyes crinkle. She holds open her hands. "Ta-da."

Gerry sniffles. "Oh, is that what this is?" She wipes her face with her sleeve.

Her mom smiles at the sarcasm, a gentle, closed-lip smile, her gaze warm and unwavering as she brushes a hand over Gerry's head. "That's what this is."

THE BOY RETURNS TO FIND THE GIRL pacing the cabin, nipples leaking into her dress. As he hands her the baby, she searches his face, grateful but wary. The baby wails until she latches, then sucks with fervour, fingers flexing. The boy circles the cabin, gathers items into a sack.

What are you doing?

He opens and closes drawers. The baby isn't safe here.

The girl looks down at the feeding child, then back at the boy, her eyes frantic. Why? What happened?

He ignores her questions, knows she will go along.

She swaddles the baby in a folded bedsheet, stuffs rags between the layers for warmth. He ties two sacks of meagre possessions across his back. They wait for night, for the huddle of men to move away from the campfire and out into the woods. The boy and girl trail far behind, then continue deeper into the forest after the men turn for the road. He braces the girl as she stumbles in the dark, tries to guide her. The white circle of his flashlight dances at her feet.

When the sky lightens, they rest, sleep against each other on the forest floor. They head east, through the cover of trees just above the water line. They walk for two nights without food, drink muddy stream water that the boy sieves through a shirt into their mouths.

The baby cries for hours, the girl's breasts flatten, her legs buckle from walking too long. As they settle again to sleep at dawn, it comes to the boy that they are walking to their deaths, the three of them wasting to skeletons amidst the deadwood of the forest. He curses his instincts, whatever tricks of mind led him to torture his own wife and child. The gun he brought, a small pistol from behind a panel in the writer's desk, he imagined for hunting, but more and more he thinks he will have to use it to end the girl's suffering if the baby dies. As the girl sleeps, the boy prays into the baby's swaddle, begs her to stay alive.

The boy's prayers are answered. The next night, a glow on the beach in front of them. A fire. They pad down softly through the trees, hide as they watch. The aroma of cooking meat brings tears to the boy's eyes. There are many, thin but not weak. Each moves with purpose, stacks wood, passes utensils, turns food on a grate over the fire. A gale of laughter rises. A group of women. Farther down the beach, more gather by the water. The baby starts to cry.

Faces turn. Those around the fire remain still. Those closer to the water hurry up the beach, stand between the campfire and the forest. The boy recognizes the slap of metal and wood: at least one has raised a rifle in their direction.

Come down from there! Now!

The girl nudges the boy. He scuttles ahead, reluctant, looks back over his shoulder at her and the baby. As they approach, the boy sees that three women have stepped forward. Two hold long loops of rope, ready beside the one with the gun.

The boy stops, raises his arm, and helps the girl manoeuvre the sandy rocks before the beach. He holds the crying baby while the girl climbs down in front of him, then passes the bundle to her. She shakes as she stands above the women in the camp, their bodies alert and sinewy. He watches as she tries to mask her fear by jiggling the baby. The baby writhes and fusses, lets out an indignant wail. Some of the women laugh, eyes blinking in wonder. The woman with the rifle keeps her gun on the boy.

The boy knows the women will invite the girl to stay, ask him to leave, and, when they do, the girl will refuse, follow him instead. But he has nothing left to offer her. The weakness he tried to escape has followed him, belongs to him. Inside he still feels like a child, a boy, unskilled at taking care. All along he has relied on the girl's strength.

He steps back into the shadows, the baby's name on his lips. With each step, a picture of who she will be through the months and years grows in his imagination, until over the rise of a hill, crouched in a nest of boulders, it explodes in his mind like a star. So that when the girl turns around, an easy smile on her face, she finds nothing behind her but a distant echo, a shiver of light through the dark stretch of trees.

$$24$$

T HE DAY BEFORE HENRY'S FUNERAL, a postcard
arrives through the mail as if through a time machine. A
massive cloud of ash erupts from the peak of Mount St.
Helens. On the back: *love, Henry* in a flourished scrawl.

Gerry and her mom arrive early, wait in the car. Buffered
against the cold morning wind, they watch each guest cross the
grass to the small white canopy.

The rows of chairs fill before the service begins. A carpet of
faded Astroturf twists and buckles under their shoes as they find
a spot along the side, stand next to a television camera. Henry's
coffin, plain, polished wood, rests on a heavy brass frame at the
front. On an easel, a blown-up version of the newspaper photograph, Henry with lean cheeks and mischievous eyes. Gerry
tries to read the program with its many thank-yous to donors
but finds herself distracted by the men in the crowd, a likeness
to Henry that unsettles her, until she places it: local talent, the
same shiny suits, the same on-air posture and moulded hair.

After a droning eulogy, colleagues rise to share their stories.
How Henry spent months in Africa covering famine relief, how
as a cub reporter on the crime beat he made a point of eating his
breakfast at the morgue, and how for two decades as an anchor
he tossed the same fifty-cent coin before every broadcast, refused

to take his seat until it came up heads. Gerry stuffs her hand into her pocket, runs her fingers over the ragged edge of the postcard, clings to the Henry she knows.

Mrs. Cross's arrival takes Gerry by surprise, her careful steps, her wiry frame in a stiff black coat. She enters alone, unnoticed except by a man on the far side of the canopy who stands to offer his seat. A ball of tissue gripped in her hand, she sits on the edge of the chair, shoulders forward, knees to the side, as if she might leave at any second. She wipes at her nose and eyes, and Gerry wonders if, in spite of everything, she still thought of herself as Henry's wife, if the feeling of family was difficult to undo. Out on the road, a car slows to drop off latecomers. Gerry turns, feels her mom turn with her, waits as driver and passengers emerge.

The tributes draw to a close, an empty pause before the minister steps forward with his final words. People stand as attendants in suits prepare to lower the coffin. Past the rows of heads bowed in prayer, Gerry gets one last glimpse of Mrs. Cross before she slips out through the crowd.

Mourners gather in the centre aisle, make their way to the front, take up palmfuls of sand to dust their good wishes over Henry. When they turn to walk back, Gerry can't help but look more closely at the men, study their faces, just to be sure. She senses her mom on guard beside her, body tense as she follows Gerry's gaze. "Too tall," her mom whispers. "Too old."

As the last handful of sand skitters over the coffin and the last of the guests leave, her mom sighs. "Your father was terrible at saying goodbye." Gerry leans against her, relieved for a moment not to hold herself straight.

Together they trudge over the marshy grass back to the car. The sky cuts blue above them, air tangy with the smell of a nearby pine grove. Gerry lags behind, drawn back by the soft shovelwork as men in suits continue the burial. She watches them, the reverent way they lift and carry the soil, tilt their shovels to let it fall gently over Henry.

"You okay?" her mom calls.

Gerry turns, surprised to see her mother already so far away, alone amid the tombstones, lifting her feet to keep her heels from sinking into the grass. Gerry nods but doesn't feel ready to move, the ground between them so yielding and fragile, she must take each step with care.

ACKNOWLEDGEMENTS

The benefits of being married to a better writer are far too many to list. This book owes everything to John Vigna, whose dedication to craft, editorial instincts, gourmet chef skills, and cowboy heart inspire me daily.

I'm so grateful to my family, especially Nancy Chen and Monica and Dave Ilett, my constant cheering section. And to the Lyin' Bastards: Sally Breen, Dina Del Bucchia, Keri Korteling, Judy McFarlane, Denise Ryan, and Carol Shaben for their guidance, support, and fearless approach to the work.

Thank you, insightful readers who helped this novel through its growing pains: Laisha Rosnau, Jennica Harper, Steven Galloway, Annabel Lyon, and Jennifer Lambert, and countless friends who provided encouragement along the way: Marita Dachsel, Charlotte Gill, Andrew Gray, and Bob Breen. Much gratitude to my fine colleagues at the SFU Writer's Studio, the UBC Writing Centre, and the UBC Creative Writing Program, and to the many students I've been privileged to teach.

I acknowledge, with thanks, the funding support of the Canada Council, Canadian Heritage, and B.C. Arts Council. Parts of the novel came to fruition during residencies generously supported by Historic Joy Kogawa House, the City of Richmond, the University of East Anglia, Ville de Vincennes, Île de France, and Centre National du Livre. A special thank you to Francis Geffard, the Festival America Association, and Dominique Chevallier for a life-changing experience when I needed it most.

Anne McDermid and Martha Magor Webb have believed in me longer than any agents should. And finally, I'm grateful for the intelligence, grace, and patience of Ellen Seligman and Kendra Ward.